FREDDY ANDERSON'S HOME

Freddy Anderson Chronicles BOOK 1

BY

John RICKS

THE FREDDY ANDERSON CHRONICLES
FREDDY ANDERSON'S HOME

First Printing May 2010
Second Printing July 2014

iUniverse books may be ordered through booksellers or by contacting:

iUniverse
1663 Liberty Drive
Bloomington, IN 47403
www.iuniverse.com
1-800-Authors (1-800-288-4677)

ISBN: 978-1-4917-5707-9 (sc)
ISBN: 978-1-4917-5708-6 (e)

Library of Congress Control Number: 2015901258

Print information available on the last page.

iUniverse rev. date: 2/26/2015

PROLOGUE

✦ ✦ ✦

I awoke having no idea where I was. I did know that I was in some sort of vat. I was immersed in thick clear liquid, and there were translucent tentacles holding my body in the center. My energy was drained, so I could not teleport out, yet strangely, I was whole. There was a large portal showing that we were in space and leaving the system very quickly. Massive banks of equipment with blinking lights and readouts were on every wall, the ceiling, and parts of the floor.

The last thing I remembered was the Mars base being attacked. A gigantic hole was blown in the dome, and our air was escaping. I was torn apart from falling debris and was bleeding to death. I had used most of my energies by helping other victims of this devastating enemy, and I was reduced to using normal means for healing myself. I was trying to stem the bleeding and make it to a special Blink Emergency Escape Ship, and then I felt something grab me, and all went black.

Now that I was awake I could hear voices and see creatures that were unholy in appearance. They were humanoid but stood on two legs with three pads. They each had leathery skin; big black eyes without eyebrows; no nose; a small, tight mouth; a long thin neck; and multiple arms on each side of the body, with pad-fingered hands. Strange voices spoke in a language completely different from anything I had ever imagined. And they were speaking telepathically.

A small green one—small? Did I think small? It had to be seven feet tall and thin as a rail, with eight tentacles, four on each side—said in a booming voice, "There. I have opened some of the doors in this one's mind. Now we will see much."

A large gray one—about two feet taller than the green one, heavily muscled, and twice as wide—asked, "Are you sure that this tiny little creature is the one that destroyed our mother ship?"

Everything went black. My eyesight and hearing were gone, but the voices continued, and I could sense everything in the room.

The Green answered, "Yes, master. All the others we captured and probed pointed to this one 'creature' being the brains behind everything that has happened in the last ten or more of their years. He is fully responsible."

The big gray creature turned to another gray and ordered, "Have the fleet return home. Pull off the engagement. We will find out what caused this catastrophe, and if needed, destroy this Earth and all its inhabitants." He turned to the small green one and asked, "How long will this take?"

"Master, I must start at his birth and work my way forward. I would guess three of our days, or twenty-two of their days, at best."

The large gray ordered, "Then get to it!"

"Yes, master."

I saw myself at age six, sitting, thinking, wondering why no one would believe me.

CHAPTER 1

✦ ✦ ✦

FREDDY

I sat back from my newest toy. It was big, and Daddy told me to put it in the back of the garage so his car would still fit. It was a jumble of wires and circuits encased in several old computers that Daddy had tossed out. I had built it from almost all the parts that were in the garage and with permission from my nanny. I had it working for only a little bit before it burned out, destroying everything. I wished I hadn't got it working. From what the toy showed me, it was very clear that Earth was doomed, but who could I tell? I ran to my nanny, shouting, "Nanny! Nanny! The world is going to end!"

"Now, Freddy, don't exaggerate. The world is not going to end."

"But my new toy showed that it is going to end!"

"That's nice, dear. You go back and pretend some more."

Frustrated, I went back to the garage. As soon as my daddy came home, I ran to him. "Daddy, the world is going to end! The world is going to end!"

"Freddy, I'm sure you're correct about this, but I don't think we need to worry about it for a few million years yet. I have papers to grade, so I need time alone tonight."

"But Daddy—"

"No, Freddy, not tonight."

Mommy was the same, and so were my friends—no one believed me. I spent weeks trying to get someone to listen to me, but no one would. I thought back on my short life, trying to determine why no one would listen to me. I remembered everything as clearly as if it had just happened …

I was born on a Wednesday. That was no reason for people not to believe me. Mommy said everyone could tell from the time I was born that I was different. My eyes were already open, and I could focus quickly. My size was smaller than most full-term babies, but I was pink and wrinkled like others. The only strange thing was my eyes. The doctor had commented, "I have never seen bright purple eyes on a baby." Purple eyes were a rarity, but would people not believe me because my eyes were different?

I didn't cry at birth, although Mommy said I did smile. And I recognized both her and Daddy as soon as either of them talked. She said I was a happy newborn, and I remember playing constantly with my toes and fingers, giggling and counting them over and over, once I could finally reach them. That was a frustrating time. Something else … I could understand words at birth. Mommy said that was not normal either. I often tried to make words and talk when I was a newborn, but my toothless mouth just would not work right.

By the time I was six months old, I could talk very well and understood most words. I could hold a pencil and write a sentence, and I colored inside the lines. Everyone gave Mommy and Daddy credit for that. Daddy is a physics professor at the local university, and Mommy is the head of the chemistry and biology departments. They were very proud of me. They took me to several groups to have my IQ tested, and it was determined that I am very special indeed, but I was too young for the tests to prove my IQ.

Daddy said that all of the exams went "up top," out to the government someplace, and even though the information showed "better than normal" intelligence, it also showed a lack of increased brain use. Daddy said the government wouldn't care—and he was right. They did tell Mommy and Daddy that I needed special schooling so that I wouldn't get bored. Mommy and Daddy took me home after that. I still didn't do anything to cause anyone not to believe me.

I remember when Daddy brought my nanny home with him. She taught me a lot of good words—she had been an English teacher. Daddy told her that I was allowed to read and do anything I wanted, as long as I had her permission and she could watch—he didn't want me "burning down the house." I never lied to Nanny or anyone, and I did everything she asked of me.

Nanny took me to the playground every day. She would not let me take any books to read. At first, I was really upset with this decision, but when she told me I needed to look at what was outside and analyze it, I realized that she was right. Nanny was good at piquing my interest. I actually started enjoying my times in the park. I found answers and examples of mathematical expressions in almost everything. I spent plenty of time with other children and learned to hide my intelligence, as knowing things usually got me beat up.

I didn't realize it, but I was developing an ability. I looked it up; it's called "empathy"—I could feel the emotions of the other children and was drawn to their happiness.

At age four, I was enrolled in a school for gifted children at the university. It was a special program sponsored by the science department, and since my parents were VIPs at the university, it wasn't difficult for them to get me accepted. The first week of school was testing. The tests were so easy; I'd read all that stuff in Daddy's library last year. Each of us children was given tests to determine where we would be placed in a "normal" school, because they said they needed a base from which to grade our progress. The other children finished testing on the first day, but the university needed to find more for me, as I had aced all the tests up through the twelfth-grade level. They talked and talked trying to figure out how I'd done it.

I think it was at this time that I started developing the ability to read other people's emotions and empathize with them. I didn't understand what was going on, but it affected my life a lot. It was actually kind of funny. I often felt tired when Daddy came home, and I would fall asleep. When Mommy came home, I would be wide awake, happy, and unable to sleep for hours past my bedtime, just like my mother, but as soon as she went to sleep, so did I. Female emotions seemed the strongest and affected me the most. Mommy loved her earrings, and Daddy had pierced ears and long hair. Therefore, I loved earrings and long hair, and I convinced my mother that I should get my ears pierced. I never had my hair cut. I loved life so much.

Nighttime was becoming devastating for me because I would sense other people getting badly hurt, scared, or dying, and that gave me nightmares. Mommy would come in and comfort me. She always knew when I was having a problem.

Four weeks after enrolling in school at the university, the professors called in my parents. I went with them when they talked with the professors.

"Susan and David, we need to inform you that Freddy has been removed from the program."

Mommy and Daddy were instantly upset. Daddy placed a hand on my shoulder and asked, "Why? Did he do something he shouldn't have? We'll talk to him and straighten it all out."

"No, he did fine. In fact, he has passed all of the tests and graduated high school. The university wants him to continue with his studies here."

It was worth all the long hours of study just to see the astonishment in Mommy's and Daddy's wide-eyed, open-mouthed faces. You should have seen them; it was priceless. They were totally flabbergasted. I decided right then that I liked surprising people. It was fun. At age four, I started my studies at the university.

At age six, I received my first bachelor's degree. The university kept it quiet, at the pleading of my parents. Also, I was becoming much more empathic and could sometimes read minds. I could also move objects a little, but no one knew this. I had read the professors' thoughts about the last person who had showed signs of being "superhuman" and what the government had done. I was getting smarter and hiding my talents, because I didn't want to be someone's guinea pig, but I practiced constantly at home, where no one could see me. I just didn't see anything in there that would cause people not to believe me.

✦

The Gray stated, "This is all interesting, but the reason why they did not believe him is not of interest to us. However, according to his memory, telepathy and telekinesis is not common in this species. Let us move on. Close this door and open another one."

The Green removed a tentacle from my head, and everything went black, but then the voices returned. The Green said, "Yes, master," and replaced the tentacle.

CHAPTER 2

✦ ✦ ✦

GOVERNMENT

Two years later, at the age of eight, I had read everything in the university libraries and a lot of stuff online. I challenged every class I could and obtained doctorates in chemistry, physics, biology, and electronics, and master's degrees in a dozen other disciplines. I had written four books and posted a dozen papers. The work I enjoyed most and at which I worked hardest was inventing. I needed to fix that Earth-destruction problem, so I invented several useful items. The university lawyers and my parents were very helpful in setting up a trust for me, and they helped sell my patents for millions of dollars. My professors would often say, "I've never seen anyone so driven."

One day, the news media got hold of my records, and they blew everything out of proportion. I was on the front page for weeks: "Whiz Kid," "Super Genius," "Smartest Kid in the World." Of course, the sleaze magazines had to do worse, with headlines such as "Super Boy—is he human or alien?" and "Alien born of human mom has super intelligence." The news media made it very hard on my parents and me, and all that attention caught the government's interest.

Mommy and Daddy were peeking through the curtain

of the front window when I came down for breakfast. When they saw me, they told me to go back to my room and stay there. I peeked out my window and saw hundreds of people with cameras and big microphones, just waiting. There were also several people, dressed in white, carrying signs that read, "Thou shalt not suffer a witch to live!" And one person held up a sign that read, "Kill the alien!"

Several big black cars drove up, and men got out and forced the crowd back. Two people got out of one of the big cars and walked directly to the door. They showed their FBI badges. They argued with my daddy for several minutes but produced a warrant for my arrest and retention, pending a government review of my abilities and human status.

Against my will, I was taken by agents of the federal government and retested. They found that I was human—thank goodness!—but also found that they could not measure my IQ, because it was way too high. They thought I was cheating in some way.

I hid my other abilities from them. The last thing I wanted was for the government to know that I could read minds, move objects, and—as I was working on—heal people. I found that out after my father slipped on the icy driveway and broke his leg. I ran out, all upset and worried, but when I placed my hands on his arm, he glowed for several seconds, and his leg was healed. Luckily, no one saw, and Daddy did not notice the glow. For several days, he said, "I thought I broke that leg, but it must have just been a painful twist." I practiced on dogs and cats after that.

After twelve weeks of extensive testing, the FBI had to let me go. My parents had finally convinced the court that I was being held against my will. I was very glad to see my parents again.

✦

The big Gray said, "You did not go far enough. Close this door and open another!"

The Green removed a tentacle from my head. Everything went black, and the voices returned.

"Yes, master."

✦

Just before my ninth birthday, Mommy and Daddy took a second honeymoon. Their plane crashed, killing everyone on board. I mentally felt my mommy and daddy die. I was devastated and cried for weeks. It took a while, but I finally started planning what I would do. I was left in a bad situation, so the county placed me in a foster home near the university until things could be worked out. I had to find a place to live, somewhere secluded, away from the city. I started researching a place to live and created a plan for a home there.

Luckily, I had a lot of friends at the university, including lawyers. Within a few months, I obtained a hearing and proved that I was more than capable of taking care of myself. As one judge admitted, I was "much better than most eighteen-year-olds I've seen."

However, the problem could not be settled in the lower courts, and it quickly escalated to the higher courts. I was ten when I was taken before the US Supreme Court as a statement on my constitutional right to freedom. Young or not, I was a collage grad and had my own funding. I did not need to stay in a foster home with people who did not really want me, other than for the government funding they received. (Note: Washington is no place for a telepath to live!)

It was a miracle that the Supreme Court saw me so quickly, but I was still in the media and constantly hounded.

The justices were very considerate and listened to my lawyers, but I could tell that they were not going to give me custody of myself. I asked to meet with them alone, and they agreed. When we were in their chambers, I asked if everything said and done would be treated confidentially, and they agreed. I had not planned on revealing my secrets, but I was left with no choice. They were astounded when they saw me raise and turn the couch they were sitting on, but my verbalizing everything they were thinking caused them to become agitated, especially when I pointed out that one judge was upset that my hair was long and my ears pierced, so I stopped that. But when I touched one judge and healed his skin cancer, suddenly they were very interested in what I could do.

People are funny. It meant little to the justices that I had to move away before I had a mental breakdown, because I'm not able to shut people out when they are in trouble or dying. Proving that I was more intelligent than they were, that I could move objects and read minds, was nothing compared to my ability to heal. It seems that elderly judges always have someone they love who is dying of something. Once I realized this, I offered to help them if they would help me.

They talked among themselves and then asked if I would heal one person for each of them. If I agreed, then they would grant me custody of myself and help me find a secluded place to live.

One of the justices said, "As you can read minds, then help us with a case." That was something else I had not expected, but I made a quick decision and said, "I agree to help with the case, in exchange for a grant of land that runs along the Pacific Ocean. It's federal property, but it's secluded enough to prevent me from going insane. The army uses the land for training and the navy for a radar system site. I have only one stipulation: I don't want to enter the mind of a serial killer or something worse." They assured me that the case was quite important but did not involve violence and that they would look into the situation regarding the land.

Over the next six weeks, each Supreme Court justice brought a person to me, and I healed each of them—nine in all. Each one sapped my strength, so I had to wait several days between each healing. It was weeks before I could help with their case. I think my showing them that I had limits helped them become a little more comfortable around me.

The justices investigated the land situation and decided it was perfect. During a private meeting, which I mentally spied on, the justices concluded that the place definitely was secluded, but they just couldn't send a young boy out there without monitoring. "We'll get the military to keep watch on him. We'll grant him the land in exchange for his services a few more times."

The next day, the justices brought me to their chambers to tell me their decision. It was less than I had hoped for, but a compromise was in order, as I did not have a good position from which to negotiate. I reluctantly agreed but put a limit of five times maximum on the additional help. I made it clear that I would do them a favor by checking in with this admiral of theirs, but that I was not in his custody and could do as I wished.

Everything was set. I was granted my own custody and the land was placed into my trust, permanently and tax-free, for as long as the trust existed. No one could take it away or enter upon it without my permission, except the navy, as it still had to run its radar station. I granted access rights for that purpose only. Congress approved the agreement by unanimous vote, and the president of the United States signed it. When the justices handed me the deed, they made it very clear that they had to pull in a couple of favors to get it. I got the idea that they were expecting a payback.

The next day, the justices had me sit behind a one-way mirror during the questioning in their case. We had worked out beforehand what questions would be asked. The US attorney was stunned by the questions but asked them anyway. The criminal answered, but I wrote down the true answers as they popped into his head, which were different than the answers he said aloud. My answers were given to the US attorney, and the evidence to prosecute the man and close the case was found the same day. The justices were so impressed that they assured me they would keep their promises. Their surface thoughts were, *Just in case we need him again.*

After everything was finalized, I had to talk to a lot of people, including congressmen, senators, and even the president. The president seemed very nervous about my being able to read minds over the phone.

I placed almost everything I owned into storage. My trust sold the family house and cars and made sure I paid the taxes. The last thing I wanted was the government having a hold on me for tax evasion.

When I was in Washington, I met a very honest man with whom I contracted to build me a special house. (One of the benefits of being telepathic is that it's easy to find the best people with whom to contract.) I had completed building the platform base for my house over a year ago, so I made a trip to his company in South Carolina, just south of Greenville, and gave him the base and plans for building the house. We talked for days about the specifications and plans. During the visit, I drifted for two days, just thinking about what changes I could make. Luckily they had seen this before and let me drift while taking notes. "Drifting" is when I concentrate so hard that all else is excluded. Many top scientists have an issue with drifting. I didn't sleep, drink, eat, or go to the restroom; I just thought about the issues. I tend to talk out loud and walk around when I drift, and that can be very dangerous. When I was younger, I drifted and fell down the stairs and didn't know until I stopped drifting and found myself in the hospital with a broken leg. (On another note, I need to learn how to control it before I take up driving.)

I did the research on my new wilderness home site and printed a map off the Internet. I had a horrible time trying to arrange transportation. First, I had to set up a one-way flight to the nearest big city and then a private plane to fly me to the nearest small airport. I wanted to arrange for a limousine to a hotel, but there were none—no limousine and no hotel. A very nice lady operator connected me with the only place to stay, the Seaward Inn. ("By the water," she said.)

The lady at the inn said she could arrange for a taxi to pick me up. I gave her my flight information and estimated time of arrival. She said, "Don't worry, honey. I'll make sure old Jake is on time."

My only real worry now was that I had promised the justices and the president that once I got settled, I would see Admiral Bates, whom the justices told me would help to oversee my new home.

✦

The big Gray ordered, "Hold there!"

Everything went black.

The Green said, "Yes, master?"

"Did we not capture an Admiral Bates?"

"I will check, master. Yes. The Body System confirms."

"Stop and read back what this Bates and any other

captives may know. I want to tie everything together. I need a case to present to the body superior for complete inhalation of this species."

The Green looked upset at that announcement but answered, "As you wish, master."

I tried as hard as I could to prevent entrance into my mind, but the Green replaced his tentacle and memories flowed. My senses were wide open, and I could clearly see Admiral Bates on a big screen in the ceiling.

CHAPTER 3

✦ ✦ ✦

GREAT NEWS

Admiral Jeff Bates was near retirement. He was sixty-seven years old, with hair as white as snow—at least, what little was left on his balding head. He had the start of a pot belly because of all the desk work, and he was tired. *I was tired ten years ago. I was tired last year, and I'm tired now. How darn tired do I need to get? I don't need this kid on top of everything else.*

His hand felt the cool smoothness of his old sea captain's desk. It was made of mahogany, with carved figures of dragons adorning every corner and leg, as well as the front. Thinking back, he said to no one in particular, "I got this in the Philippines thirty years ago. Nearly fainted trying to bring it up three flights to get it into this office last year, but I'd be darned if I was going to let those stupid movers put another ding in it." He patted the desktop. "This desk and I go back a long way."

He would retire in two more years, after a distinguished career of fifty years in the navy. He had both elbows on the desk, and his old worn hands held up his wrinkled face. He was actually happy to learn that the land near the base had been sold, but the smile on his face showed concern mixed with happiness. True, it meant that the army would not be using it anymore. The little fishing town would be very happy about that, and his base would run a lot smoother without the army personnel messing around and getting arrested. He could cut the military police force down by 75 percent, and watches could go from port and starboard to four-day or maybe five-day rotations. That meant more time at home with wives and children for the sailors and marines. Fewer fights meant fewer injuries and a considerably shorter wait at the base clinic and the dental facilities on Friday nights and Saturday mornings. The base commissary finally could be stocked and kept that way. He lifted his head, thinking, *I can start letting the veterans have access and privileges again. Oh yes, this is going to make me very popular around here. When I retire, I'll be a hero. Yes, indeed!*

Still, something was not quite right about the situation. The president herself had sent a message regarding this Freddy Anderson person:

TOP SECRET

For Admiral Bates's Eyes Only

Office of the President of the United States

Jeff,

I hope this finds you well. By unanimous decision, in payment for services rendered, the Congress, Senate, and I have granted the land southwest of your position, a total of forty square miles, to one Freddy Anderson. Copies of the pertinent papers are on the way. The army has been notified that they are not to come within fifteen miles of that area. It is now off-limits to all personnel, with the exception of your radar team and your top staff, for inspection and maintenance of the radar station only. Do not get caught spying on Dr. Anderson!

Dr. Anderson is only ten years old, but he can take care of himself. Don't let his age fool you. According to my information, he is probably the most intelligent person on the face of the planet. He is highly eccentric and very capable of doing almost anything. My God, the kid has more degrees from a highly respected university than my entire staff. His abilities are limitless. I don't know what he plans to do with the land—it could be anything. One justice confided in me that Dr. Anderson needs to be alone most of the time, but he would not say why.

Jeff, I want you to keep an eye on this one. I'm making this your top priority. Befriend the boy, help him in any way you can, but don't hamper him. Keep undesirables away from him. Frankly, his abilities and knowledge scare me. You have permission to grant him full base privileges. That should be a good way to see him and get to know him. Give him housing on base until he gets his new home built. Get someone to help him with anything he wants. Naturally, I don't expect you to do this yourself, so find someone he can learn to trust.

Best regards,
Margaret A. Kabe
President of the United States

He'd read the letter a hundred times and could well see why the president was scared. It left a bad taste in his mouth.

According to the files, this kid had invented a portable laser, an anti-gravity device, and some kind of compression system that was being used for compacting rock to make tunnels. All he needed now was a portable power source, and he would be his own army. *Impressive, but I'd be more impressed if the kid could straighten out my supply problems. Relax—what difference does it make if a kid is moving in? The army's moving out, and nothing could be better than that.*

Smiling, he rested his face back in his hands as he thought, *Now, who can I get to babysit the brat? I've got it! Another one of my problems is about to be solved!* Smiling even wider, he said out loud, "I love this kid."

✦

The view on the alien ship's monitor changed to a split screen, with the admiral on the right and an outside view on the left, showing Susan throwing knives.

Navy SEAL Lieutenant Susan James was outside her barracks when the call came. She stood tall, about five foot eleven, and weighed about 150 pounds—all muscle, solid. Her blonde hair was in a tight cut that made her look more male than female. So far, every knife she tossed had stuck two inches into the trunk of the old oak, all within a finger's width of each other, cutting the white, hand-sized circle that was painted there.

A very nervous ensign approached, stopped a good distance away, and after a snappy salute said, "Lieutenant, sir, the admiral wants to see you."

She returned his salute with a smart one of her own. "Very well, Ensign. Carry on." Her words were lost on the ensign, as he was already running away as fast as he could. *It's about time,* she thought. *I'm bored, and my team is being wasted. I hope the admiral has something a little more interesting for us this time. We've been sitting here for a month with nothing to do but pick on the army and marines—not that it hasn't been fun.*

Thinking back on her situation, she realized that the boredom was mostly her fault. *I should have realized that in proving my team is the best—that an all-female team is by far superior to male teams—we'd hurt the feelings of too many high-ranking men. It's not Admiral Bates's fault that we were forced on him.* Part of the orders from her last commanding officer had been verbal. "In a nutshell, Lieutenant, it comes down to this: you're being transferred to a little command in the middle of nowhere near the Oregon/California border. Try to advance your career from there."

When they'd reached this base, the admiral had nothing to give them. He was always trying to find something. He'd sent them out to pull some interesting things on the marines, but the admiral had kept that secret, and the marines couldn't prove a thing. He'd also had them spy on the army. For some reason, the general of the army in that area had a mean streak and so did some of his men. They were always messing with the town, parking convoys in the middle of the street, getting drunk and starting fights with the fishermen and tourists, messing with the fishing nets, and just generally being obnoxious. When the men were arrested for drunken assault, the general had enough power to get them out. They never paid for anything they damaged—they nearly put the tavern out of business due to broken furniture and light fixtures. Therefore, my team threw some shenanigans into their maneuvers. It was a lot of fun, but according to the latest scuttlebutt, there was no more army—they were finally kicked out forever.

The whole town was saying that some little kid kicked them out. I'd heard how hard the town had been on the general and his men—throwing sticks and rocks and yelling out names. Stupid civilians! That was a big mistake on the town's part, and now the general was madder than a hungry pit bull and swearing revenge. Strange—most army personnel were very good people, some of the best to know and have as friends, but this group seemed handpicked for malicious personalities.

Susan tossed the last three knives, one right after another, and they thudded into the circle on the oak, touching each other.

Within minutes, she stood tall in front of the admiral's office, waiting for permission to enter. When he finished with the yeoman, he motioned for her to come in. She entered and stood at attention in front of his desk.

"At ease, Lieutenant. Have a seat." She relaxed and sat down. "I have new orders for you." He handed the Top Secret folder to her and said, "Read it."

It took her only a minute to scan the paperwork and memorize it. She handed it back.

"Well, what do you think?" he asked.

"Begging the admiral's pardon, but I think this is a babysitting job for some yeoman or one of the enlisted men's wives."

The admiral looked upset, as one eye squinted and the other became hard and glassy. His brow wrinkled, and his mouth became tight. "I don't think you're seeing the whole picture, Lieutenant. Private, state, and federal groups have fought over that land for years. Suddenly, this child gets it lock, stock, and barrel with a unanimous decision from Congress, not to mention tax-free! When's the last time we've seen the Democrats and Republicans vote unanimously on anything, especially something tax-free that doesn't include them?"

Lt. James said, "Never, sir."

"This request was from the president herself, Lieutenant. You have a degree in human behavior. What's the emotion in that letter?"

Lieutenant James thought before responding. "I would say … worried and possibly a little afraid, not necessarily for the child's life but for the knowledge and abilities that he has. Admiral, why don't we just kill him?"

"Because he's useful in some way, so much so that everyone wants him protected, but he wants to be alone."

"So, leave him alone, sir."

"Can't do that, Lieutenant. How would you feel if you had the world's smartest person sitting in your backyard? No supervision; you can't touch him; you can't see what he's doing; and he has everything he wants to make anything he wants at his disposal. To top that off, the kid has the social experience of a naive ten-year-old. I don't care how smart he is; he has only ten years' experience with life and morals."

"I see what you mean, sir."

"This kid will see right through anyone I send to befriend him. You've always said that your team is the smartest and ready for anything. Well, here's your chance to prove it. I don't care if everyone sees it as a babysitting job. You and I know it's different. Do we have an understanding, Lieutenant?"

"We have an understanding that you were probably never at a loss for babysitters. You're a born salesman, sir."

"Good. Do your best on this, Lieutenant. I have to make monthly reports to the president, so I expect weekly reports from you. Dismissed." Lieutenant James came to attention and left. *How is she going to explain that to the team?* the admiral thought with a smile.

✦

The Gray said, "I don't understand this human admiral." Everything went black.

"Master?"

"This Bates clearly outranks James, yet he took the time to talk her into the 'babysitting' position and is wondering how she is going to talk her subordinates into the situation. She outranks them. Why explain anything? How do they run a military like that?"

"I do not know, master. Possibly they spend a little time attempting to acquire approval for what they are doing or plan to do. Some might consider getting buy-in from subordinates as a way to enhance the morale of the troops and therefore make their duty seem more worth doing."

"That's very funny, Green. There is nothing more worth doing than to do that which keeps your superiors from stripping the skin off your backs."

Under his breath, Green mumbled, "Yes, you get the job done exactly to the bare minimum required to please the Gray—or less, if you can get away with it."

"What was that?"

"Nothing, master."

"Then continue with the little one's memories."

C H A P T E R 4

✦ ✦ ✦

THE INN

After sleeping most of the way through my first plane ride, I was wide awake when it was time to land. The stewardesses were nice, and I had plenty to do, planning out what I would need at my new home. The flight was fun and the view amazing, but I had to pop my ears several times. I wanted to go up with the pilots to ask some questions, but I was told that it wasn't legal.

The second flight was much more interesting. The plane was a small single prop with a turbo. Captain Bob was the pilot. He was probably sixty but seemed much older, as if he was about to fall apart. He looked just like the grandfathers I'd seen in movies—black hair that was gray over the ears, untidy blue overalls, and a white shirt that was clean but looked worn. He looked almost like a farmer with his sun-wrinkled skin that was dark brown, like the old earthenware plate that my mother used to love. There was a pin over his chest that read "Captain Bob Nevers." After touching him on the arm and using my healing abilities to check that he was fit, I settled in for the ride. Captain Bob let me ask all the questions I wanted, and I learned everything about flying that I could in the time I had. I think I asked enough questions to drive the poor man away from doing private flights altogether. Most of my questions were things like, "Is the interior of the cockpit correct, or could you make improvements if you had the chance? Why would you do that? Would that work for someone who was left-handed?" Of course, Captain Bob had no idea that he was helping me with my next project.

Though I was curious, asking questions about the town would have been fruitless, as Captain Bob would have exaggerated everything. If he had known that I was empathic and knew he was lying through his teeth, he would have kept his stories to something a little saner, like accidentally flying around the moon—really now! I wanted to know more about the town, though. I had looked it up on the Internet and learned that its reason for existence was fishing. It also supported the navy base and the army. I filed everything Captain Bob told me away for later use. The only disappointment was the lack of speed, as the flight was very slow. There were cars below us that seemed to be passing us as if we were standing still.

We landed at a tiny airport, and Jake, the taxi driver, was waiting. The big old taxi pulled right up to the plane. Jake was the quiet type and said almost nothing. He had a small French-style mustache that he played with constantly when he saw my size and apparent age. The look on his face was amusement. He was short and very overweight but lifted my luggage like it weighed nothing and effortlessly settled it down into the taxi's huge trunk. When everything had been transferred, we took off. The taxi was a 1985 Ford, according to the license tag hanging from the window, and had so much room in the backseat that I felt almost lost. The trip was made in silence as we sped over winding mountain roads for the thirty-mile trip to the coastal town. When we arrived, Jake helped me with my luggage.

The old two-story Victorian inn was nestled against the little bay that supported the town. There were a few fishing boats at the docks but almost no people. It was an old building with a good coat of paint. My first impression was that it was warm and cozy, just like home. It smelled of fresh-baked bread and had very clean wooden floors. Large evergreens surrounded it, keeping it cool in summer and cutting the wind in winter. At this time, in spring, there was no need for a fire in the huge fireplace. There were deer heads, a moose head, and all kinds of animals hanging overhead. The woman with whom I had spoken on the phone came into the front room. She had a friendly smile and introduced herself as Mrs. Crain, the owner of the inn. She was very lovely, tall—and nearly covered in flour. Her hair was long but pulled up into a very large tight ball at the back of her head. She looked young and happy, with a pleasant smile. She was very polite and said nothing about a ten-year-old, who looked more like a seven-year-old, being out on his own. She showed me to my room and told me that dinner would be ready in about half an hour. I instantly took a liking to her.

The second-floor room was nice—open and light with a big window that offered a good view of the mountains in back of the inn. The large bathroom had an old-fashioned tub on legs—a tub big enough to swallow a grown-up. I could stand up in it and still be submerged over my waist. (I know, because I tried.) My room had pictures of Victorian people playing, dancing, and hunting. The chest of drawers had a mirror big enough that, if it were magical, you could walk through it and not have to duck. It reminded me of *Alice in Wonderland.*

By far the biggest thing in the room was the bed. It was almost as tall as me and had steps up to it. It looked very inviting with its thick, homemade quilt and gigantic pillows, but sleep was still a long way away.

Across from the inn, a young woman sat alone on a bench near the dock. She was wearing a jacket and blue jeans, but I had seen those standard-issue boots used by the Reserve Officers Training Corps, or ROTC, at the university. She looked very much out of place when I arrived. I touched her mind and learned that she was from the navy and was watching me. *Interesting,* I thought. *The navy is having me watched. I wonder why? Whatever! Unpacking comes first for now.* After unpacking, I washed up.

In exactly one half hour, I went downstairs for dinner. Everything was ready, and it sure smelled great. Four children—three girls and a boy—were helping to set the table and pour drinks. The girls wore everyday dresses, and the boy wore shorts and a T-shirt. It was just the children, Mrs. Crain, and me for dinner.

Mrs. Crain came in and the children lined up for inspection. Starting with the oldest, Mrs. Crain inspected their hands and behind their ears. I was very glad Nanny had taught me proper hygiene. Carroll passed inspection, and then it was Johnny's turn.

Miss. Crain said, "Okay, Johnny, you may sit down." The short five-year-old came next and she smiled up at her mommy. Mrs. Crain inspected her and told her she could sit down, but with a sideward glance at her oldest, she gave the little girl's fanny a swat saying, "Carroll needs to help you work on doing a better job of cleaning your fingernails."

Carroll said, "Yes, Mother. We'll start tonight."

Mrs. Crain motioned for me to sit next to her and across from Carroll.

We all sat there quietly while Becky, the middle-aged girl, said grace. Then everyone waited for Mrs. Crain to start dishing out food. Mommy and Daddy never said grace and often ate most of the food before it reached the table. Nanny let me see that others do things differently, so I held back until I saw how everything was done. Nanny taught me great manners, and I'd read a few books on the subject, so I was prepared not to eat until I saw someone else start.

"Dr. Anderson, this is my eldest daughter, Carroll." Carroll was tall for a twelve-year-old, with long blonde hair that was tied back, just like her mother's. Somewhat skinny, she had light blue eyes that shone with curiosity, but they held a kindness that was very reassuring. Her skin was tanned and smooth, nearly blemish free.

I said, "Nice to meet you, Carroll."

"Nice to meet you also, sir," she said.

That "sir" produced giggles from the rest of the children.

Mrs. Crain then said, "This is my second eldest, Becky." Becky was ten years old and taller than me by only an inch, which means she was very short for her age. She also had long hair and a twinkle in her eye, like she was trying to pull something. She was extremely pretty, and I had a hard time taking my eyes off her.

I said, "Nice to meet you, Becky."

"Hello, Dr. Anderson. It's nice to meet you," she said.

I must have blushed, as Annabelle giggled and pointed at me. Mrs. Crain said, "Annabelle! Stop that or go to your room." Annabelle stopped immediately and looked very chastened. I smiled and winked at her. That made her smile.

"This is my son, Johnny," Mrs. Crain said.

"Hello, Johnny."

"Hi." Johnny was nine years old and looked a lot different from the rest. His complexion was darker, and he had bushier eyebrows over dark blue eyes. His hair was cut in a typical boy's short butch cut. He was tall and very stocky. He had a look on his face like he was highly irritated about something.

"And last, but not least," said Mrs. Crain, "this is Annabelle, my baby."

Annabelle gave her a look that said, *I'm not a baby.*

I said, "Hello, young lady."

She smiled back at me and said, "Hello. You're nice." Annabelle was five years old, and she appeared to be a little ball of fire. Emotions played across her face like waves during a storm. Her blonde hair hung down to the middle of her back and spilled over her shoulder and halfway into her plate. She had her mother's blue eyes and a smile that would light up the darkest room.

I looked at Mrs. Crain and complimented her on her wonderful family as well as the nice dinner that was spread before us. I told her that I hadn't had a home-cooked meal in over a year.

When she heard this, she picked up a fork and started eating, and so did everyone else. I think she purposefully waited until my mouth was full before asking me the first question.

"Dr. Anderson, what brings you way out here without proper supervision?"

I had just taken a small bite of the most wonderful roll with real butter. I raised one finger in response while I continued chewing. She smiled and waited. When I had finished the bite, I said, "Mrs. Crain, this is where the government has allowed me to live. They granted me the land south of here, and I intend to build a home and settle here. The reason I am here alone ..." I started to choke up a little and desperately tried to hold back tears—memories of Mom and Dad still did that to me.

"I'm sorry," she said with concern. "I did not mean to meddle in something that is obviously painful to you."

"It's all right, ma'am. I need to get used to it. I'm sure the subject will come up many more times. I am without 'proper supervision' because my mother and father died in a plane crash. I have no one to provide me with supervision.

After they died, I petitioned the government for my own emancipation." I could hold on no longer, and the tears fell.

The table was silent after that. Mrs. Crain said, "I'm sorry, dear."

"That's okay, ma'am."

After a few minutes of enjoyable eating, I looked over at Johnny. My curiosity got the better of me, as I knew that he was upset about some punishment he earned. I looked at Mrs. Crain and asked, "May I ask what caused Johnny to be punished?"

Johnny turned four shades of red. Mrs. Crain said, "Johnny is being punished for flipping up his sisters' dresses in public."

I looked at Johnny and asked, "Are you a bully?"

Johnny started to answer but was cut off by his mother. "No, he's normally a good child, but sometimes he gets into trouble. I find that a little swat on the backside and time doing the girls chores is a good way to put him back in line."

"I personally find the idea of teasing girls appalling," I said. "I am glad you love him enough to correct his ways."

"Thank you very much, Dr. Anderson."

We ate the rest of the meal in silence, but Becky kept smiling at me.

After dinner I started to help clean up, but since I was a paying customer, I was told that I was not allowed to help. "Besides," Mrs. Crain said, "I want to talk to Johnny alone, and this is a good time." She scooted the girls and me out of the house "for a little while."

I started walking out to the beach. It was still early, and I thought I would do a little exploring. The whole group followed me. Annabelle, being little and not at all shy, asked me, "Why are you wearing earrings?"

I looked at Carroll for the right to answer, and she nodded for me to go ahead.

I told her, "At home, my mother and father were very open about what I did and what I wore, and they both wore earrings. So, when I said I wanted to wear earrings, they had no problem with that, and I've been wearing them ever since."

Annabelle smiled up at me and said, "I like you. You're not like the mean old boys we have around here."

I gave her a hug and kissed her cheek. "Thank you. That's very kind."

They had a thousand questions, and I answered them all quite candidly, even though that navy woman was quietly following us and seemed to be taking mental note of everything I said. I did not want to scare my new friends, but I kept an eye on her just in case. Her emotions showed that she was harmless, so I didn't worry much. Time passed quickly, and soon the children were called inside. I told them I would be in shortly.

After they went inside, I turned to the woman who was sitting on the bench again and said, "Please tell Admiral Bates that I'm in town and that I would like to see him at his earliest convenience, maybe Wednesday." Then I turned and walked inside. The woman never moved, and her face never changed expression, but my empathy told me her feelings screamed, "How did he know?"

I went up to my room. Mrs. Crain came up with Johnny. He looked sad, but he was very happy inside. Most confusing. Mrs. Crain wanted to check on me to be sure I had everything I needed.

After she left, I did a little testing with my equipment and set my proximity detector on automatic. Then I took a bath and went to bed. *Tomorrow is going to be an interesting day. I'll bet that in a town this size, everyone knows everything that is said and done.* I'd already planned not to hide any normal stuff about myself. I found out early in life that it only makes things worse. As my daddy once told me, "Either they accept you or not; it's their choice."

✦

The big Gray ordered, "Hold there!"

Everything physical went black, but my senses were becoming stronger, and they were far more acute than normal physical abilities. I could sense everything and everyone, including the electronics attached to this tank.

The Green said, "Yes, master?"

"I am trying to understand these humans, and I am finding it difficult. Why would this woman be surprised that the boy knew that she was from his military? I know they are not color coded at birth, as we are, and she is not wearing a uniform, but she should have a mark, something that shows she is better than the others."

"Master, most humans do not consider someone in the military as being any better than anyone else. Master, your mouth is hanging open. I do not see why you would be surprised. Even with our own race, only Gray thinks that Gray is better than everyone else."

"We do not think that we are better than everyone else! Just most everyone else."

"Still, master, it does seem that the humans feel that they are all equal in some ways. They are not born, marked, and trained as military. They volunteer to be military for a small portion of their lives."

"Green, think a little harder! How can a military have given us so many problems when they cannot keep their people more than a few years? I am beginning to believe that you understand these humans wrong! Continue."

CHAPTER 5

✦ ✦ ✦

DYING TO MAKE FRIENDS

The next day, a Tuesday, I was up early and eager to go outside. My main plan called for obtaining as much nongovernmental help as possible, so finding out about the town was essential. I would use this day to prepare for meeting with the admiral, and that meant knowing what local resources I could count on. I had received a call from a general in the army who offered a lot of help if I would let him use some of my land, but that went against having no government influence. Still, I would keep it in mind in case it was needed.

Mrs. Crain had a wonderful breakfast ready for me, and I ate alone, as her children were already up and doing their chores. They wanted to play on this first day of spring break and that meant getting chores done first.

I thanked her and headed out to see the town. As soon as I left, I could feel her start to worry.

I headed down the main street, which followed the beach in a half circle. There were a few side streets, and in the center was the exit from town. All the stores were on either the main street or the road heading out. The walkway was made of wooden planks, and there were lanterns every twenty feet on poles that held up an overhang, which kept the snow and rain off the walkway. The overhang was slanted, and there was still snow on the top in some places. Signs written in old script spelled out the types of stores—Susie's Old World Fashions, Taproot Tavern, Pale Lady's Guns and Ammo, and Tinker John's Repair.

The first place I stopped was the sporting goods store. The sign read, "The Lazy Fisherman." I needed equipment to camp and hike around my area. A guide would be nice too, someone who knew how to hike and camp, as I didn't. I walked into the tiny store and was astonished at the amount of stuff that was amassed inside. The aisles were only two feet wide, and every square inch of space was being used. I looked around for a while, realizing that I could spend a week in here and not see everything or find what I needed. Two people stood by the counter, talking, and a third person was behind it. They watched me as they talked. The man standing behind the counter was wearing a red plaid shirt and faded jeans. He finally came around and asked me if I needed anything. He was big and burly, with a mustache and beard that hung a good six inches below his mouth. His face was somewhat puffy, and he had shoulders as wide as the aisles. He had to turn sideways in one place to get to me.

In a deep voice, he said, "Hello, young man. I'm Mr. Thompson, and this is my store. Is there something I can help you with?"

"Hello, Mr. Thompson. It's nice to meet you. This is a very nice store. It certainly has a lot of equipment. I'll bet you have everything anyone would want for fishing and camping."

He smiled and bragged, "You betcha! And if I don't have it, I can get it quickly."

One of the men at the counter cleared his throat very loudly. Something was definitely up, and I knew I had to be on my guard.

I put my hand out to shake his and said, "My name is Freddy."

His hand did not meet mine. I could feel his sadness and reluctance to do something. I slowly pulled my hand back and said, "Sir, I would like to purchase some equipment to go hiking and camping south of here. I am also looking for a guide to help me explore that same area. I would like to start with a good, lightweight backpack. What would you suggest?"

Thompson was definitely upset that he had to do something and sent a mean look toward the man at the counter. Turning back to me, he said, "Look, Dr. Anderson, I can't help you. You're too young to be allowed to purchase items for camping. I can't help you with a guide either. Please leave."

I looked at him in astonishment. He knew my title and last name and was not going to help me. This was definitely a setback. I looked over at the man at the counter. He was not happy about doing this either, but I could feel his sad determination. I touched his mind and was shocked to find that he had orders not to let anyone help me. I smiled and walked toward him. I looked up at him and asked, "Are you responsible for this?"

He said nothing, but he felt sick at what he was doing. I left the store and sat down on a bench outside to think for a minute. *These two were not pulling the strings. They were definitely just following orders. I wonder how far these orders extend.*

Getting up, I went to the next store. It was a gas station/convenience store combination. A man came out as soon as I entered. His short, skinny frame had a mean face and shifty eyes. He was clean-shaven and had a look of extreme superiority. In a high-pitched and irritating voice, he said, "I'm sorry, but I have nothing here that I can sell you except candy, little boy." This man was not so friendly, and the feeling I got was one of pure irritation. *Interestingly, this man actually seems glad that I came by, just so he can kick me out.* I wondered if these people had any idea of the lawsuit I could bring against them. I talked myself into calming down, as I was almost ready to call my lawyers when I left his store. The last thing I wanted was to make things worse by coming in here with money and threatening people. *Darn! I need to get these people on my side.*

I passed some stores that were not yet open and others that closed their doors as I walked by. This "shun the little kid" plan was well made, and it was working. I touched some minds and realized that the plan was to make me leave. They were rid of the army, and now they wanted to get rid of me. "Bad mistake!"

About midday, after being turned down by half the town, I stopped in at a place called Betty's Diner. I was so mad that I was in tears by this time. The diner was an L-shaped design, with five tables—three by the windows, two toward the back—and some chairs at the counter. Everything was in dark wood, except for the red-and-white-checkered tablecloths and the lamps over each table in the shape of large red-and-white-checkered bells. I took a table in the back, as much out of the view of the public as possible, where I could calm down in private. I could feel the concern, and I knew their hearts were reaching out to me, even though their words and actions were cold and almost violent. I used some techniques I had learned from Daddy to relax my mind and think. By the time the waitress came up to me, I was beginning to form a plan. I kept up the quiet crying. I may be very intelligent, but I'm still just a kid, and

I can't control my emotions very well, and right then, I was highly frustrated.

She asked with concern, "Are you all right?" Her nametag read "Nancy," and she had to be about sixteen or seventeen. She was very pretty. She had blonde hair and even though it was pulled up in back, it still came down to just below her shoulders. She was dressed in a white cotton dress with a pastel pink apron. She knew I was crying because I was mentally hurt and that caused her to be considerate. How interesting. I could play on that. I use to play the cry game with Nanny to get my way, and I always won.

With my head downcast and in my most humble, quiet voice, I said, "Yes, ma'am." I could feel her heart nearly break right there. If only everyone was as nice as she was, then maybe I could turn this around.

She asked, "May I get you something?"

"Could I please have a glass of milk?"

"Sure, but don't you want something to eat too?"

"I don't feel much like eating right now." I could feel her become extremely angry, but it wasn't at me.

"I'll get you some milk, sweetheart."

Nancy walked back behind the counter and through to the kitchen. I took the time she was gone to devise a plan. I could hear an argument in the back and opened my mind to watch and listen. I could hear some voices, at first muted, but as I concentrated, they became crystal clear. The man from the gas station said, "Look, Nancy. I know how hard this is, but everyone must comply, or the plan won't work. The council voted on it, and even though you don't like it, you're going to do as you're told!"

Nancy said, "I'm taking that little boy an ice-cold glass of the freshest milk we have, and don't you try to stop me."

She turned away, and the man put out a hand to restrain her but suddenly backed up quickly when Betty, Nancy's mother, pressed a very big knife to his throat, saying, "Don't you ever come into my diner and tell us what to do—and no one touches my daughter. *Got that, Mr. Mayor?* Nancy, use the tallest glass we have, and tell him it's on the house."

Nancy smiled. "Thanks, Mom."

"No problem, and as for you, Mayor, get out *now*!"

The man left.

So that was it—the town council had voted to make me leave. My plan would change that. For maximum effect, though, I needed to play this completely out, and that was going to be very difficult. I used my healing ability to force my tear ducts into action. I was too darn old to play the crybaby and really disliked doing so. Still, mathematically speaking, this seemed the best percentage of being successful.

Nancy returned with the milk. "Here ya go, kid. Mom says it's on the house."

I turned a red-eyed, teary face up to her and said, "Thank you. That's very nice of you. Please tell your mommy thanks too. I hope you didn't get in trouble because of me."

She started to reach out to me but thought better of it. "No problem, kid."

She left, and I sipped my milk for a little while. I left, pretending to feel much better, and I waved good-bye as I boldly walked out. I noticed a tall woman with short blonde hair. She was watching me from a park across the street. I waved, and she waved back. *Change of watch?* I thought.

I had gone only a short distance when I sensed some people in an alley, thinking about me. I reached out and was mentally surprised. The mayor had hired them to rough me up a little—not really harm me but bloody my nose and kick me around a bit to scare me as much as possible. I stopped and looked across the street, taking my time to think about this new option. I could easily take all four of them, even though they were bigger and stronger.

When I was younger, and the bullies would pick on me, I would simply use my telekinetic ability to hold them in place. I hit one once, kicked him right in the privates, and my extreme empathy caused me to buckle over in pain; I wouldn't do that again, but I could hold all of them. It would take a lot of energy, and I would be nearly helpless afterward, but I could stop this before it started. No, that would be a mistake, as it would quickly get around town. Everyone would be afraid of me. I had seen enough TV to know what people think when something happens that they cannot explain. I wondered if these people would stone me to death because they thought I was a warlock or something equally as stupid.

Okay, so fighting back with my mind was not an option. I could make sure that my navy babysitter across the street knew what was going to happen, and she could stop them, but then I would be in the admiral's debt—not a good idea and completely contrary to my plan. I could avoid them all day, but that would also show that I had abilities. I could take a beating from these guys. They weren't really going to harm me too badly, and I could heal myself later. Being small and intelligent, I'm used to taking beatings from the bigger kids. Besides, I could cut down the pain by temporarily shutting down the senses that go to that part of my brain. I learned that trick while teaching myself to heal others. If I did this, they could beat on me, and I could fight back and make a good show of it. I would lose, of course, but that would work right into my plan by increasing the sympathy of the townspeople. I was afraid; who wouldn't be? Deciding to take a beating is not an easy thing to do, but I walked toward the alley and the next store.

As I drew even with the alley, a big hand reached out and pulled me in. They started in right away. I fought back and did fairly well, considering they were much bigger. They said things like, "Sissy! Little boy likes to wear earrings," and "We don't want you here. Get out now!" They really showed a total lack of imagination; I was somewhat disappointed. I was kicked in the head at one point, but I rolled with it. The biggest guy said, "Not in the head, stupid. You want to ..." Then he looked at me and changed it from "kill him" to "hurt your foot or something?" The last thing he wanted was for me to know this was a setup.

When they were finished and took off, I was on the ground, bleeding from my nose, and I had a cut to my face just above my right eye. Someone had stepped on my hand, and I had a gash in my knee, because I had fallen on a piece of glass during the struggle. I was hurting from a couple dozen hits that were sure to bruise up nicely. Not good enough, though. I needed a shocker. I used my abilities to open small vessels in my right eye and deep in my right ear and make that cut above my eye bleed like a river. Head wounds always bleed excessively. My knee was already bleeding badly, so I left it alone.

I slowly stood up and limped back out to the sidewalk. My babysitter saw me and quickly got up and started my way, but I motioned for her to stay back. She was good and did as requested, but I could see she wasn't happy. I started back toward the inn. Everyone who saw me wanted badly to help me, but I said, "Please leave me alone." I must have said that a hundred times before I reached the inn. When I got there, I walked out to the beach and sat down in the saltwater that was about six inches deep. Tears were mingled with the blood, and I know I left a bloody trail all the way to the water. Becky saw me heading to the water, bleeding, with people following me at a distance. I could hear her scream, but I was concentrating on what was going on with everyone else. Mrs. Crain and Carroll were out of the inn in less than a second. They were covered with flour from baking, but as soon as she saw the blood, Mrs. Crain told Carroll to run and get the doctor.

Mrs. Crain ran to me, paying no attention to the water, and nearly fainted when she got a good look at my face. By this time, the bleeding had covered half of my right side and soaked most of my shirt and pants. It was only about a quarter cup, but spread that much red paint on a ten-year-old kid, and you can cover him completely. I must have looked like I was bleeding to death. As soon as she got there, I turned the sensors up enough to be in a lot of pain so that I would cry properly. Man, that hurt! I forgot about saltwater getting in the cuts. Ouch!

She got down on my level and asked, "Freddy, can you hear me?"

I looked up, tears just pouring down my face, mixing with the blood, and I started shaking. I said, "Mommy?" and then shut my body down.

✦

"Now, that's more like it."

Everything went black.

"Master?"

"Taking a beating just to ensure his plan. Now that's more like the warriors we met in battle. Brave, willing to sacrifice themselves, capable of reacting quickly and decisively."

"And that's to be admired?"

Gray looked closely into Green's face and smiled. "We do the same every day to protect your miserable green hide. Do you think our freedoms come cheaply?"

"No, master."

"What with the undead war on the Northern Ice Gate and the rebellions on Black Patch, they cost Gray lives every day. Continue!"

CHAPTER 6

✦ ✦ ✦

MAKING THEM SEE

Passing out was a gimmick I used on my nanny once. Shut down the body, and it looks just like you passed out. My saying "Mommy" did the trick. It kicked in Mrs. Crain's motherly instincts, and she picked me up and carried me into the inn, giving everyone who had gathered a look of total disgust. She took me to my room and sat me down in the tub. She turned on the water and started cleaning me, all the time talking slowly to me, trying to assure me that everything would be all right. When she had finished cleaning me, she picked me up, covered me with a large towel, and held me in her arms in a rocking chair. I was still bleeding, and she was becoming a mess.

Becky, Johnny, and Annabelle looked on in shock that someone from their town would do this. Annabelle was crying and asked, "Is he going to die?"

Mrs. Crain said, "I hope not, dear."

Carroll came running in with the doctor. The cut on my forehead required four stitches, and I needed six stitches in my knee. What worried the doctor most was the bleeding from my ear and eye. It had stopped, but she couldn't find any external reason for it, which meant there was an internal reason. I turned my body back on and woke up as they were stitching up my knee. The doctor appeared to be a very friendly but "no nonsense" black woman. I could feel the intelligence almost radiating from her. She was probably the most intelligent person in the town, and her dark eyes held concern and empathy. Her thick, smooth hair hung down her back in a tight braid. She was beautiful.

I said, "Ouch!"

That startled everyone. The doctor looked up and smiled. "The dead arises! Hello, I'm Dr. Karen Jenson. I apologize for the pain I'm causing you, but you were out cold, so I saw no reason for giving you any anesthetic at the time."

I flinched at every stitch but asked, "How long was I out?"

"Oh, for about thirty minutes or so," the doctor said as she tied off the last stitch. "How do you feel?"

"I feel like I was beaten to death by four big boys in an alley." I looked at Mrs. Crain and saw my blood all over her. She also had a burn on her arm from setting a pan of hot cooking oil down a little too quickly while trying to get to me. I pretended to panic, and with tears in my eye I asked, "Are you all right, Mrs. Crain? You're bleeding! Doctor, she needs help too."

Mrs. Crain hugged me, saying, "No, dear, don't worry. I'm okay." She handed me over to Carroll and said, "Get him into some clean clothes while I clean myself up. Bring him downstairs when you're done."

Carroll washed me up a little more before putting me into some fresh clothes. I was a little embarrassed about having a twelve-year old dress me, but what could I do? She was just like a mother, taking care of a child who had fallen down. She talked to me in soothing tones and let me know everything would be all right, just like her mother had done earlier.

While Carroll was taking care of me, the doctor told everyone that she did not want me going back to sleep for the next six or so hours—she believed that I had a mild concussion. When she was sure that everyone understood her instructions, she picked up her equipment and left. I watched her mind, and she was furious about what the boys had done to me. I thought that the mayor had better stay clear of that lady for a while.

Carroll brought me downstairs and told the rest of the kids to keep me company. They were to be careful, as I could not go out or play rough for a few days. I felt relief come over me and looked around for the source. I saw the doctor outside, talking to the navy woman, who seemed very relieved to hear that I was going to live. I got up and walked to the door. She saw me, and I motioned for the navy woman to come over.

"How you feeling, kid?" she asked.

"Better, babysitter." This got a laugh from the other kids. "Next time, do me a favor—save me before the beating, please."

"I'll do my best."

"Thanks. I have a feeling your best is much better than most people's."

She smiled. "I have a message for you from Admiral Bates. He'd like to see you tomorrow morning. He'll send a car around, if that's all right with you—say, ten o'clock?"

"Tell him that's good for me and that I'm looking forward to it."

Looking around, she added, "This town is not acting right. Normally, the people here are really friendly. I don't understand it." Then she said, "Tomorrow."

I went back inside. Johnny was having a hard time sitting

down. I asked him why he'd gotten another spanking. He looked surprised but said, "I messed up on my chores. Want to play a card game?" When he said this, I noticed that Annabelle started to pout.

I answered, motioning toward Annabelle, "Only if everyone can play."

Becky smiled and asked, "Annabelle, where are the Old Maid cards?" Annabelle laughed and ran from the room to find them. Becky looked at me and said in an analyzing tone, "You care a lot about how others feel. You were worried about the blood on my mom, with little thought about yourself. You care about how my brother feels, and you care that Annabelle is happy, because you included her in the card game. You have not said a word about wanting revenge for the way the townspeople—and especially the boys who beat you up—have treated you, yet I bet you have the ability to harm them. I saw you talking with that navy woman. She's been watching you like you're someone very important." She had obviously been analyzing things for a while. I was beginning to like this girl.

Annabelle returned with the cards, happy and ready to play. We sat around the coffee table and played until we were called in for dinner. Becky never took her eyes off me, and I'm sure she caught me cheating so that Annabelle could win. When she did, I smiled and winked at her. She smiled back. Most of the time, I was not paying much attention to the card game. I needed to get on with the next part of my plan, so every once in a while, I let a few tears fall.

Dinner was wonderful, but I was still working my plan, so ate hardly anything and would shed a tear every now and then. I told Mrs. Crain, "The food is great, but I'm just not hungry right now."

Annabelle asked the needed question: "Mommy, why is

everyone treating Freddy so bad? I'd cry too if they treated me like that."

Mrs. Crain said, "I'm not sure, baby, but I bet the mayor has something to do with it."

Carroll said, "I asked some people. They said they were trying to make him leave town. They don't want anyone using that property, not even one little boy."

I looked at her with surprise and asked, "Why?"

"The town has had some bad problems with the army and wants to be left alone."

I pretended rising panic. "They don't understand. I have no choice. I don't want to be forced to live alone, way out there."

Mrs. Crain touched my arm to calm me down. "What do you mean, you have no choice, dear?"

"I'm …" I hesitated, wanting them to draw it out of me.

"You're what, dear?" Mrs. Crain gently asked.

I could feel the anticipation and fear start to form in her mind about why the government would force a little boy to live in the woods, away from everyone. I figured I had better answer before she drew the wrong conclusion.

"Because I'm intelligent."

Everyone relaxed, and Mrs. Crain said, "I can see that, dear."

"No, you don't understand." I looked directly into her eyes and said, "My IQ is so high that they can't measure it. I have four doctorate degrees and a dozen master's degrees. I have invented things that are making me a lot of money. I can build almost anything. When I went to Washington, DC, they found out I can heal people." I reached out and touched her arm where she had burned herself earlier. The red was gone instantly and the pain with it.

"My goodness!" said Mrs. Crain. Everyone started talking at once except Becky. She just smiled. Mrs. Crain said, "That's very good, dear, and thank you very, very much, but why don't you heal yourself?"

"I can't," I lied. "I can just barely do the little I did for you. It takes a lot of strength that I just don't have. Please don't tell anyone … please."

"Dear, being intelligent and having this wonderful ability is no reason to send a little boy into the wilds by himself. And yes, people should know, and in a little town like this, it will get around anyway, so I won't make that promise."

I looked embarrassed. "Mrs. Crain, the government knows that I am still growing. I'm inventing things that they don't understand, and they don't want me doing it in Washington, DC, or where other governments can find out just how smart I am, but I can't stop. I love inventing things. They wanted me to invent things for them, but I said no. I don't want to invent things that hurt people."

Mrs. Crain said, "But that's good, dear."

With a little indignation, I added, "The people in the government weren't happy about my decision. They drew the wrong conclusion. The politicians do not like that idea one bit. Because I refuse to build what they want and do what they want, it makes me a possible national security problem. They can't just kill me to get rid of the problem, because they might need me someday. My little healing ability can do wonders when used around the heart or liver, and I healed someone with enough power to get them to agree that I was useful to them, They decided that putting me out here keeps me under the eye of our government, yet keeps me out of trouble and hidden away from other countries. The choice was given to me: live out here or have an accident." The gasps from everyone broke my train of thought for a second, but then I said, "Now the whole town is against me too. I've never harmed anyone, so why do people hate me?"

"Oh dear, it does look like you're between a rock and a hard place. I'm so sorry."

"I don't hate you," Becky said, and I smiled at her.

✦

"Interesting."

Everything went black.

"What now, master?"

One of the Gray's tentacles reached out and slammed into the Green's head, knocking the Green away from the vat. *"Don't you ever use that tone of voice with me! Ever!"*

I was drifting down in the gel-like substance of the vat, and the Green quickly reinserted its tentacles to hold me very gently. The Green asked sincerely, "Master, if this one dies due to your interference with my process, how long will you live?"

"You wouldn't dare!"

"Master, this vat is shielded in such a way that it keeps his energy drained to a point that he cannot use his mental abilities. I am holding him in the center to ensure that he does not touch the sides or bottom. If he does touch the shielding, his energy will be drained completely in a single count. He will instantly die. You nearly made me kill him just now."

I could plainly see the fear in the Gray's eyes.

"Someone would be dispatched, and I would not live very long, Green, not very long. Why is that light blinking?"

"Master, it is a warning light and alarm. The boy was only a fraction of a drop from touching the left side. We will have company very soon."

"Continue when you are ready. We must have something to report when they arrive."

CHAPTER 7

✦ ✦ ✦

PLAN B

"It's not your fault," I told the people at the table. "You've been very kind to me, all of you, and I appreciate it very much. The town has ruined everything, but I have a way out, a Plan B that I'm going to have to fall back on. It's guaranteed to be successful, but I was hoping not to have to use it, because it goes heavily against my not wanting to be involved with the government."

Everyone was quiet for a little while, and then Mrs. Crain asked, "What does your Plan B entail, dear?"

I looked up at her and said, "Nothing hard. A general from the army called me up just before I came out here. He said he'd trade me workers, materials, and anything I wanted if I would do him a favor. He seemed very nice to me and quite upset with this town—he said they were a bunch of ... pardon the expression, 'hick fools.' He told me they would hate me here because I'm different and that they would do everything they could to make my life miserable."

"That's not true, dear."

I looked at her with wide eyes and said, "Other than this family and a nice lady named Nancy at the diner and her mom, the general hit the nail right on the head, as far as I can see."

Annabelle said, "Aunt Betty and Cousin Nancy."

Her mom smiled and looked at me. "Family."

Carroll said, "I can see his point, Mom. I think the mayor just played right into the general's hands. Freddy, what did the general want from you?"

"Oh, nothing much—something I can easily give him but that will cost me hardly anything at all. It really seems like the best way to go, considering the circumstances. I'll call him tomorrow."

Mrs. Crain looked worried now. "Sweetheart, this is very important. What did he want?"

"He wants ten square miles of land on my northern border to set up a permanent compound. Since my land borders this town, I would say that's right at the backside of the last street in the south part of town. When I asked him why, he said he had some undesirables that the town near the base begged him to transfer. He needs a new town to keep them in, about two hundred of them."

Mrs. Crain nearly fainted, and I could see the look of terror on the kids' faces. I knew this information was about to explode though the town, so I needed a little insurance. "I don't see what all the fuss is about. The land reverts back to the army's use if I leave or get killed anyway. That almost happened today."

Mrs. Crain turned white. She got up and told Carroll to please watch the younger kids and clean up the dishes because she had to go somewhere right away. Before she left, she asked, "Freddy, why are you going to see the admiral tomorrow?"

"Oh, I'm supposed to check in with him. He's having me watched to ensure I don't try to leave. I'm sure the president, or Congress, or the FBI ordered him to make sure that I stay here or die, one or the other."

She looked outside at the woman who had been watching the house for days. I got up and came to her. "Haven't you noticed that the navy SEALs—trained killers—have been watching me since I arrived?"

"Oh dear, she can't want you dead."

"It's like I said, ma'am; either way is all right with them. They'd prefer me alive because I can be useful to them, but dead will work too. You notice she never tried to help when I was being beaten up, even though she was right across the street. She could have easily stopped it, but that's not what she was ordered to do."

"That's cold-blooded," said Carroll as she walked up next to us.

"Don't worry about the kids, Mrs. Crain," I said. "She doesn't have orders about them. She'd never harm anyone unless she was ordered to do so. She'd probably protect them with her life as long as it didn't interfere with her orders regarding me. I know her kind. She can really be nice, but she'll do her job with perfection."

Mrs. Crain bent down and looked at me with tears in her eyes. Then she straightened up and left. Carroll immediately took over, and the kids listened to her without issue. She let me help with the cleanup, as she wanted to keep an eye on me like the doctor said to do. This made me very happy. Becky quietly helped and watched me very closely. She noticed I was happy with helping, and this made her smile even more.

✦

The Gray said, "Hold."

Everything went black.

"Master?"

"So, their military is intelligent enough to know that

the boy is dangerous. No wonder we had such a hard time getting to him. He was protected by far more than their president."

"Yes, master."

"Where is the lady going? She has the boy and her children to watch after."

"Just a moment, master." The Green's expression went blank for a second. "We scanned that entire family. As you know, most humans are weak-minded, without the mental protections this boy has. They are evolving and developing mental protections that will stop our ability to grab information. However, this family has none, so we copied and recorded their memories and let them go. The Body System has everything on file. Would you like me to play the female's memories back for you?"

"Absolutely!"

CHAPTER 8

✦ ✦ ✦

TOWN MEETING

On the overhead screen, I watched as the scene fell into place. I smiled, as I had several ideas on how to improve on this mental copying ability. And their screen was not the best. Still, information flowed across the viewer, setting up the information from Mrs. Crain.

A town meeting was called right after the doctor left the Crain's bed-and-breakfast. The doctor went straight to the police and spread the news that the mayor's little game had possibly gotten Freddy killed. She told the police that if Freddy died from a concussion, she would personally call the state police and have the mayor and the boys arrested for premeditated murder.

Posters went up and the word was passed: "Town Meeting Tonight—7:00 p.m."

Mrs. Crain was very upset when she walked into the town meeting. The old wooden church was packed. People stood and sat wherever they could. Children were sitting up in the rafters and on their fathers' shoulders to get a good view. The meeting had just started when Mrs. Crain arrived, and already the mayor had humbly stepped down. He and the boys were not feeling so well, once his wife and the boys' mothers learned what they'd done. In fact, the mayor and the boys were grounded permanently, and all of them were sitting very quietly on the hard wooden benches in the back.

When Mrs. Crain reached the town hall, she went right to the front. Devin Miles, owner of the lumberyard and hardware store, as deputy mayor, had stepped up as acting mayor until they could elect a new one. Devin Miles was a good, kind man. He was in his early forties, but was already showing some signs of age. Tall and extremely well muscled from hard work, he looked more like an old-fashioned blacksmith. His face was clean-shaven, and he had brown eyes that smiled even when he frowned.

When Alice Crain walked in, Devin motioned for quiet and then motioned her forward. He filled her in on what had happened during the day and at the beginning of the meeting. She asked for the floor, so Devin introduced her and stepped back.

Mrs. Crain addressed the entire town. "Friends, I have good news and very bad news. Freddy … Dr. Anderson … looks like he'll be all right." That got cheers from everyone and sighs of relief from the boys in the back. Devin motioned for everyone to quiet down. Mrs. Crain continued. "The boy has problems—life-or-death problems—and doesn't need us compounding the issue. And the general is on his way back here."

It got deadly quiet. Devin Miles stood up and said, "You'll need to explain that one. We've been working hard to ensure that degenerate stays out. My goodness, Alice, that's what this is all about."

"Well, let me tell you what you've just done. A little boy, an orphaned boy, all alone in the world, has caught the attention of our wonderful government. It turns out that he's extremely intelligent, so much so that he can do minor healing using his mind. I burned myself with hot grease today, and he healed it with a touch."

The whole town started talking at once. Devin stood up and motioned for everyone to be quiet again. When the group calmed down, Alice continued. "He begged me not to tell anyone this, as he has been persecuted for it ever since the government found out about his abilities. I believe he thinks we'll regard him as a freak—or worse, that we'll try to kill him like we almost did today." Most of the group turned to stare at the boys again.

"Just like any of us would, he refused to work for the government and build things that harm others," Mrs. Crain said. "This child would never harm anyone who wasn't directly trying to kill him." Everyone glared at the boys again. "The government thinks he's a threat to national security. First, because he can do this healing with his mind; second, because he can build and invent things that no one else can; third, because he won't work for them; and fourth, because they can't afford for him to fall into the hands of some foreign country."

Devin said, "Man, that's a lot to put on a child and an orphan at that."

Mrs. Crain turned to him and said, "That's not all." Turning back to the group, she continued. "He was given this land and a choice—live here or have an 'accident.'" The entire town was shocked into total silence.

Betty stood up and said, "That sounds like something you get from TV. How can you be sure of this?"

"Let's look at the facts," Mrs. Crain replied. "One, the government gave him the land. I saw the grant on his desk in his room. People and government agencies have been trying to get this land for decades and haven't come close. Now, all of a sudden, it's his, free and clear and tax-free to boot. Two, it was important enough that the army was thrown out to make room for him. The general would never have let this happen if he had any choice, so it had to come from way up—say, presidential level. Three, the boy was sent here and has to go to an appointment with the admiral tomorrow. He said he has to check in. And four, a different navy WAVE has watched my hotel for three days. It seems they were waiting for Freddy. The only time they left was to follow Freddy through town today."

One of the boys in the back, the one who had kicked Freddy in the head, stood up and said, "I saw her. She watched us beat up on him, and she did nothing." He was happy to get some of the townspeople upset with someone other than him.

"Freddy told me he was being watched to ensure his compliance with staying here."

A marine stood up. "What does this navy WAVE look like?"

"She's about six feet tall, with blonde hair cut real short," Alice answered. "She looks like she could uproot a tree with her bare hands, yet it was several days before we even noticed her. She's very good at not being seen."

The marine nodded. "I know her. I've seen her on the base, and everyone is saying that her team is doing a babysitting job now."

"So she's watching him. So what?" asked a girl in the back.

The marine answered, "This is a team of the navy's best SEALs—they're specialists. They don't talk to the rest of us. We think they were responsible for the notes attached to the marine commandant's pillow said that read, 'You're dead.' We could never prove it, but once a week, the note showed up, even with live guards and our best Green Berets trying to catch them. They go to bars just to get exercise by beating up on the marines and the army. We know they're the ones responsible for stealing the general's clothes on his last outing, but we can't prove it. No one can; they're just too good. When we see them coming, we walk on the other side of the street out of complete fear."

Devin stood up. "Do you know what their specialty is?"

"Yes sir, I do. Although there's no proof, of course, I heard our captain say that they're assassins and to keep the men away from them. If these SEALs are watching the boy, then he's extremely important. If their orders are to keep him here or kill him, then he has no choice. He stays here, or he's as good as dead."

It took ten minutes to calm down the town. Devin finally gave the floor back to Alice.

"This is an awful lot to be placed on a child's head," she said, "and what did we do to help the poor boy? We practically threw him out of every store in town and then tried to kill him! But now for the bad news."

Devin whispered, "That wasn't that bad news?"

"The boy came here with a plan. He was going to stay away from the government as much as possible and get all his supplies and help from this town. We said no, so he's going to implement what he calls Plan B tomorrow. He says that Plan B will be much easier for him, and it will cost him nothing. I bet he's wondering why he didn't do it in the first place."

"I hate to ask," Devin interrupted, "but do you have any idea what Plan B is?"

"Sure, I do. He trusts me and told me all about Plan B. You see, the nice general has offered to get him anything he wants if he'll grant the general ten square miles of land right next to our town. Seems the general wants to build a compound to house his 'most undesirables'—all two hundred of them. To top that off, you almost killed Freddy today, and the land reverts back to the government's use if he dies. You nearly gave the land to the general, and now

Dr. Anderson is going to make the only choice left to him and give it to the general for you."

It took a moment for the shock to wear off, and then a voice could be heard saying quite loudly, "David McConnelly, it's the couch for you tonight." That broke the tension and the whole group laughed.

Alice sat down, and Devin stood up. "People, calm down, please. It's very clear that we really messed this one up badly. As my mom always said, 'Hurting people never does a person good,' so how can we fix this situation?" He looked back at Alice and asked, "Or can we?"

"The boy's the nicest, kindest boy I've ever met," Alice answered. "I think we can change his mind, but it's going to take some planning, and it has to be done tonight. Tomorrow, he sees the admiral. I'm sure that Betty, Nancy, and I can talk him into not calling the general right away, but we need to get him to think about giving us a chance before he leaves for the base."

The meeting went on from there.

✦

"Hold!"

Everything went black.

"Yes, master," the Green said as he flinched.

"The mayor made a bad mistake. Why is he still alive?"

"Master, I do not think the humans kill as indiscriminately as the Grays do."

"Be very careful where you're going with this, Green."

"Yes, master. We have found that the humans allow for mistakes, both in their lives and in their planning. Thus, they learn from their mistakes and try not to make the same one again. Have you not noticed that the fighting is becoming harder with every battle?"

"Yes."

"They try something. If it does not work, they try something else, but they never give up. They don't kill the one with the bad experience. They learn from him and try again. They will continue to try until they find something that works, and use it until we develop a defense, and then try something else. With this type of planning, they could win this war eventually, if they are not totally destroyed. Humans are very stubborn. They would make a great ally."

"Yes, tricky race to fight against, as we are finding out the hard way. But that does not get us any closer to finding out why and how they destroyed our mother ship. Continue."

CHAPTER 9

✦ ✦ ✦

CHANGE OF MINDS

Back at the house, we had just finished cleaning up the kitchen and settled down to watch TV. Becky was still watching me, and it was making me a little nervous. Her emotions were very strong. She was falling in love with me. It didn't help that she was very pretty, really sweet, and slightly empathic. I felt flattered and happy that someone cared about me, and her emotions were affecting me, so I admit that I was a little taken by her too. I smiled at her and sat down. She sat next to me. We talked a lot, and I learned that she was very smart for her age. I let her know that I liked her being intelligent, and we talked about her studies and math and stuff for over an hour before her mother came in.

Mrs. Crain had brought Nancy and Nancy's mom with her. "Freddy, you know my niece Nancy?"

"Yes." I smiled and put my hand out. "Hello again. This must be your mother. I have you to thank for the kindness today, don't I?"

"It was nothing, Dr. Anderson. My pleasure."

"Please call me Freddy."

"Thank you, Freddy, and you can call me Betty."

Betty was a short woman who looked just like I pictured a cook would look—short and round with permanently rosy cheeks from standing over a hot stove all day. Her head was covered in permed, short brown curls. She had a nice, easy-to-give smile and a pleasant, motherly voice with a big-city accent. She sounded like she came from New York.

I hadn't realized it until Mrs. Crain and Betty looked at my left hand and smiled—I was holding Becky's hand. I looked at Mrs. Crain and said, "Becky and I have been talking about her studies. She's very intelligent and has some great ideas."

Mrs. Crain smiled and patted Becky's head. "Yes, she is intelligent. Freddy, if it's all right, we need to talk with you."

I looked at Becky, and she smiled and nodded her head. We all sat down at the kitchen table. Mrs. Crain indicated that Becky should sit directly across from me, but I focused my attention away from Becky. I had an idea what this was going to be about, and I did not need to mess it up because I had a case of puppy love.

Mrs. Crain said, "Freddy, I was just at a town meeting."

I visibly stiffened. They all saw this, and Nancy placed a hand on my shoulder, saying, "It's all right, dear."

Mrs. Crain continued. "The mayor, who ordered your beating and also ordered the rest of the town to shun you, has been dismissed and is being punished, along with the four boys who attacked you."

"Punished?"

"Yes, Freddy, the rest of the town is very sad about what this man did. The town is willing to fully support you in any way you need."

I looked at her and settled back in the chair. "What made them change their minds? Please don't tell me it was this guy's fault entirely. I now know how stubborn the town can be. These people will do what they want. What really caused them to change their minds so quickly?"

Betty looked hard at me and said, "Okay, here's the deal. First, you're right about us not putting up with much, but we were fooled for a little while, and the old mayor was a smooth talker."

"He didn't fool you," I said.

Nancy touched my arm. "Mom doesn't take orders from anyone. She would rather spit at a rattlesnake."

I smiled.

Betty continued. "When the town saw what had happened, the support for that fool died right there. He resigned, and the deputy mayor took charge. The new mayor and the town were about to decide what to do next when Alice showed up and told us everything."

"Everything?"

"Yes, sweetheart. We know you can do some minor healing. We think it's great."

"Really?" I purposefully started crying, and Becky came around to hold my hand. I don't know why, but that actually helped. It must have showed, as her mom encouraged her to continue.

"Sweetheart, half the people in the town are from families that use old-style remedies for healing," Alice explained. "Almost every family here had a granddaddy or great-grandmother who could heal or move small objects or something. You should have heard the tales that went around the room. Everyone is thinking you're some long-lost relative come back to us, and we don't treat our own that way. I know it's a little late, but the town is yours."

"That's not all that changed their minds, is it?" I felt it coming, and I had to prepare my body for it. I hated using Becky this way, but she was the best choice.

Betty looked at Alice, saying, "You said he was smart." She looked back at me and said, "When they found out that the general had contacted you and that you were going to give him some of your land, the town nearly freaked out."

"I don't understand … why would they care? I would think that the revenue would be good for the town."

Betty frowned. "You don't know, do you?"

"Know what?"

"The general hates us," Betty said simply. "The two hundred men he wants to send over here are people who would tear this town apart and hurt everyone in it, just for fun. They are a bunch of misfits and troublemakers who would destroy everyone and everything in this town."

As she spoke, I slowly increased my look of shock. I looked at Becky and saw that she was crying. "These people … would they harm Becky?" I asked Betty.

She said, "Yes, they would and everyone else at this table."

I said, "I wouldn't allow that to happen. I can't do something that would harm her—I mean, the town. I won't do it."

"That's good news, dear," Mrs. Crain said, "but I think too much has happened to you today. It's time for bed. Girls, you too."

With that, Mrs. Crain took me upstairs and placed me in bed. I then heard her tell Carroll to watch the kids. She had to let the town know.

When they left, I listened to their minds just a little. "That boy has a crush on your daughter, Alice."

"Yes, I see that."

"I think your Becky helped make a hard job a lot easier."

"I don't think it was just Becky. That boy would never knowingly do anything to harm someone. It's just as we thought; we only needed to make him aware of what he was doing." Then she added, "Of course, his liking my Becky didn't hurt matters any."

After that, I fell asleep.

✦

The big Gray said, "I don't understand."

Everything went black.

"Master?"

"I don't understand what 'it's the couch for you tonight' means."

"Master, there are a lot of things that we don't understand about these creatures, but I believe it is a mating ritual of some sort."

"But the man was being punished!"

"Perhaps mating is a punishment in this species. Look at the Conacor—the eggs are planted within the male and when they hatch, he is eaten alive. Perhaps it is the same with these creatures."

"Perhaps. Continue."

CHAPTER 10

✦ ✦ ✦

FRIENDS

I awoke early the next morning and went outside. The navy woman was out there, hidden but extremely alert. She didn't bat an eye when I walked right up to her hiding place. She stood up, waiting for me to speak.

"Good morning, miss."

"Good morning, Dr. Anderson." She didn't offer a name.

"Did you sleep okay?" I asked.

"I slept yesterday, Dr. Anderson. That was a smooth move, letting the boys beat you up. The town is on your side now." She smiled.

"I'm glad you appreciated it. It hurt a lot more than I thought it would."

"Still, it showed a lot of guts."

"Thank you. I'm sorry, but I had to allude to your team being my watchdog. I'm afraid the townspeople got the idea that you have orders to kill me if I try to leave." This did not seem to bring out any emotions and helped to confirm that I was correct in my guess. "I do have a concern—I would like to know exactly what your orders are."

"Why, Dr. Anderson?"

"I need to know that the people in the house where I'm staying are safe from possible harm."

"If harm comes to them, it will not be from us, sir, unless someone attacks you again. New orders are that anyone attacking you is fair game. If you want us to take care of the four who did this"—she motioned to my head—"we'd be more than happy to do so."

"No, just tell me what your full orders are, please."

"Watch and protect. Give you any assistance you need, whether you want it or not, and ensure that you stay put. The admiral is not willing to report to the president that we let the townspeople beat you to death and did nothing. He was very upset."

"Interesting. Very well, thank you. Is my appointment still on?"

"Yes, sir. A car will come for you at 9:45 a.m. Are you going to call the general?"

"Everyone's been talking, haven't they?"

"Yes, sir."

"No, I won't call him, now that I know that could cause harm to the people inside the house."

"Good. The general would chew this town up and spit it out, just for fun. No one wants that. We like this town and the Crain family. They are good people."

"I don't want it either. I'll see you for the ride into base then?"

"Next watch will be here, sir."

I turned and headed back inside, where Mrs. Crain and Carroll were waiting for me.

"May I ask what that was all about?" said Mrs. Crain.

"I couldn't sleep last night, worrying about what their orders were," I said. "I was worried that they were less than friendly toward the townspeople and, therefore, this household. I had to find out."

Mrs. Crain said, "That was very brave of you. Let's get you something to eat. The other kids will be up soon."

As I sat at the table and watched her fix breakfast, Carroll asked, "What did she tell you?"

I explained what the navy woman had told me and then added, "She was real concerned about the town."

"What? Are you sure?"

"Yes. She did not want me calling the general, as she said it would hurt the town. Apparently, her team likes you guys. She also likes your family and promised that her team would never harm you. She really is very nice; she just has a bad job."

Mrs. Crain asked, "She's not here to kill you?"

"Not if I don't try to leave, and I'm not going to try." I could see Mrs. Crain was thinking hard on this information, and then a light seemed to go off in her head. Her face scrunched up in determination, but there was a little fear deep in her eyes.

"Carroll, please set another place at the table," Mrs. Crain said and then went outside. I listened with my mind as she walked up to the woman who was sitting on the bench. "Hello," said Mrs. Crain.

"Hello. How can I help you, ma'am?"

"You're here to watch over my guest and protect him?"

"Yes."

"Don't you think you could do a better job if you were inside?"

"Yes."

"Then please join us for breakfast."

"I'd be delighted, but that would be against orders."

After talking with her for a while, Mrs. Crain returned to the house alone.

When the younger kids came down for breakfast, everyone seemed highly excited, so I asked them why.

Becky said, "Daddy comes home today!"

"I'm sorry; I don't even know what you father does."

"He's a fisherman," said Carroll. "I hope he had a good catch."

Annabelle said, "If he did, maybe he'll stay home a little longer this time."

Mrs. Crain said, "Don't count on it, dears. It's spring, and the salmon are running. He'll be out most of the time, I expect."

Becky said, pouting, "If Daddy had been here when you came, he'd have put a stop to this town nonsense right from the start. He doesn't put up with nonsense. He'd tell that navy lady where to go too."

Mrs. Crain winked, letting me know not to worry. I'd hate to think Captain Crain would try to straighten everything out and cause my babysitter to have to hurt him.

After breakfast the kids went out to do their chores. I was going to help Becky, but Betty came over to ask if I'd please come over to her diner. Some people wanted to talk with me. It was only eight fifteen, so I said, "Okay, as long as I'm back by nine forty-five. I have an appointment with the admiral at ten o'clock."

We walked to Betty's Diner, and everyone we saw said hello to me and welcomed me to the town. The store owners came out to tell me that I could have anything I needed. Guy Thompson came out and said he had a couple of people who would love to take me camping and to explore my new home. He offered to loan us a couple of horses for our explorations.

When we reached the diner, the whole place was full. I pulled back, but Betty reassured me that it would be all right and that no one would harm me. Nancy came over to me with a big glass of cold milk and said, "They all want to talk to you." I spent the next hour or so answering questions about my mother and father, my genealogy, my life, and being in Washington, DC. At one point, the four boys and the ex-mayor came in and apologized. I shook hands with each one, forgave them, and said I would like to be their friend.

When it was time to go back to the inn, I felt very much at home.

✦

Green pulled out the tentacle. Everything went blank. "That's strange."

"What's strange?" asked Gray.

"There is a feeling at this point. A small feeling, but something I've never seen in any species besides ours."

"Hatred? Determination? Spite?"

"No, master. Love."

"Love? Oh, for goodness sake. Pay no attention to any of that trash, and continue."

"Yes, master."

CHAPTER 11

✦ ✦ ✦

ADMIRAL BATES

Nancy walked me to the inn, where the car was waiting. I went to my room to get something and then came back downstairs and got in the car. The kids and half the town were watching. The driver was one of the navy SEALs. I asked her if any of them had gotten into trouble for what happened to me yesterday.

She looked at me in the rearview mirror and said, "We can handle it. Not to worry." She showed no emotion, but I could feel her feelings—she liked me. Of course, liking me and not killing me were two different things.

The ride to the base was short but breathtaking. The road wound around a mountain and from some vistas, I could see the ocean. The base was nestled in a little valley that was nearly filled with buildings. There was a short runway and several planes on the ground. There had to be at least twenty helicopters. The driver told me that the base was a watch for weather and a radar-tracking station. I didn't interrupt her, but I had already done research on the base and knew exactly why it was located here. The planes were reconnaissance and could spot submarine activity miles away. The helicopters were for everything from rescue to assault. Normally, a captain or some lower-ranking officer ran the base, but this was the admiral's retirement tour; he had only two years to go until retirement, after a fifty-year career. When we pulled up to the gates, a guard motioned for us to stop. "So this is your babysitting job?" he said to the driver. "Change his diapers yet?"

I quickly got out of the car and started walking back toward the town. The guard laughed, but the driver got out and came after me.

"Where do you think you're going, Dr. Anderson?" she asked in a panic.

"I'm going back to town," I said loudly. "Please tell the admiral that the first person I met on the base insulted me, and I no longer wish to see him." I winked at her, knowing the guard couldn't see it.

She smiled and then put on a worried face. "He's going to be extremely pissed off at someone," she said in a loud voice.

"I hope so. I hope he busts that marine down a few notches. You just tell him that his guards don't care if the president of the United States wants me to see him, so I don't care either. I was doing this as a favor to the president. I don't have to check in with anyone."

"This could ruin the admiral's career. Please don't go."

"Look, I don't know the admiral. As far as I know, this is the way everyone here is going to treat me, including the admiral. I won't put up with it." I looked over and could plainly see the guard was getting very worried, so I poured it on. I whispered, "Quick, ask me a favor."

She looked back over her shoulder. "Please, Dr. Anderson. I'll get into trouble too. Please don't do this."

"Well, I don't want you to get into trouble so … well, okay." She looked at me strangely, as if to say, "That's it?" I winked at her again. We walked back to the car slowly.

Just before getting back into the car, I said, "I think you're right. It's much better to tell off the admiral to his face and then go back to town." I took my time getting in the car and buckling my seat belt. When we pulled away, the guard was almost white with fear.

As soon as we drove around the corner, she pulled the car over long enough to have a good laugh. She said, "I think that's the first time I've ever seen that sergeant tremble, much less turn white!"

I smiled but said, "I wasn't joking."

"I don't understand. He'll be in fear for days. You don't really need to tell the admiral."

"I was hoping I wouldn't need to. I agree with you that telling the admiral is a little much, but I don't want people thinking that I'm all bark and no bite. That's a reputation I can't afford. We took our time getting back into the car so that he'd have plenty of time to apologize, and he didn't. He's left me with no choice. I have to carry through with what I said. Are all marines that dumb?"

"No, most are very intelligent. He's an exception to the rule, what we call a 'Cat 4.' A category 4 is a person who had to get a waiver to join, due to scoring low on the entrance test. All four branches of the military feel a pinch for recruits sometimes and lower their requirements."

"I'm very glad to hear he was a bad example and not the norm."

"Tell you what; you need to save face, and I'd love to have the sergeant owe me," she said. "You don't tell the admiral, and I'll tell the sergeant that I pulled a favor and he owes me big time."

"Works for me."

We drove across the base and pulled up in front of a large white building with flags and banners and big brass ornaments. There must have been thirty or more sailors and marines in dress uniform standing at attention—sailors on one side of the walkway and marines on the other. Another marine in dress uniform opened the car door. When we climbed out, the admiral was heading toward the car. He shook my hand and welcomed me.

"Nice base, sir—very clean and neat," I said.

"Thank you, Dr. Anderson—or may I call you Freddy?"

I remembered what my father told me about seeing government officials: *"Don't introduce yourself as Freddy. Use your last name and make them do the same. Keep it professional. If you allow them to call you by your first name, and you still have to call them by their title, it gives them advantage over you."*

"I apologize if this seems a little unfriendly, Admiral Bates, but at this point, I would prefer to keep it on a professional level. I have not yet determined why I was asked to see you, other than as a courtesy to the president, and I seriously doubt that you want me to call you Jeffrey in front of your men. So unless we find a mutually agreeable relationship somewhere down the road, I would prefer that you call me Dr. Anderson."

He was very quiet as we walked into the building and went up the two flights of stairs to his office. When we entered his office, he immediately went to his chair and sat down behind a desk that had dragons carved into it. He said, "Please have a seat, Dr. Anderson."

I sat down, and a marine offered me coffee or milk. I asked for water and quickly received a glass. There was one other person in the room, leaning against the wall in the back. I almost didn't notice her. Her relaxed stance and total lack of emotions screamed deadly. On her blouse was a name tag: Lt. Susan James. The insignia on her collar told me she was a SEAL and an officer. I assumed she was in charge of the team that was watching me.

I put my hand out and said, "It's nice to meet you."

She smiled and said, "I've heard a lot about you. It's nice to actually meet you in person."

"What? The pictures your team took didn't do me justice?"

She frowned.

I turned to the admiral and said, "Thank you for your concern and for providing me with twenty-four-hour security, but I assure you it's not necessary. Please have it stopped immediately."

The admiral's eyes opened ever so slightly. "Do you know why you're here, Dr. Anderson?"

"If you mean in this room, it's because I decided to allow your person to drive me here. After all, I did promise to drop in and let you know that President Kabe says hello."

"So you met the president, then?"

"No sir, we talked over the phone for a little bit. She seemed very pleasant, but it's hard to tell what's on the mind of a politician. I had the distinct feeling she wants me watched, so that she knows I'm not going to blow up Oregon and northern California."

"After reading your stats and meeting you in person, I can see why she might feel that way, Dr. Anderson. The reason she asked you to see me is simple. She wants me to keep an eye on you and protect you. I think you can figure out the reasoning behind this, sir, considering the reaction of the town yesterday and the fact that you've been all over the media, gaining your emancipation. You are a target for child predators and kidnappers. You're inventing things that could make people rich, and just being a kid who's alone raises a lot of concerns. The president knows you are extremely intelligent, and she does not want you falling into enemy hands. She is putting her career on the line by sending what the media would see as a poor helpless child into the wilderness. If anything were to happen to that child, and the media found out, it could be very damaging, politically speaking."

I smiled and said, "Admiral, I'm not going to fall into anyone's hands unless I want to, nor am I likely to die anytime soon. The president wants me watched closely. Not because I may be kidnapped, but because I invent things that the government wants first shot at or can claim national security rights to. Please don't get me wrong; I know she's worried and has pressure from Congress and the Supreme Court to keep me from harm and watch me closely, yet at the same time, leave me alone. It'll be a good trick. I expect a satellite will watch me at times. What do you plan to do to carry out her orders?"

"I am prepared to offer you some concessions in exchange for allowing me to keep a watch on you, and I am willing to help you in any way necessary, in exchange for your cooperation and permission to enter on your land as guards and a watch."

I thought about this for a second, just to give the admiral the idea I might be interested in his proposal, and then I shook my head. "The answer is no, not at this time, Admiral, but thank you for your offer."

"Dr. Anderson ..."

I held up my hand for him to stop. "Please wait and let me finish. I don't wish to have the government watch what I do in my own home. I don't think anyone does, do you?"

"Actually, no."

"Honestly, I can do nothing about someone watching me while I'm outside my property, especially people as quiet and covert as the SEALs you've had watching me since I arrived. However, I do ask that you please don't trespass on my property. I have reasons not to allow anyone near me while I'm building my home. I plan on using inventions that I have not yet patented to build it. After my home is finished, I have plans to invent things that I don't want copied or looked at until I get them patented. I think you can understand this requirement. Watchful guards would report what satellites cannot see. It could cost me hundreds of millions of dollars if I allowed watchers, and information got out, so I'm politely asking you to leave me alone. Don't get me wrong, Admiral. I would love the company and the benefits you're alluding to, but at this time, I just can't afford it."

"This is the navy, sir, and we can keep a secret."

"Really? Then please explain to me why only one hour after you received orders regarding me, the whole town knew I was coming? Were those orders not Top Secret?"

His face became quite red and a little mad. "How did you know that?" After a minute of quiet, he calmed down. and with a determined look on his face. he said, "Yes, they were Top Secret, and I'm looking into it."

"Admiral, you have a security problem, and I can ill afford to have your problem transferred to me."

"I understand, Dr. Anderson, but the offer still stands, even without our watching you while you're at home. If you could simply let us know when you're leaving your property and when you're having visitors, I could still offer our help in return for your cooperation."

I knew what he was doing—trying to get a foot in the door—but in truth, I needed his help. Dad always told me, usually after losing an argument to Mom, "The key is not winning or losing, son. The key is getting what you want while giving up as little as possible."

I used this tactic now. "Admiral, I understand that you have a need to follow your superior's orders, and I truly would like to help you, if for no other reason than to keep the channels of communication open and create a mutually beneficial friendship. I suppose that I could possibly check in with my *babysitters* under certain conditions," I said with just a touch of disdain to let him know this did not sit well with me. I could tell from the emotions emitted that Lt. James didn't like the idea any more than I did.

"What conditions would those be, Dr. Anderson?"

"First, I need some supplies that could be alarming to simple townsfolk. I suppose it would be helpful to have a place where the supplies could be delivered until I can pick them up. Second, I may need to test some inventions, and a naval base would be a good place to do such testing. Of course, this means that you will have first view of some of my new toys, and I will need some sort of security maintained. Last, I may need potentially dangerous materials that you can get from sources I simply do not have."

His eyebrows rose on that final one, but I really did not need this; it was a bargaining chip.

"Storage space is not a problem, Dr. Anderson. I can easily find a place for some materials to be stored on occasion. I will even entertain testing your inventions, if I first understand what they're to be used for. It may be interesting to actually see some of them in use. However, I do have a problem with ordering potentially dangerous, perhaps restricted, materials for you."

"You will have veto power regarding anything I request, Admiral."

"We'll see, but I will not approve hazardous materials without knowing how and why they're to be used, and I can assure you right now, I will never approve radioactive materials. I would like to extend base privileges to you—commissary and exchange, medical and dental, and living quarters, if you wish. It has already been approved, and I can give you an ID card that will allow you access to almost everything."

"That's very nice of you, sir. Any chance they come with a price tag?"

"No, they're yours, but I would like a favor."

"Go ahead."

"You could stay on your land for extended periods of time, but I need to report monthly."

I smiled. "You have a dilemma, then. I suppose it would look fairly bad if your report was, 'Sorry, I haven't seen him lately.'"

"Yes, it would."

"You already have two opportunities to see me at home, Admiral. I don't see why you need another excuse."

"What two opportunities are you talking about, Dr. Anderson?"

"Don't you need to do monthly maintenance on the radar station?"

"Yes."

"Before the maintenance team comes out, they're supposed to let me know, correct?"

"Yes."

"Good, I have no problem showing myself when they come out, as long as a member of the SEAL team is with them."

That raised his eyebrows. "Why one of the SEAL team?"

"Security, of course. I trust they will keep the maintenance team at the radar station and off the rest of my land. They're into babysitting; they can babysit the radar team too. The other time to see me is during a neighborly visit. I would expect anyone who wishes to pay me a neighborly visit to let me know beforehand so I can clean up. I would also expect that such visits would not occur very often."

"Of course, but it's the neighborly thing to do. I may be sending a representative on the visit, as I'm not always here."

"That would be fine, as long as I know who it is. I would

love to have Lt. James visit now and then, now that we've been introduced."

The admiral looked at her and smiled. "I think that could be arranged."

"I have a cellular phone and will call you when I have visitors or if I am leaving my land. Is that acceptable?"

The admiral stood up, and so did I. "Good," he said, "it sounds like we have a workable understanding. Dr. Anderson, it has been a pleasure. The lieutenant should be able to take care of your needs from here on out."

"Thank you. It was nice meeting you, Admiral."

✦

"I'm totally lost."

Everything went black.

"Master."

"He says he does not want government involvement, yet he just invited the government into his home for visits."

"Simple, master. He must be watching them as much as they are watching him. The humans have a saying: 'Keep your friends close and your enemies closer.'"

"Yes, they have a lot of good short-ranged weapons. Fighting hand-to-hand is something they do well, considering they only have two hands. They are highly limited. Continue."

CHAPTER 12

✦ ✦ ✦

NAVY SEAL TEAM

It was eleven thirty when Lieutenant James and I left Admiral Bates's office. Once outside, the lieutenant stopped me and said, "Let's talk." She led me to a bench under the shade of a tree, and we sat down.

"You don't like being babysat do you?" she said.

"It's not a problem with being babysat as much as it's a problem with people thinking I need to be."

"I see. I would like to thank you for not telling the admiral that you saw our watch the first day."

I shook my head slowly. "Lieutenant, stop playing games with me. You've had three women watching me at all times, one in the open so that I—and the rest of the town—could see her and two hidden, using long-range cameras and infrared scopes." She said nothing, but I could feel her increased emotion. I expect some heads were going to roll.

"Very well, Dr. Anderson, where do we go from here?"

"If we can agree to be honest with each other and not play these silly political games, then we do exactly as the admiral said. If not, then all bets are off."

"Very well, the political games stop here."

"Good. You give me a phone number to contact you when I'm coming out and when I'll be having guests, but you stay off my land. You provide me with security, the storage space, and an ID card, and in return, I'll make watching me easy. For some reason, however, I sense that you would prefer a challenge of sorts. Do you think your team's talents are being wasted here, Lieutenant?"

"That's not up for discussion. You're going to comply with the admiral's requests, then? I had a feeling that you would renege."

"Right now, Lieutenant, the agreement stands. This agreement may and probably will change in the future. When it does, I will try to let you know, possibly before I change my mind."

She smiled and said, "Understood."

"One other thing, Lieutenant."

"What's that?"

"I have a list of the personnel who work on the radar station maintenance team, and none of them are female. Your entire team is female. Please ensure that when on my land, one of your team—someone I would recognize—is with the radar group at all times. I will be setting up some defenses, and if I don't see someone I recognize, then I will trigger those defenses. There are issues on this base, and someone is leaking information. I cannot afford to have those issues."

"Understood. I think the admiral will ask us to find the problem with his security. Before your conversation, it meant very little to him, but your finding out about it in just two days and then turning him down on something he wants and was ordered to get will cause him to make this his top priority."

"I would hope so," I smiled. "Did you see the color in his face change when I brought it up?"

She smiled. "Yes. I hope you don't mind, but that's one I'd like to tell my team."

"Not a problem. They need to know where we stand in order to do their jobs anyway."

"Come on, let's get lunch and then set up the rest," she said.

Lunch was in the officer's mess. It looked neat and very clean, so I had no idea why they called it a mess. After lunch, Lt. James got me an ID card and showed me the exchange and commissary facilities. Eventually, we made our way to the barracks to meet her team. They were living in an old building that they had converted into living quarters. The placed looked really nasty on the outside, but when we went inside, the change was remarkable. The paint was fresh, the floors were polished to a high shine, and everything looked like it was new. We entered through a "quarterdeck" and went into the lounge to meet the rest of the team. While I was waiting for them to "muster," I asked Lt. James, "If you fixed up the outside of this building, would someone of higher rank get jealous and take over the place?"

Her eyes opened wide as she cocked her head. "You're a veritable Sherlock Holmes, aren't you? The answer is, yes, they would, and that is exactly the reason we don't fix up the outside. It keeps the others thinking we have a bad deal, staying here."

By this time, the whole team was in the lounge. I was introduced to all twelve of them, including the lieutenant. Lt. Susan James was in charge, just as I thought. Ensign Daphne Morgan was the only other officer. She had a nice smile and seemed extremely intelligent. Gunnery Master Chief Jacquelyn Uniceson was the top enlisted person. With a shaved head and hard-muscled shoulders, she looked like a man and was built like a tank. She didn't seem to have a sense of humor.

The rest of the team were a mixture of every color and size, and all were extremely professional.

✦

"I thought you said they had no coloring."

Everything went black.

"Master, he is reminiscing about his first impressions. Interesting thing is that he does not really care where someone comes from or what race they are. He simply files the information away for later recall. Other humans had strong feelings about such things, just as we do. Still, this one thinks all are the same and should be measured on their actions, not by their religion, color, ancestry, or—strangely enough—their words."

"Green, you seem surprised. We of the Gray determine rank on prior accomplishments. Not words or shades of Gray but on deeds."

"Greens are the same way, but other colors are measured on promises that are mostly not kept."

Both said in unison, "Blues."

Gray looked around like they were in trouble and mumbled, "Continue. Quickly."

CHAPTER 13

THE CHALLENGE

After introductions, we retired to the lieutenant's office. It was a big room, so the lieutenant, the ensign, the master chief, and I were fairly comfortable.

"Dr. Anderson, I find it hard to determine just how you knew my two people were watching you from a distance. Could you enlighten us, please?"

"No."

"I see." She thought for a second. "Let me put it another way. I would like the opportunity to correct their actions, so that we will not have this issue with others. It could save their lives some day."

I thought about this for a minute, and then I reached into my pocket and pulled out my portable scanner. I turned it on and handed it to the master chief. "Lieutenant," I said, "this is one of the items that I have not yet patented. Please do not allow this information out of this room."

"Agreed."

I showed her how I could see anything within a twenty-mile range, using my scanner. I explained to her that when I saw her decoy out front, I naturally scanned for any others. I knew they had to have long-range equipment to see me from that distance. One of her girls moved with me as I crossed my room, so she could see through the walls; therefore, she used an infrared scope. The other girl lost me as I moved away from the window; therefore, I knew it was long-range equipment, possibly photography or optical. "I'm sorry if I got anyone into trouble, but it really is not their fault. They can't hide from me as long as I know to look."

The ensign looked at my scanner. "I can see the town and everyone in it. I can pick out Janice from here. She's still in the church tower, and she's watching the road for Dr. Anderson's return. This scanner is way beyond anything I've ever dreamed of—I mean, that if—"

"That's enough, Ensign. Call her in, Master Chief. Let her know her position has been compromised. Dr. Anderson, I would—"

"Lieutenant, you and your team can call me Freddy, if I can call you by your first names."

She smiled. "Freddy, I must admit this gadget of yours is impressive. I can see why trying to watch you without being noticed would be difficult. I hope you don't mind if we continue to try."

"Susan, I would be delighted if you can find a way to fool my scanners. I will let you know when you're not successful. Please let me know when you are. Here's a challenge: if anyone of your team can sneak up on me at any time that I am awake, I will grant you one request, within reason. This means actually touching me before I acknowledge your presence. It cannot be while I'm here on base, as I expect to be near you then."

The lieutenant looked at the others and said, "We have a challenge placed before the team, Master Chief, and a prize that could be very useful—a concession the admiral could not get from him. What say you?"

"We accept the challenge, Lieutenant," said the master chief.

I took the scanner from the ensign and said into it, "Computer on."

"Welcome, Freddy."

"Computer, did you scan the people in this building and file them in your memory?"

"Affirmative."

"Good. Did you also include the team member in the church tower?"

"Affirmative."

"Good. Set for continuous scan and report each time any of them approach me within one hundred feet. Continue to report that person's progress toward me each ten feet or until I let you know to stop."

"Set and calibrated. Warning—there are twelve of the thirteen targets within one hundred feet of you now."

"Affirmative. Please do not report again until we leave the naval base. Also, do not report when I am in bed or sleeping."

"Affirmative."

I looked up at the lieutenant and then turned to the master chief. "I doubt that you would wish me to make it easy for you, would you?"

The master chief smiled. "Of course not."

I turned back to the lieutenant. "As I understand it, when in company, you normally use titles to show respect. Is this true, Lieutenant?"

"Yes, it is."

"Good. I would not wish to break that standard, so I will continue to call you 'Lieutenant' in the presence of your team and the same thing for the ensign and the master chief."

"That's very thoughtful of you."

"I try, Lieutenant, but sometimes I simply don't know when I'm doing something wrong. Just let me know so I can think about it."

She smiled. "It is apparent that watching you from a distance is useless, so do you mind if we join you when you are out and about?"

"I don't mind, but there's something you need to know. The town has the idea that you are here to take me out if I try to leave."

"We're to follow, watch, and protect, but if you try to leave without permission, then it would make some people very nervous."

"I understand this, and your reputation precedes you. The town believes that you're assassins. They will not take kindly to your presence there. We need to do something to prevent possible violence toward your team."

The master chief quickly picked up a walkie-talkie. "Watch One, this is home base. Come in."

"I'm here, home base."

"Watch One, where are you?"

"I'm just coming out of the tower."

"Well, go back up and wait for a jeep to pick you up."

"What's up, Master Chief?"

"The town is unfriendly—repeat: the town is unfriendly. You wait right there until the jeep arrives. Got that?"

"Roger that. I'm not moving. How long?"

"Fifteen minutes. Out."

The master chief opened the door and sent two girls out to pick up the watch. "That was close. I'm glad she was still there."

"I really don't think the townspeople would harm her, Master Chief."

"I'm not worried about her. I'm worried about the townspeople. If Janice has to protect herself, a lot of people could get hurt. With two additional SEALs showing up, it may make the townspeople think twice before they start anything, and the two I sent will keep Janice from doing anything rash."

I could feel her emotions, and she was not kidding. She was genuinely worried about the townspeople getting hurt. "Then I hope nothing happens, Master Chief."

"So do I, Freddy."

"Back to your question, Lieutenant," I said. "I think it would go a long way to pacifying the townspeople if we were hand in hand, so to speak. I do think it will look like a bodyguard, but considering what the town did to me yesterday, I think they would understand the admiral's insistence on this. Will that make it easier?"

"Yes, it will. From now on, you have bodyguards twenty-four hours a day."

"I like being a bodyguard a lot more than being a babysitter," said the ensign with a pout. Everyone looked at her.

"One other thing, Lieutenant. I am going into the woods on horseback soon. I need to scout out an area to build my house. I would accept it if two of your team members came with us."

"You could cover more territory in a helicopter."

"Are you offering to take me up, Lieutenant?"

"Of course, and when you have decided on a couple of possible sites and want to check them out on horseback, we'll go with you."

"That's a great idea. Thank you."

"I'll send a car for you tomorrow at 0700. Wear warm clothes; it gets cool over the mountains."

"Thank you, Lieutenant. I'll look forward to it." We talked for another half an hour before the admiral called. He wanted to know how things were going, so the lieutenant had to leave. I took my pocket scanner back from the ensign, who'd been sitting in the corner, spying on people at marine headquarters with it.

My next bodyguard, Petty Officer First Class Colleen McMasters, was already dressed in civilian clothes and ready to go. The entire team, except the master chief and Colleen, were gone in seconds.

She turned to me, saying, "The leak will be found shortly, and when we get through, there will be no more leaks, not even people talking to their spouses. We will fix the admiral's problem ourselves. If another country finds out you have equipment like that scanner, you'll either be dead or kidnapped. They would want to make sure that they had the equipment first or that we never got it, and that would mean your capture or death."

"I think you people are a little paranoid, Master Chief. I think the only ones I have to worry about are people in my own government and their being overly protective. Why do I get the feeling that this was already planned before I even stepped foot on this base? It seems to me that your team was prepared for this possible change in plans and that I was manipulated by someone who's just a little smarter than me."

She smiled and said, "She's good, isn't she?"

"If you're saying the lieutenant set this up, then I must agree."

"She didn't set it up, but she did her homework and now understands you a little bit better than most. She said that this would be the best possibility, with a 93 percent probability index. That's a high rating, so we prepared for it. I hope you're not mad."

"On the contrary, Master Chief, I like working with professionals. I find them easier to understand. I'm a scientist, as you said. I enjoy a good challenge, just like you do, and I like the fact that the lieutenant can figure me out. Not only will it make things interesting, but it could save me a lot of time and effort. I also noticed that things went very smoothly today. I am pleasantly surprised, and now I know who was responsible. Please give the lieutenant my compliments when she returns."

"I'd be more than happy to, Freddy."

I climbed into the car with Colleen and the master chief, who drove as we headed back to town. While going through the gate, the guard snapped to attention and saluted us. That was a definite change in attitude.

As soon as we left the base, my scanner let me know that two navy SEALs were nearby, within ten feet. I ordered it to not include Colleen and the master chief at this time. Colleen played with my scanner for the rest of the trip.

✦

The big Gray said, "That's interesting."

Everything went blank.

The Green asked, somewhat annoyed, "What's interesting, master?"

"They've only had scanners for a short time."

"Yes. All of their technology is new."

"How long have we had scanners?"

"Master, the first scanner was invented in the year of the Forgometa, approximately eight thousand years ago."

"How could such a primitive creature destroy our most advanced ship?"

"We will soon find out."

"Good. Continue."

CHAPTER 14

✦ ✦ ✦

BODYGUARDS

The car dropped me off at the inn. The difference this time was that Colleen stayed with me. As I went into the inn, Becky and Johnny were waiting for me.

"How did it go?" asked Becky. "And who is this?" she inquired with just a hint of jealousy.

"This is my bodyguard. Colleen, this is the beautiful Miss Becky Crain and her brother, Johnny Crain."

Becky's eyes gleamed, and I could feel her crush on me increase. Colleen shook hands with the two of them.

"Where's your mom?" I asked.

Johnny motioned toward the kitchen.

We went into the kitchen, where Mrs. Crain was kneading bread, and Carroll was at the oven, checking on the pies. "Hi, Mrs. Crain. The navy SEAL team has been assigned to watch and protect me. I'll need to rent a room for my bodyguard, if that's okay with you."

She had a great big smile and said, "Sure it is, sweetheart. The room adjoining yours is empty. Can you please show her where it is, dear? I'm up to my elbows right now."

She sure was making a lot of food. There were pies, breads, rolls, pastries, a stew, and huge roasts baking. This was going to be a big dinner for a lot of people. I said, "Sure, and thanks."

As soon as we left the kitchen, Colleen said, "I don't think this is necessary. We'll be changing watch often enough that the room won't even be used."

"Actually, the master chief and the lieutenant thought that this would be better, and I agree. The room is not the most important part of staying here. The meals are included, and most of the time I will be eating here. Please don't tell me that navy SEALs don't eat. I've watched your team for the past two days, and you change watch every eight hours, like clockwork. When do you eat in that time? Also, why watch me at night if you know I'm sleeping? The media lost interest once I won my emancipation, and few know where I am. The risk is minimal. We agreed that sleeping right next door is good enough. In short, I'm doing what the lieutenant and I agreed on. Another benefit of making it look like you're my friend is that it will make it easier for the townspeople to get used to you. This is important if you want to be with me. I don't want the townsfolk to feel intimidated, and you must admit, some of you are extremely intimidating."

"I understand," she said with a smile.

"Good. I also do not want to be awakened each time you change watch, so it was agreed that the watch stays the night. Now, that doesn't mean you can have pajama parties." I looked up at her with a smile. She was looking at me in shocked silence, but it changed to a smile when she saw I was kidding.

I showed her to her room and pointed out the amenities—clock radio, TV, dresser, bath. Colleen said, "If I go to sleep on that bed, I may never wake up. I may not want to."

I saw Becky at the door, just watching and listening, and I asked, "Where's Annabelle?"

"She's in the front room, playing Chutes and Ladders by herself. She's trying to keep her mind off waiting for Daddy."

With excitement, I said, "Chutes and Ladders is a great game! Let's go!" I took Becky's hand and headed downstairs. I could feel Colleen's mirth. When I saw Annabelle, I knew she wasn't happy. "Hi, Annabelle!" I greeted her. "Mind if we join you? I love to play Chutes and Ladders."

She got up and gave me a big hug and said she'd love to play with me. Becky and I sat down, and Johnny came over to play too. Colleen went to the front door, where she could look outside and keep a watch on us at the same time.

✦

"Chutes and Ladders. Another game."

Everything went black.

"Master?"

"Chutes and Ladders. I can see on the screen that it is a game, but what are chutes and ladders in real life?"

"I believe that a chute is a form of downward passage that allows people to descend quickly. A ladder is an item used to climb back up."

"I knew it. They are trained from an early age to traverse all kinds of terrain. Look at all the games they play, and everyone has a winner and a loser. Every living room must have training equipment, and these games are the start. Military trained from birth—no wonder they are so difficult to fight on the ground. Continue."

CHAPTER 15

✦ ✦ ✦

THE FLEET'S IN

We played the game for about an hour, and then the church bells rang. Everyone got up and headed for the door. Becky grabbed my hand and ran with me out the door. She seemed very excited and said, "Daddy's coming home!"

Outside, things were getting busy. The whole town was on the docks, setting up supplies, preparing for repair, and refueling. I looked out to sea but saw nothing. Of course, I knew about the curvature of the earth and realized that someone was up high, keeping watch.

Becky explained everything to me. Most of the children were on the beach. Everyone older than age fourteen was on the docks, working. Becky pointed out the weighing and separation area, the cleaning and scaling area, the freezing area, the preparations for trucking, the people setting up smokers, and the dock supervisors who would pay the fishermen. Boat crews were preparing to work on the boats, doing cleanup and repair. Repair included paint, motors, nets, and lines—anything for the smooth operation of the boat. Apparently, they had radioed ahead that it was a great catch and that they needed to go right back out. People were stacking food and cooking fuel on the docks, out of the way of the fish preparations. Becky made it very clear that getting back out to sea was important, but the current catch was the first priority.

I said, "A bird in the hand is worth two in the bush."

"Exactly," she responded.

These people were experts at what they were doing. Everyone worked in unison, and there were no arguments. Though the work was hard and time-consuming, they were all happy, in anticipation of the great catch.

I stepped back to look at the overall picture. A great catch meant more work and a better income for the fishermen, and in this case, it looked like more money for everyone. If everyone who was on the docks made more money, then the stores made more money, and the town thrived. I wondered what it was like when the fishing was not so good.

"Becky, this is great!" I said enthusiastically. "Do they ever have a bad year?"

Becky's radiant smile vanished and a frown came to her face. "One bad year is not too bad," she said, "but two bad years will hurt everyone. It's not so bad for us. Mom has the inn, and that makes enough to support us, what with the hunting parties that come through in the fall, but when fishing is bad, the whole town suffers. Mommy does what she can by feeding people and passing out food. We eat a lot of soup and stew that Mom prepares all year, just in case. We work at canning food and keep a large amount of supplies ready, year-round. Some people have to close up their shops, as no one is buying, and some left after we had two bad years in a row. Mom said that three bad years would close the town and put us all out on the street." Now she smiled again. "But we don't have to worry this time. Dad had a great catch, and that means the boats are full to the top rail." The bells clanged, and she jumped up and down. "They're in sight of the tower now. They'll be here in about an hour."

Sure enough, about fifty minutes, later six boats came into sight. They were bigger than I imagined and sat low in the water. The people on the docks were still very busy, but the children were getting impatient.

Becky said that the boats still had to dock and then unload before her daddy would come home. It would be another hour, and dinner would be late.

"Interesting sight," Colleen said.

"Yes, it is. This town works well together. I can see why they don't want live-in strangers."

"It's not so much being a stranger," said Colleen, "as your possibly causing fishing problems. The army used many boats that polluted the waters. They wanted this town shut down so they could have increased staging areas for their war games, full use of the docks, and more housing for army personnel and families. They constantly ran through the fishing nets and created havoc whenever they were here—and they did it on purpose. The townspeople have accepted you, Freddy, but they're still worried that you may somehow pollute the area south of here even more."

"I get the message loud and clear, thanks. I don't intend to do any damage, but I'll be extra careful."

The boats were pulling up to the dock now, and I could see the salmon from the beach. The kids, including Annabelle, were waving toward one of the boats. Johnny was at the dock, waiting. The name on the boat was *Daddy's Dream*. I pointed toward the boat. "Is that your daddy's boat, Annabelle?"

"Oh yes, *Daddy's Dream*. Isn't it a wonderful boat?"

"Yes, it is. How long has he been out?"

"Oh, forever."

Becky interjected, "The boats were in just last week—a

fair catch but low poundage, not much meat. Now that the salmon are running, things are picking up, but they need several good catches like this one to keep the town going. This is a good sign, but it's just the beginning. The people will pay bills at the local stores with this catch. The next catch will stock the shelves, and a third catch would give them a little extra to make repairs to homes and possibly have a nice Christmas. A fourth catch would be put in savings in preparation for a bad year. This is the first good catch this year. All others catches broke even—enough to stock the boats for another outing, but that's about it. That leaves the wives and children living off the little they make in the town or using the credit at the stores."

"They don't make money off tourists or anything else?"

"Very little. Fishing is it. Your staying at the inn will make our family enough to make it through the winter, even with bad catches. Paying for two rooms is going to be great. It will take a lot of pressure off Father, but he will still be doing his best for the town. Notice that almost the entire town is here?"

"Yes."

"Many of the people will not get paid for helping out," Becky said. "They do it because the town needs the help. If the town had to employ people to do all this work, they would be sitting around most of the time, doing nothing. There would not be enough money to pay them, and the cost of the fish would be sky high. Instead, they all work for the common good of the town. Most have everyday jobs, but who is going to be at Betty's Diner right now? Maybe a few military people, but that's it. The base isn't that big, only three hundred people. They eat on base and do most of their shopping at the exchange. There are no real reasons for the military to come into our town when the other town has restaurants, movie theaters, a small mall, a bowling alley, and the main highway leading to other places. The choice for them is at the crossroads coming out of the mountains—ten miles west to this town or twelve miles east to the other one."

I said thoughtfully, "No one is in the town, so no one is buying anything—no shoppers, no one eating, no one needing building materials. The store owners are left sitting alone. Being here and helping makes them part of the town, and the town will take care of them, if and when the need arises. Say no one buys anything for a long time, and they have no food."

Becky added, "Actually, most of the store owners have husbands who work on the boats, but if the catch was lean long enough, then it would hurt them both, and so what you said is true. The few male store owners are mostly retired military. The gas station gets most of its money from the base, but it's not much. The navy was going to put in a gas station on base, but the admiral protects this town and put a stop to it. He has land north of here and plans to retire there. We like him, and he wants to keep it that way. His wife works on base but does all her shopping and ordering in town. She is very much loved here."

"How is my ordering stuff going to affect this town?" I asked.

"Depends on how much you order. A little won't affect them much, but a lot would be highly welcomed, and the money would be put to good use. They won't count on it continuing, so don't worry about having to keep it up. Our people are very conservative when it comes to saving. Most of it will go into the bank for that time when fishing won't keep things going. Some of it will go to repairs in the town. They've been trying to get the money to build a new school for years. The navy would help, but the town refuses to take charity."

"A new school … interesting."

We were watching the boats, but now, Becky was watching me. "What are you thinking?" she asked.

"I was just thinking that there are a few things I could use too. Maybe I could use that information to do some good. For example, I may need a boat dock somewhere in this bay."

"You might have difficulty getting permission for that. It's one of the things the army wanted, and they were turned down."

Annabelle looked at me and said, "You're going to help us build a new school?"

I looked at her and whispered, just loud enough so Becky could also hear, "Annabelle, no one can know what I was just saying. Do you understand? If they find out I'm doing something like that, they may try to stop me."

"If they stop you, then no new school?"

"That's right, sweetheart."

"I won't tell. It sure would make my sisters happy. The school is cold in the winter."

"Well, if you can keep this a secret, then we'll fix that, okay?"

"I can keep secrets," Annabelle insisted. "I'm keeping a secret that Becky loves you, so I can keep your secret too."

I blushed slightly and said to Becky, "I think I need to watch what I say in front of this one."

"I think that would be a good idea," Becky responded, looking at Annabelle disapprovingly, yet with a hint of laughter in her eyes.

I could not believe how much fish was packed in ice on those boats. All six of the boat crews worked as one. They worked on two boats at a time, and when they were done with the first two boats, the crews all moved to the second two boats, and then the last two, until all of the boats were unloaded. Then they each returned to their own boats and started shoveling out the ice.

By the time the fishermen could come ashore and the cleanup and repair crews could go on board, it was turning dark. When Captain Crain, a big, rough-looking man with big eyebrows, came off his boat, he headed toward the dock supervisor. They talked for what seemed like an eternity while Annabelle was jumping up and down in anticipation. Finally, he started off the dock toward the inn. Annabelle ran toward him but then stopped short so she would not get that fishy smell on her. She started talking, and I don't think she stopped until her daddy was entering a door to an outbuilding. When he saw his little girl, he wanted so much to grab her and hold her, but he didn't. He just patiently listened and told her how much he missed her.

Becky said, "They don't touch anyone until they're scrubbed down. Fishing can be a smelly process, and going by the depth that they sat in the water, I'd say the hold was filled to the top. It was a great catch. This is a good time. Dinner will be ready just as soon as their baths are finished. The entire boat crew will be here only a few hours, so the wives are in the scrub house, taking care of their husbands in more ways than one. These men have a lot to come home for, and their women make sure they know it. Even if it's a bad catch, the men know they're loved."

We went into the inn to wait with the children. I went into the kitchen and asked if I could help with anything. Carroll nodded. "Yes, bag these sandwiches and double-wrap them. When you're done, put them into that cooler." She started slicing more roast beef.

Colleen then took over the slicing, freeing Carroll to do other chores. While bagging the sandwiches, I watched Colleen work with the knife. She was extremely fast. I was expecting her to cut a finger off, and I saw Carroll was thinking the same thing. When Colleen passed Carroll more meat to put into the sandwiches, I could see the meat was sliced very thin and even. I think this put a little fear in Carroll, because she could only stare at Colleen.

"Carroll, please check that meat for bits of fingers and bone," I teased. "Don't look for blood because navy SEALs don't bleed!" When Carroll saw I was holding back laughter, she started laughing. After that, everything was all right. She actually started singing a little. She had a good voice, and I enjoyed listening to her.

✦

"Fishing. It sounds like illegal slavers caught a boatload of slaves and are planning on making a lot of money."

"Master, I don't think that fish are slaves. I get the feeling they eat them."

"I don't like slavery. We abolished it thousands of years ago. Still, we find creatures like these humans. Remember the Wansacks?"

"No, master."

"The Wansacks were completely terminated, so it's no surprise that you don't remember. They took slaves, but like these humans, they ate more than they sold. Sad, and a good reason for complete destruction. Continue."

"Master, I don't think—"

"Continue!"

CHAPTER 16

✦ ✦ ✦

DRIFTING

The dinner table was set for sixteen people. This required putting leaves in the table. I'd never seen a table that you could climb under and turn a crank to separate it. The leaves were stored underneath, and after you placed them on top, you cranked in the opposite direction to close the gaps. I could think of a hundred ways to make it easier. I took out the pad and pen I always carry with me and started talking out loud. I must have drifted off. I did not realize anything was going on until Becky kissed me on the cheek. I looked up from my drawings on a new table design and saw that everyone was at the dining table, including Captain and Mrs. Crain. I said, "Sorry," and blushed deep red.

Colleen said, "As I was saying, in college I learned that some top scientists have a tendency to forget everything else when they get an idea. The more intelligent the person, the more he drifts. This may include forgetting to eat and sleep. They simply drift off to another world. Einstein, I am told, drifted for an entire day once. They need looking-after to keep them from walking off a cliff. I am very surprised that Becky could rouse him at all."

"Especially since we've been yelling at him for ten minutes," said Johnny.

Captain Crain sat back. He was clean and freshly shaved, and there was a happy, satisfied look about him. He wasn't smiling, but I could sense his amusement at the whole situation. I went to the table and sat down at the place Becky indicated, right next to her. Everyone bowed their heads, and Captain Crain gave the blessing for the food. His prayer was long and meaningful, and I could tell he meant every word he said as he thanked the Lord and asked for guidance. He included a wish for me to find a good home site and build a fine house. When he was done, I thanked him.

"Freddy, is it?" Captain Crain asked.

"Yes, sir."

"This is Bob Allen; his wife, Deborah; and his two daughters, Pamela and Misty. Bob's the captain of our sister boat, the *Pay Day*. This is my second mate and his wife, Martin and Nancy McDermott."

"It's nice to meet all of you. Have you met Colleen?"

"Yes, we all met while you were out," said Mr. McDermott.

I blushed again. "I'm sorry about that, sir. I do have this tendency to drift off a little."

"Really? What's the longest you've ever drifted off?" asked Captain Crain.

I blushed even deeper. "Five days, I think. I can't remember when I started drifting off, only that I was really hungry by the time I finished jotting down my ideas."

"Well, I hope you're hungry now." He picked up the potatoes and took a big spoonful. As soon as the food hit his plate, the talk started, and the food went around the table. Many questions were directed to Colleen and me. I asked only one.

"Captain Crain, who is the best person to talk to about

things I want to do—stuff like building a home, which may upset the surrounding waters?"

The table talk came to a dead halt.

He put his fork down and said, "Depends on the purpose of the talk."

"I want to make sure that I don't change the environment in any way. I have an interest in making my home completely safe, while helping the environment at the same time. I am interested in consulting with someone knowledgeable before I do anything that may adversely affect the surrounding waters."

He smiled. "I like your attitude, Freddy. When you want to do something that may affect the waters, we'll get the boat captains together and take a look at what you're planning. I assure you that between the six of us, we'll know what will be bad or good for the waters." He put his hand to his chin and rubbed. "Come to think of it, if you want to do anything with your land that would help us now, get the army back in here to clean up the dumping they did in the canyon."

"Dumping?" I asked, a look of disgust crossing my face. "What dumping?"

Colleen said, "The army has been using the canyon, where the river flows into the ocean, as a dump site for years. I'm sorry to tell you, but it's right in the middle of your land."

"The dumping has caused the fish in the area to be inedible," said Captain Crain. "We have to test all the fish now, because they may have fed off the fish from that polluted area. We see fish coming from there all the time, floating belly up. It's a mess. Thanks to you, at least they're not dumping there anymore. We tried to put a stop to it, but the army gave the courts a list of the things they dump, and the courts ruled that the materials are not illegal to dump there and that they have a license. We could not afford to hire outside help with this, as you can't sue the army, and so there would be no profit in it for the lawyers. For this, they would work on a profit margin, but because it's the army, they would make no money. We sent letters to congressmen and senators and even to the president. We have heard nothing. A group talked to them in person, but the answer from each was no comment. The site is off-limits, so we have never been able to get in there and prove they were dumping anything caustic or illegal."

My eyes narrowed; I was very upset. "I want to see that area tomorrow during our flight please, Colleen."

Colleen nodded.

"Captain Crain," I said, "I will not put up with pollution on my land. It will be cleaned up." I sat quietly for a few seconds, deep in thought. "I may need to do some burning and construction that will temporarily cause some mud and soot in the water in order to fix the problem. After I'm done, though, the water will be clean again."

"If someone doesn't do something soon, then the fishing here will be closed down permanently. This poisoning of our fishing grounds is the biggest reason that the townspeople wanted you and everyone else out. If you can clean up the mess with just a little mud and soot for a short time, then you'll be doing more than anything the government has offered to do so far. The current drift is south from your land to the deep water, and then it turns west and finally picks up the current north. The mud and soot will settle before it gets out there. Right now, we're fishing north and out, so it won't affect us for the summer. If you can do something before the winter fishing season, we would be most appreciative."

"I'll try, sir. Let me think about it some more."

I immediately started drifting off, forming plans in my head, but Becky took my hand and said, "Think after dinner." Everyone laughed.

When dinner was over, we all helped clean up. The captains sat around, enjoying their kids, while Colleen and I went upstairs. I had a lot to think about, and when I had finished making plans for a cleanup project, I went back downstairs. It was dark, and everyone had gone to bed. Colleen came down and asked what I was doing.

"I'm looking for the captain so I can show him my plans for the cleanup."

Colleen took my hand and led me back upstairs. "Freddy, the boats left a couple of hours after dinner. It's two o'clock in the morning."

I looked at my watch and said, "Oops, sorry."

"It's okay. Becky was going to get your attention, but Captain Crain thought it was more important for you to complete your work. He did tell her that she was to make sure you didn't starve to death. Please go to bed."

"Okay. Good night."

"Good night, Freddy."

✦

"Typical politicians."

Everything went black.

"Master?"

"Typical politicians. Allow something to become messed up and then throw it on the military to clean up the problem. They are more like us than I suspected."

"Master, he was saying that the army—their form of military, though they seem to have several—was the cause of the problem, and the politicians found out and did nothing. Then, they allowed this creature to have the land in the hopes that he would be able to fix the problem."

"Yes, but did we not find out their military is run by their politicians? Was it not their politicians that forced the military to change tactics, just as they were pushing us back, granting us some victory? I am sure it was not the 'army' that caused the mess. The foolish politicians must have ordered them to dump their pollutants."

"Master, there are no facts to back that up."

"I don't need facts. It's the same with our species. The politicians try to run everything according to their own agenda and end up ruining everything instead. Continue."

CHAPTER 17

✦ ✦ ✦

THE LEAK

I was still sleeping when Colleen came in the next morning. "Well, you're up when you're supposed to be asleep and asleep when you're supposed to be up."

"What time is it?" I asked.

"Six thirty. The car will be here for you in thirty minutes, so let's get going!"

"Yes, ma'am." I climbed out of bed and took a quick shower. When I came back to my room, Colleen was looking at my drawings. I started getting dressed, while watching her out of the corner of my eyes.

"Can you really make all this stuff?" she asked.

"Yes. That plan is based on existing technology."

"Really? Whose? Not any I've ever heard of."

"Mine. Ready?" I grabbed my bag and started for the door. It was very heavy, so Colleen helped me carry it.

There was a different look in Colleen's eye. I touched her mind a little to see what was going on. The feeling I got was respect. She was starting to understand why I was sent out here, and she had respect for my work. As we were descending the stairs, I asked, "Where did you get your engineering degree?"

"Stanford University. How did you know I have an engineering degree?"

"How else could you read and understand my drawings so quickly?"

"Freddy ..." She put her hand on my shoulder and gently turned me around. "Look, I'm sorry for snooping. I won't do it again."

"Why? Good minds are always curious. If you're going to be my bodyguard, then you're going to see things. It can't be helped. I'm just counting on you to keep quiet about what you do see, and that includes not telling the admiral. If not, then you won't be my bodyguard anymore."

We went straight to the kitchen to grab a bite to eat. Mrs. Crain was already making the morning meal. When she saw me, she said, "Is it all right if I set up an appointment for you this afternoon? Mr. Thompson, the owner of the sporting goods store, would like to talk with you about your camping trip. He called last night."

"Great!" I said enthusiastically. "After the helicopter ride this morning, I'll have a better idea of where I want to go. Yes, please set up a time for us to meet."

Colleen and I left as soon as the jeep pulled up. It had no doors or top and the windshield was folded down. The driver was Petty Officer Second Class—or PO2—Denise Potter, and Petty Officer First Class—PO1—Betsy Donet was sitting in the front passenger seat. Colleen put my bag behind the rear seat.

Betsy asked if I'd like to sit up front. I said, "Sure, thanks."

"I hope you don't mind the jeep, Freddy," said Denise, "but it was the easiest transportation to obtain."

"I don't mind at all. How does it corner?"

"Not very well. It leans a lot, so buckle up real tight."

I did, and so did the rest of them. "Betsy, I take it you're my next bodyguard?" I said.

"That's correct, Freddy."

"Cool! Please don't take offense, Colleen, but it will give me a chance to rest my neck." They all laughed. The ride was uneventful. When we went through the front gate, we were saluted in a snappy fashion. I asked why.

Betsy said, "Apparently, the stupid marine guards told their commander what happened yesterday, and he called the admiral to apologize. This was before we could get to them and fix the issue. The admiral went ballistic and blamed his failure with you on the marine guards. The commander really went off on his men when he found out that you are 'presidential priority.' He called a full-dress inspection and reamed everyone, making sure they knew why he was upset. I think you'll find all of the marines on the base will be very nice to you from now on."

"So how long have you had the admiral and the marine commander's phones tapped?" I asked. I must give credit to the girls—not one of them showed any sign that they were surprised that I knew.

"Since the day we got here," said Colleen.

"So it's possible that your whole group knew about me even before the rest of the base?"

"Yes."

"Then one could assume that a member of the SEAL team is a likely suspect for being the leak on this base."

Total silence, and then Betsy said, "Freddy, I don't think that one of our people is the leak."

I shook my head and said, "Before the flight, I would like to see all of the navy SEAL team members, please—one at a time in the lieutenant's office, starting with the lieutenant, then the master chief, then the ensign, and down the chain of command."

We pulled up in front of the building, so no one said a thing. When we reached the quarterdeck, Lt. James was waiting. "The helicopter will be ready in about half an hour," she said. Colleen took her aside and told her quietly of my request. The lieutenant nodded and said, "Tell no one. Just send them up as we call for them."

Lt. James motioned for me to come with her. When we entered her room, I motioned for her to keep quiet. I pulled out my scanner, made a small adjustment, and then scanned the room. I found two electronic bugs and pointed them out. We went into another room. I scanned that room, and everything was clear.

"Lieutenant, why do you allow your room to be bugged?"

"I didn't allow it, Freddy; I didn't know—a tactical mistake that will soon be corrected." She was definitely not happy; in fact, she was fuming, but not at me, thank God. "Why did you wish to talk to each person individually?"

I took out another device and turned it on. It was a simple antigravity belt unit, about the size of a deck of cards. I felt that if I was going up in a helicopter, I wanted something to ensure I would land softly if things went wrong. Right now, I was going to use the device as a lie detector. The last thing I wanted Lt. James to know was that I am telepathic, because it would be reported instantly.

"What's that, Freddy?"

"The answer to your question, Lieutenant. May I ask you a few questions, please?"

"Shoot."

"How old are you?"

"Twenty-eight."

"That was a lie, Lieutenant."

"Thirty."

"That's better."

"Let me see that." She headed my way. I deactivated the device and used my mind to move the needle. She pointed it at herself and said, "I weigh 180 pounds."

Nothing happened. "Sorry, Lieutenant. It's keyed into my body code."

I took it back, and she repeated, "I weigh 180 pounds." The needle jumped. "I weigh 142 pounds." Nothing happened. She looked at me and asked, "How?"

"Not patented yet, Lieutenant. Now, do you know who is leaking information from or around this base?"

"No."

"Good enough. Next person."

She opened the door and called the master chief in.

"Master Chief," I said, "I need to ask you a question."

"Go ahead."

"Do you know who is leaking information from or around this base?"

"No."

"Good. Send in the ensign."

We continued this until we got to PO2 Bunny Taylor. When she entered the room, I knew right away that she was the leak, but I still asked the question. "Do you know who is leaking information from or around this base?"

"No."

"Really?" There were now thirteen people in the room, including me. Eleven of the people started toward her. I held up my hand. "Petty Officer Taylor, this is a lie detector, and it is physically impossible to tell a lie without my detecting it. Let's try my question again."

"I don't know what you're talking about."

"That was a lie. Is it you?"

"No."

"That was a lie. Anyone else?"

"No."

That got my attention. "That was also a lie. Is it someone in this group?"

"I didn't do anything! This is illegal. I'm requesting Captain Mast. This is wrong."

I told her, "One more time, Petty Officer Taylor. If you don't answer truthfully, the lieutenant and I will go up in the helicopter and leave you here alone with your teammates."

The lieutenant looked at the master chief, who was looking like she wanted to kill someone. "I'm leaving soon, Master Chief," the lieutenant said, "and I don't expect Petty Officer Taylor to be here when I return. I don't care where or how or in what condition she leaves. We'll call it absent without leave—AWOL. I'll let you decide, though. I don't want to know, and we'll never talk about it." The master chief smiled a big, evil smile that caused me to tremble.

I could feel the fear pouring out of Petty Officer Taylor. I asked, "Did anyone help you?"

"I'm really Army Sergeant Nettie Davies. I'm working directly for General Johnson. He set it up for me to be placed in your group just after the incident with his lost clothes. I work with a civilian, and I pass messages to the general through him."

"What's his name?"

"Harry Dellavechia. He works at the gas station."

"That's why you volunteer to get the gas all the time," said the master chief. "I thought it was just because you like to drive."

"Anyone else?" I asked.

"No, that's it," Petty Officer Taylor answered.

"Finally, the truth. Thank you," I said. "Master Chief, next person, please."

"I don't see why we need to continue this. We've found the one responsible, and she said there was no one else."

Lt. James said, "And, if you were the general, would you have only one spy?"

"I'll get her," said the master chief. She motioned to two of the girls. "Take this one to my office and watch her."

I added, "Please don't harm her. She was under orders. I think if you want to harm someone, get the general."

The next girl came in, but no others were guilty.

"My apologies, Lieutenant, for needing to do this. I know it's embarrassing, but as you can see, it was necessary. Do we have a minute to scan the rest of the building and vehicles?"

"I think we should make the time," said the lieutenant.

We scanned and removed twenty-one passive and active devices from the building and two from each vehicle. Some were built into the walls, and one was in the lieutenant's toilet. They called the toilet the "head"—figure that one out.

Back in her office Lt. James said, "I'm glad that's over, but she's not the base leak; it's someone else. She was just a plant from the general. He would never let her make the mistake of giving out information and possibly being caught. The base leak is someone else. Ensign, the priority is still to find that leak. It's in the admiral's office somewhere. I want that information, and I want it now."

"I'm on it, Lieutenant. Any chance I can borrow that little device?" the ensign asked.

The lieutenant shook her head. "Sorry, it's keyed into his body code. He's the only one who can use it."

"Lieutenant," I asked, "any chance you can get the admiral to throw a little party—say, one to welcome me to the base? If he put the word out that he had some very important information for me, and if he hid that information in a briefcase and let no one see it, I bet the person would show up. Since I'd be the guest of honor, naturally I'd be talking to everyone. With a few well-placed questions, I might be able to find out who the leak is."

Colleen said, "Lieutenant, I think that would be placing Freddy in unnecessary danger."

"I agree," said the lieutenant.

"What if this leak is not only to the townspeople but to others as well—like some people who would be interested in my inventions?" I suggested. "How dangerous would it be then? Besides, who's going to know except your team? You and I both know that they're clean now. You keep it that way, and there should be no danger to me at all. I feel safer already, but I can't check the entire base. This device works off my body, and it can cause problems that I don't need."

"What kind of problems?" asked the lieutenant.

"Headaches, loss of equilibrium. You can see why I don't use it very often."

The lieutenant laughed and said, "I very much understand, Freddy."

So did everyone else. They even thanked me for helping them. The master chief had calmed down by then and assured me that she would not allow the spy to be harmed. She said to the lieutenant, "This cannot go unpunished."

The lieutenant said, "When I get back, we need to talk about what should happen to get the general's attention. He needs to understand that this was a bad idea, and Master Chief, we make all of our own repairs and upgrades from now on. Understand?"

The master chief exclaimed, "We'll need a bigger budget."

"I think I can get that past the admiral after I tell him what we found and who found it." She looked at me and said, "I may need to embellish a little about your attitude. You've been helpful, even apologetic through all this, but I think it would get the admiral's attention if you were just a little upset instead."

I motioned for her to get closer, and she leaned down. I said in an angry tone, "Don't ever make me do your job again." Then I winked, saying, "I didn't want you to lie to the admiral about my being upset."

Everyone laughed at that, and the lieutenant said, "Time to get you in the air. Master Chief, take care of our friend, but don't let her go. I have an interesting idea that I'll explain when we get back. Ensign, you're in charge. Betsy, you're with us."

"Yes, ma'am."

"Let's go."

"Denise, you're driving."

✦

"Ahhh."

Everything went black.

"Master?"

"It seems that their military has spies that watch other aspects of their military. It is not a cohesive force. Good-to-know information."

"Master, this may be an isolated case. The army commander, in this case, seems to be somewhat of an 'Uoopfordiss.'"

"Uoopfordiss! That's something you call a politician, not a military commander, unless ..."

"Unless? Master?"

"Unless sometimes the politicians make their way into the ranks of the military. No. That cannot be. The species would have destroyed itself long ago if that happened."

"Our records show that most life on this planet was destroyed several times."

"Makes sense, then. Continue."

CHAPTER 18

✦ ✦ ✦

MY LAND

The lieutenant explained that the helicopter was used for the transportation of troops and supplies. Due to its size we likely would not be landing in the forest. I must have asked a hundred questions about the helicopter. The lieutenant finally told me, "Get in, or we'll never get up." I blushed and climbed in with my bag. Once in the air, I started unloading my equipment. Now it was Betsy's turn to ask questions.

"What's all this, Freddy?"

"This unit here"—I pointed to the biggest unit with a flat screen lying next to it—"is a portable scanner. It's considerably more powerful than the pocket version you've seen. It has a lot more flexibility and provides better information and details. This is the power supply, and it goes right here." I shoved it in, and it clicked into place. "This is the color monitor that goes right here." I placed the flat screen in position. "This tiny crystal bank is the memory unit, and it goes right here." I placed it into the holder. "Ta-da. All put together. And now, the add-ons. When I patent this invention, I expect to sell the main unit for an outrageous price but give buyers a break with the add-ons. That way, when other companies come up with more attachments, I won't have any problem with them trying to undersell me. This prototype can take up to ten additional pieces of specialized equipment." I held up several small devices, each about the size of a pack of cards. "This unit is for measuring gravitational fluxes. It adds on in this slot here. This unit is for measuring radioactivity and all forms of ionic activity and goes into this slot. This one measures density, this one is for types of life, this one measures temperatures in five different modes, and last but not least, this unit is for checking the air, ground, and water quality."

"This is an environmentalist's dream come true—if it works," Betsy said.

I stuck my tongue out at Betsy and then turned back to my unit, mumbling, "If it works? Of course it works! Why wouldn't it work?" I turned it on. The screen came up, but it was garbled. I adjusted the unit from one thousand miles down to five hundred feet and pointed the scanning gun toward the ground. Instantly, I received a view and readouts of the ground below us. I explained to Betsy, "I can touch the heat-activated trigger and get a continuous reading on wherever I point the gun, or I can let go and it holds the last recording. All information is stored in this crystal bank. Lieutenant, when will we be over my property?"

"We have been over it ever since we left the base."

"Great! Please take me to the center section that borders the ocean. I plan to use a boat to go back and forth from my home to town so that I don't have to build any roads on my property."

"We'll be there in just about ten minutes."

I continuously scanned the areas that we passed over. There was an underground river flowing from the mountains behind us, directly through my property. The water quality was excellent. Most of my land was dense forest and mountains—difficult to travel through, I would think.

"I don't see any roads. What did the army do out here?"

"Mostly they played games—Hide and Seek, Go Fish, Old Maid," said Betsy. We all laughed. "Actually, they practiced war games. They had a setup for forest survival that they ran several times a year. They also practiced running scenarios that required the use of helicopters and boats. The terrain is too dense and steep for land-based equipment. One dirt road goes from our base to the radar unit. They used it to bring tanks, trucks, and other equipment in for their games and to evacuate anyone who became injured."

Lt. James added, "They also used it to bring in their contaminated waste and then transferred it to helicopters and dumped it in the canyon, where we're headed now. It's exactly in the center of your property on the other side of this mountain and just back from the shoreline."

I scanned the mountain; it was exactly what I was hoping for—hollow, although not completely, with several caves that ran deep into it. Some of the caves ran on a winding path that took them all the way to the center. Just off center toward the ocean side was a large, open cavern. The river ran along the left side of these caves. It appeared that the river had made the caves while trying to reach the sea, but sometime, eons ago, the river apparently had been cut off from the main caves and forced to reroute itself around them, leaving them abandoned. The mountain itself was mostly granite, which was ideal because granite condenses really well. There were other mineral deposits but nothing worthwhile.

As we reached the other side, I could see several rivers running down the snow-covered mountain toward the ocean. They all seemed to flow into the ground. As we traveled closer, I could see that they were flowing into a deep canyon. The lieutenant pointed out the area and said she was going to bring us directly over the canyon.

The canyon was enormous. Two waterfalls flowed over the edge and plummeted down the sheer cliff to the bottom, where they splashed on the rocks over a thousand feet below. Another waterfall came out of the side of the cliff. The bottom of the canyon was about two-thirds rock and one-third deep lake. The scanner showed that the water at the bottom was highly contaminated. The underground river exited near the top of the canyon wall, and the caves were right at the bottom. I could see what years of dumping by the army had done, as virtually the entire canyon floor was littered with junk. Some of it was in drums clearly labeled as hazardous materials. The canyon was so beautiful and the damage so extensive that I nearly cried.

"Please fly over the ocean end," I said. The lieutenant moved us over so that we could see the ocean but still see into the canyon. Here, the cliffs thinned to only one hundred yards across, with a river running through the middle. This is where the river met the ocean. The river was very deep, and there were several spots where the water had to go under the cliff to continue its flow, making natural bridges from one side to the other. The scanners showed that there were many kinds of contamination all the way to the ocean and out into the currents.

I stared across my land, saying to myself, "The president, Congress ... I guess everyone knew about this. Just like politicians to pass this kind of problem to someone else. Now I understand why they voted unanimously to give it away. Probably thought I'd need the money to clean the place up. I do not doubt they have some plan to cite me for having all this pollution on my land. Darn them!" I was mad and realized that I had been talking aloud.

The lieutenant said, "Knowing politicians, I'd say you hit it right on the nose. Want to see the rest of your property?"

We traveled the rest of the shoreline, seeing the radar station and many natural wonders. The lieutenant said, "People say that seals and otters used to play along here." We didn't see any and I could guess why, but we did see deer, a black bear, a gray fox, and all kinds of birds but very few near the shore and none around or below the river.

"Let's head back, Lieutenant, and thank you." I was becoming extremely angry very quickly. The general was not making a good impression on me and neither was Congress.

The trip back was in total silence. When we landed, I asked to go right back to the inn. I thanked the lieutenant for her help and told her that I would contact her shortly. I also told her that I would not be making a trip on horseback, as I already knew where I was going to build my home. I promised to contact her soon and let her know when I was leaving.

✦

"So, I have to wonder again how such a primitive race could put up such a grand battle."

Everything went black.

"We have wondered this also. Their technology is far inferior to ours. Scanners like the one he describes were toys, hundreds of years ago. Today, any child has two or three class-eight scanners implanted in his body."

"True, but these toys are not what destroyed our mother ship."

"No, we have studied his scanners and determined that they could not penetrate our illusion device."

"Continue."

CHAPTER 19

✦ ✦ ✦

HAVING A MENTAL GIFT HAS ITS PITFALLS

Once back at the inn, I called Mr. Thompson, the owner of the sporting goods store, to say that although I no longer needed his camping equipment, I would have a list of quite a few products that I needed from him by tomorrow. After a short conversation, I went upstairs to my room. I tossed out the cleanup plans and started over on new cleanup plans.

I felt something warm on my cheek and realized I'd just received a kiss. I focused, and it was Becky. I was not finished with my planning yet, so I asked what she needed. "Did I miss dinner?"

Becky took my hand and pulled me out from in front of my computer. "No, dinner is on the table. You're going to be late if you don't come now."

"Why did you disturb me?" I asked, looking longingly at my computer. "I'm not finished yet."

She put her hand on my cheek. "Oh, Freddy, you have to learn when to work and when to play. It's time for dinner now, and that's that." Becky took my hand, and we headed downstairs—followed by Katie, one of the navy SEALs.

I couldn't read any feelings from Katie. Her concentration was too strong. An ant could have crawled under a chair and not escaped her view. This woman was all business and no friendliness. She was probably the only one on the SEAL team of whom I was actually afraid—at least a little bit.

Everyone was waiting for us at the table.

During dinner, I said to Mrs. Crain, "The dinner is really great tonight, as always. I really like this creamed spinach." Then I looked at Annabelle and said, "I hope you'll come to visit me when I finish building my new home."

"Oh Mommy, can we? Please can we?"

"We'll see, dear. Right now we need to clean up this mess."

Everyone except Katie helped to clean up. She had disappeared for a few seconds but returned and stood in the doorway. Becky and I were doing the dishes, and I called to Katie over my shoulder. "Find anything when you checked the perimeter, Katie?"

"Just a dark brown cat with white boots on three of its legs."

"So where are you from?" I asked, trying to strike up a conversation.

"Where I'm from is none of your business," she retorted. "I would prefer not to talk about myself."

"As you wish. I suppose it makes no difference whether we talk or not." I said it with just a hint of mischievousness, which caused her to have a surprising emotion—hate. I reached out and read her mind. She didn't hate me in particular as much as she hated all men—age, ethnicity, or appearance made no difference; she just simply hated men. I looked a little deeper and found out why. It seems she'd had a lot of trouble while she was growing up. I felt sorry for her. I'd personally had a great childhood, but I had met some people when I attended college who'd had some very bad experiences. This lady had been betrayed too many times. It wasn't her fault that people treated her badly, but it was her fault that she reacted to it as she did. She had an ability, one that probably caused her some emotional troubles when she was young—she was telepathic. It wasn't very strong; she couldn't pick up emotions or thoughts, but she could feel and hear things that others could not. I understood how she felt. It was difficult to hear people talk about you, especially when you know that they're only trying to get something from you. As beautiful as Katie was, I could guess what that "something" was. I could tell that her father and brothers were nasty. It must have been devastating to find out that her husband was cheating on her by hearing him on the phone, three rooms away. This woman had an outstanding mind, probably one of the most organized I'd ever met, but she had no mental shields. She had no choice about what she heard; she simply heard it all. It was amazing that she hadn't gone insane. She just shut off her emotions instead, which was a neat trick. I can't do it. In fact, I tend to be overly emotional.

As I continued drying the dishes, Becky whispered, "She's very cold."

I whispered back, "There are lots of reasons for people to be cold. I can see it in her eyes. She has a hard time trusting people, especially men." I knew Katie was listening, but I continued anyway. "When she looks at you, Becky, I don't see the same hardness. She softens considerably."

"But she seems so mean," Becky argued. "What are you going to do?"

"I'll treat her just like everyone else, with respect for her abilities and the job she does. I'll be nice to her, just like I would be to anyone. She could use a little kindness, I think."

"Do you trust her?"

"Very much so. She's the type who would die trying

to do her job, and since her job is to protect me, I think I'm probably safer right now than I've ever been in my entire life."

"What if her orders change, and she has to kill you?"

"Then I'll be dead." I could see that Becky was going to start crying. I hugged her and kissed her cheek. "Don't worry. I'm not about to do anything that would cause a change in her orders."

Becky relaxed a little, and we finished the dishes. As we were heading into the living room, Katie said, "You can see a lot by looking at a person's eyes."

"Just between you and me," I responded, "you were born able to sense things and hear things when no one else can. Do you hear the two people walking this way right now?"

Her eyes widened and then narrowed. "Yes, I can."

"It's a hard life, being different, isn't it? I can sense emotions. That's how I can see your ability as well as the two people walking up to the front door right now. I've always known when people say one thing and mean something else. It's hard when someone says 'I love you' and his or her emotions say it's a lie. As for me, it hurts to lie to others, knowing what it will do to them when they find out."

"So you don't lie, then?"

"Seldom. Sometimes it's better to lie than to tell the truth, but that's seldom the case. I won't tell the truth if it will hurt someone's feelings when there is no need. You can say what you want, but sometimes lying is best."

Becky had gone ahead of me and was waiting for me in the living room. There was a knock on the front door, but it wasn't for me. I told Becky that I needed to get back to my work and thanked her for her help. She gave me a hug and said, "Don't work too late." I smiled and went upstairs.

I could tell that Katie was trying to think things through. I knew she was going to report this to her superiors, and that's why I left it at emotions only. It was about five thirty in the morning when I finished my new cleanup plans. I took a shower and then put a note on my door said that read: "I've finished the plan, but I'm tired and need some sleep. Please wake me for lunch."

✦

"Again, I think I am lost."

Everything went black.

"Lost, master?"

"I did not study this enemy yet. The words 'hug' and 'kiss'—what do they mean?"

"Hug and kiss are physical forms of communication, allowing an understanding that they are upset. We know that this species is not normally telepathic and cannot confront each other without openly stating so either verbally or physically. In fact, they are so primitive that they are just reaching that stage of development. We cannot remember when we were nontelepathic and therefore have lost all knowledge of what it was like. If we could take the time to understand how they live without such abilities we may understand much more about our lost past."

"Still, hug and kiss seem to mean hit and hit harder. How else would she get his attention?"

"On this one, I tend to agree. Although in this case, they do tend to hit each other a lot."

"Of course they do. You should spend some time in the Gray pads. Children continuously fighting are a good way to weed out the weak. Continue."

CHAPTER 20

✦ ✦ ✦

SURPRISE PROTECTION

I was awakened at 9:10 a.m. It was the changing of the guard, and a heated discussion on the other side of the door woke me. I listened in.

"No, you don't understand. The kid is sleeping. You can't go in until he wakes up."

Cool! Katie is getting protective.

"Standard procedure states that during the pass-down, I check the area to ensure that everything is proper. I trust you, but I can't take over the watch until I see the merchandise."

"No problem. I'll simply stay here until I hear him get up."

I took exception to being called "merchandise," so I decided to put a stop to it. I yelled loudly enough for them to hear me, "Hey, you two! Shut up! I'm trying to sleep in here."

Both were silent for a couple of seconds, and then Katie said, "Well, he's awake now, so I guess you can go in."

I heard a knock on the door, so I opened it and said, "I'm not merchandise." Then I quietly shut the door.

"Whoops, I take it he likes his sleep."

"He didn't get to bed until 5:23. He's tired, and I would bet a little cranky too."

"Okay, I'll take over from here. I don't think I started out on the right foot."

"Yeah. See you back at the barracks … and good luck."

I got dressed but remained in my room, making a list of the items I would need from Mr. Thompson's store. Becky came to get me when lunch was ready. Maggie, the navy SEAL, followed right behind.

"Freddy, I'm sorry about waking you up, but orders are orders."

"Tell the lieutenant I said to change them. I don't want to be disturbed when I'm inventing or when I'm sleeping. I think she'll understand."

"*Warning, Freddy! Two persons.* Petty Officer Frist Class Katie Swanson and Petty Officer Second Class Marian Smith are within one hundred feet. *Warning Freddy! Two persons.* Petty Officer Frist Class Katie Swanson and Petty Officer Second Class Marian Smith are within ninety feet."

The warning continued each ten feet until finally, at fifty feet, I said, "Position, please, and stop reporting."

"Straight up."

I went outside and looked up. They were just getting to roof level, parachuting in. They saw me, and I waved.

Becky, who had followed me, asked, "What's going on?"

"The master chief of the SEAL team and I have a challenge going on. She's trying to fool my equipment and sneak up on me. If she succeeds, then I'll grant her a reasonable request."

"Then why don't they just walk up to you when you're drifting?" Becky asked.

My eyes went wide. "Becky, I hadn't thought of that. What a good idea. Thank you for warning me. I'll guard against that from now on."

Becky smiled. "Happy to help, Freddy," she said, with a smirk at Maggie.

After lunch, I went into town and talked to the shopkeepers. They assured me they could get everything on my list. It all would be sent to the base for pickup, packed in the large, closed trailer that I had rented from Devin Miles. I paid in advance, which made everyone happy. I was assured that my items would be there within twenty-four hours.

The next day I received reports from the shopkeepers that everything was ready, so I let the Crains know that I would be leaving the next morning. I needed to pick up some items on the base and then go out to my home site to do some surveying.

We played games that night. Pretty Pretty Princess was one of the games, and we made sure Johnny won, which meant that he had to wear the princess jewelry and tiara. We laughed and laughed, and Johnny laughed with us. Then we watched the news for the weather report. At bedtime, I asked Maggie to have a car ready to take me to the base right after breakfast.

The next morning, I packed up all my belongings and paid Mrs. Crain, thanking her dearly for her help. She gave me a bag lunch. There were hugs and kisses from everyone, but Mrs. Crain had to pull Becky off me. I promised I would visit her soon. Becky handed me a small box and said, "Please don't open this until you get to your new home." I thanked her and left with tears in my eyes.

✦

"I'm beginning to like this Becky person."

Everything went blurry. I was getting stronger.

"Master?"

"He decided to leave, and she beat him, until her mother pulled her off."

"It seems a strange way to say good-bye. However, you seem to be right again."

I noticed that the Green's face changed to controlled laughter every time it turned away from the Gray. I tried to use my mental powers to find out, but those abilities were not there. Still, I was adjusting. I would find a way.

Green's face changed, looking upset. "None of that, creature!"

Everything returned to black. Darn.

CHAPTER 21

✦ ✦ ✦

CLEANING UP

The car was there and already packed with my stuff, so off we went. When we reached the base, they drove me directly to my supplies, as I had requested. I packed most of my stuff in the sixty-foot trailer and took out twenty little black disks. I placed them around the trailer and then shook hands with Maggie and Janice, my driver, and climbed on top of the trailer. I took the controls and energized the disks. I had never done this before, so I was a little shaky at first, but I raised the disks, and everything within their perimeter rose with them, including the dirt. (Note to self: work on that.) I was too busy working the controls to watch Maggie and Janice, but their feelings were nothing short of total astonishment. I ascended two hundred feet and slowly moved everything toward my new home site. Last night, I'd downloaded my big scanner into my pocket scanner and then tied it into the controls for the antigravity disks. Thanks to the lieutenant, I had complete directions and terrain data.

Once I reached the mountain peaks, I was glad I had worn a coat, as it did get cold crossing the mountains. It took me only fifteen minutes to reach the canyon. I set my load down in one of the few sections that was not contaminated. When I climbed down, I was standing on a rock only fifty feet from the water. The place stank, but my scanners showed that the air would not harm me. I started unpacking my equipment first. I took all the disks I had and placed them around the area. That was harder than I thought it would be, because the land area was over a mile wide at its widest point. I then went back to the trailer and took the controls. I turned on the disks and raised all the trash and junk. Of course, the disks took all the trees and bushes too, but they were also contaminated and would have to be destroyed anyway. I drove the disks together until I had one big pile. I set the pile down where it would cause no more damage by draining into the water, and then I removed the disks.

Next, I took out my laser and my tunneling unit. My tunneling unit was different from the ones I had previously patented; it had a reverse mode. Normally, I would drill a small hole with the laser and then point the tunneler into the hole while on its narrowest setting. As I slowly widened the beam, the hole would expand by condensing the rock molecules. What was left was a tunnel that had a condensed rock surface that was as hard as steel and many feet thick. It was almost impossible to collapse and wouldn't rust or erode.

The reverse mode started out wide and moved inward, condensing everything into a little round stick. With the device on its widest setting, I pointed it at the trash pile. I set the distance for fifty feet and pressed the remote button. It only covered about 30 percent of the pile, so I shut it off and adjusted it to take out the right side. When I pressed the button again, it was in the correct position, but I had to adjust the length to include another fifty feet. This time, when I turned it on, it covered the entire length. I set the unit to Auto-Close slowly and then started unpacking my supplies.

I looked into the package that Becky had given me and to my surprise, there was a set of 14-carat gold dangly earrings, with tiny bells at the ends. A hair ribbon was wrapped around a note.

> Freddy,
> I find it most intriguing that you wear earrings. I have always liked boys that are different. They seem to be so much nicer. I truly hope you like these earrings—they are my favorite pair, and they will remind you to come visit me every time they ring. Use the ribbon to tie your hair back out of your face when you are working.
> Enjoy!
> Hugs and kisses,
> Becky

This was a very nice thing to do for me. I could not wear the earrings just yet, as I might lose them in the trash, so I put them aside for later.

Some of the equipment I purchased was so heavy that I had to attach the antigravity disks to lift it. I spread everything out so that I could get to what I needed quickly. When the trailer was empty, I leveled it and then set it up to live in temporarily. By the time I had finished leveling the trailer, the tunneling unit had completed condensed the first section of trash. I adjusted it to set the trash down. When I turned the Molecular Condensing Tunneling Device (MCTD) off, the condensed trash started to roll toward the water. I panicked, running back to my equipment, trying to find something to stop it. Luckily, the trash stopped against a small raised area. It was completely solid; even the liquid was solid at that point. I had condensed a seventy-five-foot long by thirty-foot wide section down to only seventy-five feet by four inches, exactly one-ninetieth its normal size. I set the tunneling device to do the same thing with the left side and went back to my camp.

By nightfall, I was completely ready to spend a month out here by myself. The trash was condensed, cut into three-foot strips and piled onto eight steel leak-proof skids that I had ordered and had my supplies packed on. I chained everything down and then placed the disks around the entire group. For dinner, I ate one of the sandwiches that Mrs. Crain had given me.

✦

The Gray said, "It sounds to me like this tiny one has something we could use."

Everything went black.

"Yes, master. We have no condensing device. It would help on some planets in building dwellings."

"Dwellings! Think of the power such a device would have in war. You scientists are all alike. You are always thinking of yourself and not the greater good of expanding our race. Continue."

CHAPTER 22

✦ ✦ ✦

VISITING THE GENERAL AND CLEANING, CLEANING, AND MORE CLEANING

At midnight, I called the lieutenant and told the SEAL on duty at the quarterdeck that I was leaving my area and would be gone for about four hours. She had several questions, so I told her I was visiting the general, as the admiral did not have the proper equipment to handle my gift. Climbing up on an empty pallet and taking the controls, I started up the unit and checked the power supply to ensure there was still plenty of juice. I had thought of using the helicopter at the base but decided it would be too noisy. At first I flew close to the ground and very slowly. As I became better at controlling the piles of compressed contamination, I sped up and flew just a little higher. I didn't want to get too high, as radar could pick me up and panic someone. The map showed me where I needed to go, so there was no problem finding the army base. I called the general on the way there but got his answering machine, so I dropped the piles on the largest, greenest lawn I could find, hoping that it belonged to the general. I climbed off, removed my disks from the piles, and then placed a sign on them that read: "Merry Christmas, General! Caution: Possible Hazardous Material." After that, I climbed back on my skid and left.

I was seen leaving. As I waved, I heard gunshots, and one hit the skid. Thank the Lord I was now a thousand feet up and moving away quickly.

Once I was back home, I called in to let the SEALs know I was safe. The lieutenant got on the line and asked me to let them know at what point I would be coming out next time. She wanted to know what I was up to, but all I said was, "Ask the general; he shot at me!"

I went to bed. The trailer was a little cold, so I set up the portable heater that I'd bought from the sporting goods store and drifted off to sleep. Since I still had a lot of work to do, I got up early that same day, after having slept only a couple of hours. I ate another sandwich and went to work.

Removing the cause of the contamination was only part of the problem. I had to clean up the entire canyon, and that meant making some temporary changes. After mounting my tunneler and laser on a skid, I flew it up to the top of the canyon. Once there, I created a new path for the rivers, so that they flowed around the canyon and emptied into the ocean from the right side. That took most of the morning, especially since I had to dig down to the center waterfall and then block the entrance so the water would flow up, out, and around my property.

When the rivers were not flowing into my home site anymore, I cut huge slabs off the contaminated rock at the canyon bottom and condensed them into little cubes, only three feet wide. When I had made about forty cubes, I attached the disks and sent the cubes, twenty at a time, up and away. Following them with my scanners out over the ocean was boring. These rock cubes had little contamination left in them, and I knew the junk would disperse quickly, but I did not want to ruin the fishing, so I set my disks on full and let them drift straight up. When they were at the limit of their abilities, about two hundred miles, I hit the release button. The cubes were moving fast enough that they continued to travel up and out toward the sun. It would take a long time, but eventually, the sun would incinerate them.

I had miscalculated and lost two disks before I could reverse the polarity and have them drift back down to me. The movement of the earth and the pull of the moon were taking effect, so I had to work hard to get eighteen of them back, and they were hot from friction. The other two traveled along with the rock cubes. I did not make the same mistake with the next load of cubes. I sent only ten disks up and then eight more an hour later, and I took my time so there was little friction. That gave me time to get the others back. By dinnertime, I had jettisoned all forty cubes toward the sun and retrieved seventeen of my disks. One was crushed when I moved the cubes too close to each other.

Now I had the entire land section, including the riverbeds, clean. I checked with the scanner and found only one place where I needed to go deeper due to a crack in the rock. The next day, I took that section out and sent it on its way. Next, I went to the opening where the saltwater and fresh water met. This was going to be harder. I placed several disks on the side of the rock wall, and using the laser, I cut that section off. I moved it out and placed it in the ocean, just past the contaminated area. I continued this cutting and moving of rock until I had a wall blocking out the ocean. I filled in the cracks with sand, using disks to grab big sections of contamination off the beach. It took eight days to make a dam to hold back the ocean.

I used the disks again, this time to drift down to the

bottom of the lake. When I turned the disks on and raised them, they took most the lake with them. Using this method, it took another three days to empty all the water from the lake, and then it was just a matter of cutting off the sides and bottom and sending them to the sun.

It took weeks, but when I was finished with the first phase of my plan, there was not even a hint that the area had ever been contaminated. The lieutenant would be getting worried about me. Time for me to check in. I called and told her I would be coming out the next day to pick up supplies. Then I called the stores and arranged for another delivery. I picked up my supplies the next day and came right back because I was eager to begin phase two.

While the water was out, I deepened the channel using the laser and tunneler. I evened up the sides and made them straight up and down. I condensed the surrounding rock so that it was better than having a fortress. The result was more wonderful than I could have expected.

As I flew on my platform from the ocean toward my canyon and into the lake area, I saw cliffs going straight up about eight hundred feet that were as smooth as glass. The area was over five hundred feet deep and straight down to a smooth-as-glass bottom, making it a total of 1,300 feet deep from the top of the cliff to the bottom of the riverbed. The colors were amazing. I left the three natural bridges in place, but I did condense the bottoms so that they would never collapse. If I had wanted to, I could have built my house on any one of them, and it would provide support for it, but that wasn't my plan.

Upon entering the canyon from the ocean by boat, one now would see walls of polished rock. I left a couple of sections in the rock jutting out for a dock and three landing pads. I also left a walkway around this whole section of cliff. I evened out the sides of the canyon and condensed them.

I made a stairway from the top to the bottom and set areas for waterfalls to plummet straight down. I dug out areas for the rivers to flow into the lake with a minimal amount of noise and almost no splash. I had rock bridges across the rivers and a lip of rock separating each land area, so if one flooded, it would not flood all the others.

I took sections of dirt from the riverbeds and the mountain to fill all my land areas. Sifting the dirt to get all the rocks and tree limbs and junk out of it was difficult, but I did it. I readjusted the disks to a low level so that they could not pick up anything over one pound. This left me with topsoil covering my entire canyon land area, which was terraced in three levels.

Each terrace level was twenty feet above the one below and had six feet of topsoil and fourteen feet of rock. I drilled holes in the rock for drainage. The top level had nine ramps leading down into the middle level, and there were six ramps leading from there to the bottom level. Each ramp was solid rock that went up over the lip of the next higher level. The bottom level had three large places where the terrace ramped down to the water, twenty feet below.

I placed the disks on my dam and removed it slowly, allowing the ocean to rush back in. I was glad I was sitting on top of the cliffs, because the force of the returning water would have knocked me down.

Because the dam was contaminated, I sent it up to the sun. I now had a deep channel that any ship could navigate; bringing in supplies would not be a problem.

I then set the rivers back on course and watched as they plummeted over the sides of the canyon into deep pools before flowing into the lake. While watching, I realized that something was wrong—I had made the sides too smooth! The water went over the sides of the cliff without enough turbulence to create white water. Bummer! I decided I had to redo that section, because I prefer whitewater falls. I did not redo the terrace waterfalls, preferring to leave them smooth.

I traveled my shoreline and removed all the contamination I found there too.

✦

"I need this boy to work for me!"

Everything went black—well, almost everything.

"Master?"

"How many of my men could do what this boy did in just a few of his weeks?"

"Even if we had the equipment, none."

"Exactly! Something is driving this child to a near-death pace. He is literally working himself to death."

"Master, I think it's that planet-destroying issue."

"I would like to know what that issue is. Our scanners have picked up nothing."

"Perhaps, master, he has already alleviated the problem."

"Perhaps. Continue."

CHAPTER 23

✦ ✦ ✦

GENERAL TROUBLES

Phase two took four weeks, and I was now almost ready for phase three. I had ordered some things via the Internet several weeks before, and I called the lieutenant to check if my order had arrived. She advised me that I had eight very large generators and several trucks full of cable and other equipment; it had arrived a week ago. I let her know I was coming out the next day and that I would come to the base first.

I next called the inn and asked Mrs. Crain if they had two rooms for a couple of nights. I needed to rest and could think of no better place to do it.

She said, "Of course we have room for you, and we're all glad to have you stay with us again." I also asked if I could do my laundry there, as I didn't have the facilities for that yet. I didn't want to admit that I had forgotten to allow for this in my plans. "The best laid plans of mice and men," as my father used to say. I did reserve one set of clothes, and I planned to wear them tomorrow. She said she would be glad to take care of it for me. I also called the stores and made some purchases, including some furniture. I loaded everything on the extra skid and went to bed.

The next morning, I ate some cereal—dry, as I'd drunk all the milk in the first week. Then I climbed on my skid and headed for the base. I called into the quarterdeck to let them know that I was coming out and would land at the barracks. When I started my descent on the base side of the mountain, I could see the lieutenant in a small helicopter, heading my way. When she was close, she motioned for me to slow down and get on the phone, so I came to a stop and called her cell number.

"Hi, Susan. What's up? Why the escort?"

"Freddy, you made a big splash with the general. He knows you were the one who placed those bars on his front lawn."

"I figured I was spotted. I'm not the expert at this like you are. They shot at me! Did you know that?"

"Yes, I did, and so does the admiral. He's looking at replacing our team if we can't keep a better watch on you."

"Oops, sorry."

"Not a problem, but the general found out you're coming, and he's here now. He wants to have a talk with you."

"What if I don't want to see him?"

"That's your right; he has no proof that you were the one who placed those bars on the lawn. And he's not upset about what you did. He's ecstatic about it."

"He should be, but … why is he?"

"Those bars can be burned for fuel. He had his people analyze them, and they discovered that the bars are no longer hazardous waste; they're solid materials. They tried several ways to get rid of them, but when they set them on fire, the energy output was remarkable."

"Of course it was, and I'll bet that the bars lasted a long time too."

"Each bar burned for days. Freddy, they gave off enough heat to run a generator at full output—six thousand kilowatts for two days—before having to add another."

"Really? My estimates were somewhat better than that. If he can't use them right, do you think he'd give them back?"

She laughed. "I take it that you knew."

"Yes, but I need to patent the process and the unit's ability. So why did you come out here to warn me if the general isn't angry at me?"

"After hearing that they shot at you, the admiral did not want you to see the general's car and staff and decide to skip this visit. He sent me out here to pave the way, so to speak. Both of them are interested in the use of the antigravity disks and the scanner. Besides, calling me once a week is not enough to help my reports. You are supposed to show up when we do maintenance on the radar. Where were you?"

"Very busy, that's where. The admiral and I can talk about my equipment later. I fully intend to ask him to permit me to place a scanning system in his radar tower, and of course, I will supply him with the necessary equipment to use it, but I'm not ready for that. He still has a leak, doesn't he?"

"No, the leak was locked down. I'm confident that there is no more leak."

"How did the general find out that I was coming? Only your group knew. What's going on?"

"Freddy, let's talk about it later."

"Very well, but we definitely need to talk about this. Last one to the base is a rotten egg."

"You're on." She started heading that way, so I dropped down to fifty feet and flew well below her before I left her behind. I was at the barracks three minutes before she landed and eight minutes before she got there. In fact, I already had the car loaded with my dirty laundry before she showed up.

Smiling and with a little laugh in my voice, I said, "Hi, Lieutenant, nice to see you."

"I'm glad you were tied down, Freddy. I saw you almost fall out. You must be more careful—that's an order!" She was smiling, so I took it in the fun way it was meant.

I snapped to attention and saluted, saying, "Yes, ma'am."

The girls on the team were all laughing. I saw that the general's spy, Sgt. Davies, was still with the team. The lieutenant and I had a lot to talk about. I was getting hugs from everyone, and that was nice, but they all stopped when the watch pointed out that the admiral's car, the general's limo, and two jeeps of army personnel had appeared in the distance. It was just like them to ruin a good reunion. I looked at the lieutenant and said, "Just in case, I would like it made very clear that I'm being protected and that the general won't be touching me."

"Got it." She made a tiny hand signal and everyone scrambled. "Master Chief, you're with me." The master chief loaded and cocked her sidearm, and then she took two knives out from somewhere under her clothing and placed them in full view. Before the cars pulled up, there were SEALs on both flanks, some in the barracks, and some across the street in what had to be a position designed to place the army in a crossfire. The rest of the team I could not see, although I knew they were there. I knew where they were, but I didn't think it was right to give their position away by turning my head to look.

When the admiral's car drove up, the lieutenant went over to it and opened the door. She whispered to the admiral, and he smiled. "Thanks for the warning, Lieutenant. Your orders stand. Your team is to watch and protect. Those orders come from the president of the United States directly to you. The general and I could not revoke them, even if we wanted to, and I don't. If the general pulls something, shoot him.

Do us a favor, though, and try for a leg or something fixable, will you? It would look bad if we killed the SOB on navy property. Now, let's go see the boy." They walked toward me.

"Hello, Dr. Anderson."

"Hello, Admiral, sir."

"You've been out in the canyon for some time. How's the preparation coming along?"

"Fairly well, actually. I'm almost ready to pick up the house I'm having built. It's not ready yet, but I'll need to do an inspection on it soon, probably next week."

By that time, the general was getting out of his big black limousine. I went telepathic instantly, all shields up and ready. The general walked up to us and put his hand out, saying, "So this is Freddy." He pulled his hand back very quickly when the master chief was suddenly between us, and her facial expression said, *Don't!*

He backed up a little and looked around. He noticed the SEALs and saw that they were armed. Even though they looked like they were lounging, he knew better. His mind sized up the situation quickly, and he wondered where the other SEALs were. He saw Sgt. Nettie Davies but kept his mind off her, as he did not want to give her away. The army personnel in the jeeps were getting fidgety and started fingering their weapons, so the lieutenant told the general, "Sir, call off those men. I would hate to have to report to the president that we had a massacre here."

He motioned for them to stand down. "Why the tight security, Lieutenant?"

I was impressed with her acting. She actually blushed when she said, "We have a leak, sir, and I don't have it locked down yet. The orders are to protect Dr. Anderson at all costs."

"And you interpret those orders to mean killing my men if they start something?" he said with a sneer.

"No, sir, I interpret them to mean taking them and you out, if necessary, to maintain security. They don't need to start anything." She said this with such a flat, matter-of-fact tone that the general stopped thinking about his men and started worrying about himself. He started sweating.

"Lieutenant, this is a peaceful visit. The kid did something that I would like to talk to him about, that's all."

"Then let's move inside out of the sun and talk, if that's all right with you, Dr. Anderson."

"Fine, Lieutenant, ma'am." I took her hand and let her lead me inside. We went right past the quarterdeck. The general and the admiral were stopped, and their ID cards were checked. The two men with the general were not allowed to pass. The master chief purposely picked the smallest SEAL, Petty Officer Donet, and instructed her to watch them.

"Orders, Master Chief?"

"If they start anything, take them out. We need an example for the others, so make it especially bloody." She smiled a wicked smile and stood only three feet from them. They left quickly, abandoning their general.

The lieutenant, the admiral, the general, and the master chief were the only ones in the lounge with me. The master chief stood right behind the general. The lieutenant sat to my left and the admiral to my right, around a small table.

I started the conversation. "General, you wanted to talk with me. I am sorry for the inconvenience of this security, but I don't trust you." His thoughts were, *"And well you shouldn't."*

"Well, Freddy, thanks to you I seem to be the proud owner of several hundred bars of hazardous waste."

"First of all, General, I have not given you permission to call me by my first name, so please address me more appropriately. Second, you already owned the material; I just put it into a more useful form and placed it at your disposal. I thought I was doing you a favor, yet you fired a weapon at me. If you want me to take the bars back, I would be more than happy to do so. Bars like that are very expensive, and I can think of several applications for their use. I initially thought about keeping the material, but that would be stealing because it belonged to the army when it was dumped, and I'm not a thief."

His quickly made up a plausible story. "First, you were piloting an unregistered aircraft over an army base at night, which is certainly provocation enough to warrant gunfire. Second, you did not file a flight plan. Third, it was the middle of the night.

The lieutenant interjected, "Dr. Anderson does not look at time like we do, sir. It was simply the most convenient time for him. In fact, he called me at midnight to let me know that he was going to pay you a visit."

"Why didn't you contact us and let us know, Dr. Anderson?"

"I did call you, General, but I got your answering machine. I also waved at the man who yelled hello to me, but I was too far away to hear what he was saying, although I'm sure he saw me. I would have talked to someone earlier, but no one was around. Your security is very lax, you know. Why did your men shoot at me?"

The general took a deep breath and let it out with a sigh. "Now I understand why the lieutenant has such tight security while I'm around, Dr. Anderson. We had no idea who it was that got past our security, onto our base, dropped off what could have been a bomb, and then flew off without making any sound. The guards shot into the air to give warning, not to shoot you. At least, that's what they told me."

"Really? Then please explain the hole in my skid. I doubt your people are such bad shots." I took out my little antigravity device and turned it on.

The general looked at it and asked, "What's that supposed to be?"

The lieutenant answered. "General, sir. That is a lie detector."

"It works?"

"Yes, sir, it does. I tried to fool it and could not. Lie, and see what happens."

"I don't want the bars." The needle nearly jumped off the scale.

"I would think you would want them, General. They're a great fuel resource."

"I found that out, Dr. Anderson. Please, the next time you want to give me a present, give us some warning. We only found out by accident."

"You didn't toss any in a standard burner, did you?"

"Yes, we did."

"Did the burner melt down?"

"Exactly."

"That's my fault. Next time, I'll make a little more effort to contact you. It's just that I get carried away when I'm working, and I don't think about all the little possibilities, like your not wanting unannounced visitors."

"Good. I'm glad we have that all straight. We saw you using your antigravity disks … very impressive. It took a heavy-duty forklift just to pick up one bar. It has also come to my attention that you have something called a 'scanner,' and now this 'lie detector' also?"

I shot the admiral a dirty look. "I do, but they are not ready for use at this time. The admiral and I have an agreement that I can test them on his base, with his prior approval, of course."

The general thought, *Lucky man. Too bad one of my plants was discovered.*

I asked, "General, are you responsible for the leak on this

base?" The lieutenant smiled, and so did the master chief. The general was not smiling.

"I am. The lieutenant caught my plant just two weeks ago."

He was so happy that he was able to scurry around the subject that I got upset and wanted to ask if he had any others. I touched the lieutenant's mind and knew she hoped I would not expose the sergeant, so I let it drop.

"Dr. Anderson, I would like to extend an invitation for you to test anything you want on my base. Just ask."

I perked up and smiled, acting really happy, "Lieutenant, can I please? Oh, can I?"

The lieutenant was surprised and asked, "What do you need to test?"

"I invented this small thermonuclear device, and if I can get the parts, I was planning to test it over the ocean, but that would start a major tidal wave. There will be no radiation. It would be much better if I tried it on land first. His base is just about the right size. We could move everyone away for about fifty miles, and I could see if my theory works. Or we could just leave them there and make it a big surprise."

The general turned white.

The admiral said, "Now you see why I'm approving all testing first?"

The general stood up and said, "The invitation is withdrawn." Pointing at me, he said, "Admiral, this child is a disaster just waiting to happen. I'm leaving. Good luck, and I hope this base is still here the next time I visit."

I looked at the general with a pout. "Does that mean I can't play on your base? The admiral and the lieutenant are way too restrictive."

He turned around and stormed out saying, "No way!"

As soon as he was out of sight, I started laughing. The lieutenant smiled, but the admiral was not amused.

"Admiral, I'm not stupid enough to develop or even write down my theory on thermonuclear detonation," I told him. "I wouldn't want someone like the general to get his hands on it."

The admiral asked, "Then it was a joke, meant to cause the general discomfort?"

"Yes, of course. He dumped a lot of contaminated stuff on my property, and I owed him for it."

The admiral smiled.

"Sir, I'm sorry, but I may have just made your job a little harder. The general is not happy with having me around."

"Don't worry about that, Dr. Anderson. I'll point out to him that I'll take all the responsibility and share some of the 'gifts' with him—maybe a little testing too—but only on things that are already patented. He'll let me do the work if he thinks he's getting some of the benefit."

"Admiral, I like you. Please call me Freddy."

He smiled and said, "Okay, and you can call me Jeff."

"Thank you, Jeff. Susan and I have a lot to do before I get back. I understand you want to talk to me about some of my toys."

"Yes, the navy is very interested in them. I'm sorry, but I do have to report what I see, and you did use the disks here on base—the scanner too."

"I was hoping to talk to you about the scanner and disks, as well as a few more items, but I didn't plan for it on this trip. I will be going back home in just a couple of days, but I will be coming out in another week or so. I will set aside some time to sit with you over lunch and discuss our mutual needs. Is that all right?"

"That'll be fine, Freddy. I'll report to the president that things are working out between us. I'm sure she'll be happy about that."

"Tell her I said hello."

"Will do." We all stood up, and I shook his hand. We walked back outside, and he got into his car and left.

I asked the lieutenant, "Did I handle that okay?"

"I think so, Freddy. It's hard to tell at this time. Be careful about giving the admiral too much information at one time. Take it slow."

"One more thing, Freddy," said the master chief, "don't ever use your eyes to give away our positions. The army people with the general were Green Berets, and they're not stupid."

I looked at the ground, where there was a little fresh blood. "Did any of the SEALs get hurt?" I was sad, thinking that they might have been wounded because of me.

The master chief could see I was upset. She put her arm around me, sat down on the bumper of the jeep, and said, "No, the Green Berets are good, but we're better. Petty Officer Henderson came back from picking up supplies at the exchange, and she was dressed in her Class A uniform. It's a nice outfit that we'll have to show you some time. When she bent over to unload the jeep, she showed a little too much leg, which caused several wolf whistles. Petty Officer Henderson took exception to it and broke the nose of the closest man. She's very quick and did it so fast that you would have been hard-pressed to see it. In addition, three knives stuck deep into the metal of their jeep from directions they were not expecting. They were very quiet after that."

"I'm glad that none of your team was harmed. They get very touchy about things like that, don't they?"

"Most women do, Freddy. No one likes to be picked on because of his or her sex. It's just not the right thing to do. The problem with doing it to this group is that they don't have to put up with it."

"Please, Master Chief, if I'm making that kind of mistake, point it out to me, and I'll stop. You don't need to hurt me."

"Don't worry, Freddy. We look at you like our little brother. No one here will hurt you. They may get angry and chew you out if you do something stupid, but they'd never hurt you."

That cheered me up a little. Most of the SEALs were standing around us now. I said, "I can take a chewing-out, and I learn quickly, so I won't make the same mistake twice."

The lieutenant said, "We know, Freddy. That's why we like you. You never try to hurt anyone, and you're kind to a fault, except maybe to the general. Please don't take offense, but you're almost the opposite of us and of most men. Normally, we are the opposite of what most men think a woman should be. We are all aggressive, while you are passive, and that works for us. Every woman here knows you need her help, and they all want to protect you, mostly because you are not like other men. You look at the women with respect for their abilities and intelligence, and you treat them as if you care about them. They return that respect and care."

"So they treat me nicely because I treat them nicely, and I treat them nicely because they treat me nicely?"

They all laughed. "That's about right," said the lieutenant.

The master chief stood up and said in a commanding voice, "You didn't come out here for this mushy stuff, so what can we do for you, Freddy?"

I smiled at her and then gave her a big hug. She patted my back gently. When I let her go, I told her that I had reserved two rooms in the inn for two days. "I plan on talking to some of the store owners today, but mostly I plan on relaxing. Tomorrow morning, I need to come back to the base and inventory the stuff in the trucks and check the generators, and then I'm going back to the inn to rest, because I leave for home the following day."

The lieutenant asked, "What about that trip you spoke about?"

"Oh, I'm coming out in a week or two. I need to fly to South Carolina to check on the house I'm having built. It needs to match some very exact measurements, and I need to ensure that everything is going well."

"Freddy, we have to come with you on that trip."

"Really?" I looked down at the ground. "I suppose your orders would include that, wouldn't they? And I did say you could watch me when I'm not at home."

"Yes, they do, and yes, you did."

"I'll be out there for seven or eight days, most of which will be sitting around. How many people will you have to send with me?"

"I have business here, so it will be the master chief and three others."

"Okay, I'll set up the hotel, car rental, and flights. Can you get us to the airport and back?"

"You bet," she agreed. Then she looked over at one of the SEALs. "Freddy, would you mind doing a little sightseeing on that trip?"

"Why?"

"One of the girls has family next door in North Carolina. She'd love to see her children again."

"How old are they?"

Marian Smith walked up. "I have two girls, ages three and five. I haven't seen them for almost a year."

"Why? Don't you get vacation?"

"We each get thirty days leave a year, and I have over sixty days on the books, but things are not always that simple."

"If it's a money problem, I can buy you a ticket."

"No, dear, but thanks. It's very nice of you to offer. The problem is that their father died, and I had no choice but to leave them with my mom and dad. Dad's a tobacco farmer and doesn't approve of my being in the navy. He thinks I should be at home, helping on the farm. He makes things very hard for me when I'm there."

"I'm sorry about your husband, and I don't mean to meddle, but I don't understand. Why not bring the kids out here?"

The lieutenant answered that one. "She'd love to, but we never know if we're moving or being sent somewhere. This is a quick-response unit, and she can't take the time to find a babysitter at the last minute."

I put my hands on my hips, as I'd seen my mother do, and said, "Well, that sucks! You must miss them a lot."

"I do, and if I can combine work with a chance to visit my children, I'd be very grateful."

"Sounds good. Can I meet them too?"

She looked at the lieutenant for confirmation as she said, "I don't see why you can't, as long as everyone goes with you. We still have a job to do."

"What's the name of the town where they live?"

"Goldsboro."

"I'll set it up. This actually may help me, too. I wasn't looking forward to being stuck in South Carolina for eight days, doing nothing, so I was trying to think up fun things I could do there. The plan was to check out my house, make a list of things to correct right away and things that need fixing before shipment, and then fool around for six days until I can inspect the corrections they made. The only change I'll have to make in my plan is that I'll be vacationing in North Carolina instead of South Carolina. I found out that there are lots of things to do in South Carolina. Are there things to do that the master chief can take me to see while we're in North Carolina?"

"Yeah, bunches of stuff."

"Great! This will work out much better than I thought. Thanks, Marian."

She hugged me and thanked me.

"Time to head to the inn," said the ensign.

I glanced at the Sergeant. "One more thing, Lieutenant," I said. "Can we talk in private?"

"Sure, Freddy, but it's not necessary. Everyone knows what I'm doing with our friendly spy. She has agreed to do our bidding, and the general will get only the reports that we want him to get and nothing else. If I turn her in, he'll just replace her, and we'll be back to square one."

"Well, you're the expert. Good luck. Let's go. Who's my bodyguard today?"

Everyone moved away, and most of them were very easy to read. The lieutenant answered, "PO2 Bunny Taylor."

"Do you mean the spy, Sergeant Nettie Davies?"

"Yes, Freddy, but I would ask you not to call her that. She's 'Bunny' or 'Petty Officer Taylor.'" While staring at the lieutenant, I read Bunny's mind. She was silently begging me to give her a chance. She really wanted to do this, and she was sincere about protecting me.

"Very well, Lieutenant. Like I said, you're the expert, and I trust you. Time to wish me good luck, I think."

We climbed into the car, and Janice drove. I was quiet. I had no idea what the lieutenant was trying to do, but I definitely hoped she did.

✦

The big Gray said, "This I understand. I know exactly what she is doing. It's something I would do myself."

Everything went blurry.

The Green looked a little upset and said, "And I am sure you are very good at it, master."

"You bet I am. Continue."

CHAPTER 24

✦ ✦ ✦

ORDERING SUPPLIES

When we reached the inn, everyone ran out to greet me. I introduced everyone to Bunny. After hugs all around, we unloaded my laundry and took it inside. Carroll and Becky insisted on doing my laundry, saying I was here to rest, not to work. Who was I to argue?

I thanked Becky for the present, and I must have been blushing, as she touched my face and smiled. Johnny, Annabelle, and I skipped rope outside and played hopscotch until we were called in for lunch. Annabelle was surprisingly good at both games, but we laughed until our sides hurt when Johnny tried to skip rope.

The food was great, and I started thinking that staying at the inn more often would be nice, especially since I would get to see more of Becky. During lunch, they asked me many questions, and I answered all of them. I don't think they believed me when I told them the entire pollution mess was cleaned up, but Bunny let them know about the bars I'd dropped off at the general's house.

Becky squeezed my hand, asking, "Wasn't that dangerous?"

"Honestly, Becky, I was never in any trouble."

Bunny raised her eyebrows. Mrs. Crain saw her, and so did Carroll and Becky. Becky looked at me with fire in her eyes. "What you consider trouble and what everyone else considers trouble seem to be two different things. You be more careful. You hear me?"

"Yes, I'll be good."

"You'd better be or else!"

Mrs. Crain cleared her throat. "Young lady, I don't think that's a proper way to talk to our guest. Apologize right now."

She bowed her head and said, "I'm sorry."

I looked at her with a mischievous smile. That cheered her up and got a laugh from everyone else.

After lunch, I went to visit the shop owners and thank them for their help. They were glad to see me, and we went down to the courthouse to talk and split up most of the items I needed—specifically, sheets of stainless steel, titanium, copper, gold, and over a hundred other minerals in large quantities. I also asked for a restaurant-sized refrigerator/freezer that I could connect outside, something that could take the weather, had a light bulb inside, and was safe. I didn't want to lock myself inside accidentally. I asked for several hundred heavy-duty electrical outlets in one size. I also wanted five hundred gallons of sulfuric acid.

Zoë Ledbetter, owner of the grocery store, asked, "Why sulfuric acid?"

"I need it for a little toy I'm working on." No one asked anything after that. They assured me that they could get everything except the acid. For that, I would need to contract with someone outside, and they asked me to please not bring it through the town.

The rest of the day went smoothly, and the next day was very restful. I woke up very early and went back to the base. I placed my disks around the trucks and flew them out to my home site, and then I came back and took all eight generators home.

✦

"What does he need the acid for?"

Everything went black.

"Master, I have no idea. He did not mention it, and it did not come directly to mind."

"Can't you dig a little deeper?"

"No, master. Not without destroying his mind entirely, and then we would not know how he destroyed our ship."

"Yes, well. That is the most important information. Continue."

CHAPTER 25

✦ ✦ ✦

WORKING AT HOME

Once I was back in the canyon, I started right to work. I measured the waterfalls and then diverted them again. I built a tunnel into the cliff directly behind the largest waterfall and mounted the generator. Getting it up to the tunnel was easy, but locking it down was difficult. It took me three days with the first one. The second one was much easier, as I had learned a lot about drilling the holes first and setting the anchors before I blocked access to them. I mounted four of my generators, two behind the main waterfall from the underground river and two behind the next biggest waterfall.

While I was mounting the generators, I also drilled several tunnels that connected the generators together. All I had to do was set the tunneler, hit the button, and wait. I made sure that the tunnels were on a slight incline, so that the water would not flow into my main connection room, which I made quite large.

I ran a tunnel, only one foot in diameter, from the main connection room to the base of the cliff, nearly six hundred feet down, and curved it toward the edge, where the cliff met the first terrace. I went outside and drilled an eight-foot hole into the area where I planned to have a junction room. The one-foot hole I drilled from the connection room wasn't there. I had to redrill to open it up, as my tunneler had closed it, trying to compress and combine the molecules for the junction room. Work and learn. After that, I knew to drill the destinations first.

From there, I drilled a hole in the ground where I wanted my house to be and then holes out by each bridge, the landing platforms, the pier, and several other places where I might need power. Then I went back to the junction room and drilled smaller holes that went all the way out to the different spots, so that I had cable runs.

When it came time to run cable, it proved to be very difficult. Getting the larger cable straight down was easy. I just put a long rope on one end and attached a disk to the other. I sent the disk down the hole, and it came out the other end, pulling the cable with it. The problem was the smaller holes and cable. I could not use disks, as they traveled up and down really well but not side to side. After trying several different things, I finally settled on using a toy.

I called into the base to let the SEALs know that I needed to go to the exchange to get an item I needed for my cabling job. The lieutenant was waiting for me and took me there. I remembered seeing this item when she took me through the exchange the first day. I met her and luckily it was still there. In the toy section, there was a small four-wheel-drive, remote-control truck. I purchased it and lots of extra batteries and took them home.

After that, my job was easy. I attached a small rope to the truck. The holes I sent the truck down were straight and smooth as glass, no snags, and that little truck shot through the holes like a rocket. When it got to the other side, I removed the truck and attached a disk to the rope. I sent the disk straight up until it pulled the cable out that side.

I redirected the flow of the water to its natural movement, so that it turned the generator turbines. Now I had power available for all areas of my home. Most things were completed, including mounting the connector boxes and preparing for installation of fixtures. Everything was ready; the generators were tested and ran fine. The connection room and junction rooms worked out great after a little modification. In all, it took two weeks to complete, and it was time to report to the lieutenant. I was so tired, and my arms hurt from all the screwing, wire stripping, weatherproofing, and cable connecting. This was not a job for a child; I was determined to make a robot as soon as I could.

I called the lieutenant and let her know it was time to leave. When I reached the base, everything was ready for our flight to South Carolina. There were several issues with the house, which I brought to the builder's attention, and then we went to North Carolina, where we rested and played.

I simply do not understand why people watch car races. I received a stiff neck, watching the cars go around and around the track. It was noisy. The most annoying thing was that some people kept hoping for a crash.

Before long, it was back to South Carolina, where I checked out the house again, and then home. Everything went smoothly. Back at the base, the lieutenant asked if I needed help with anything. At that time, I said, "No, but thank you for the offer."

✦

"Why do it all on his own? And what are car races?" Everything went black.

"Master, I believe that some of the military and most of the politicians of this species are not trustworthy. At least, that seems to be his thoughts. I also believe that 'car races' is a form of insanity. Why else would the people continuously run around in circles?"

"I understand the Blues—I mean, politicians not being trustworthy. But the military? I can't believe that. Why would these creatures watch the insane?"

"I think they are watching the insane in hopes of seeing them run into each other."

"What? Why?"

"They must be very bored, master."

"Interesting. Continue."

CHAPTER 26

✦ ✦ ✦

THEY DECLARED WAR

I went home and found it trashed. I checked my scanners; which I had left concealed, monitoring any activity while I was gone, thinking that I might get animals visitors like bears or cougars. Instead, I got army animals. It was easy to see where they had come in, and obviously, they stayed only a few hours. I called the lieutenant and asked who knew I was going to be away.

"Freddy, anyone could have found out by simply watching and by checking transportation data," she said. "Why?"

"My place is trashed. The army destroyed almost everything, including my power junction room and four of my generators. I have a week's cleanup and a lot of things I need to reorder, including a new trailer to live in."

"How do you know it was the army?"

"I hid my scanner and left it on. Lieutenant, they took my disks and a couple of other things—things that would not be good in their hands."

"Freddy, let me handle this. You make me a list of what's missing, and I'll do everything I can to get it back."

"I'll have the list to you within an hour—with pictures."

Four days later, I received a call from the lieutenant. "Good news, Freddy. We retrieved everything. Come pick it up."

Everything was waiting for me at the barracks when I arrived. "How did you do it, Lieutenant?"

"It wasn't hard to find when they blew a hole through six buildings. We simply went in during the chaos and grabbed everything."

"Was anyone hurt?"

The lieutenant raised her hand, and the master chief placed a twenty-dollar bill in it.

"That was a sucker's bet, Master Chief," I said. "Lieutenant, what exactly happened?"

"We received information from our source, Bunny, where they were keeping the stuff. They had it altogether in one place while they studied it. Apparently, someone set off something and in just a flash, it tore a one-foot hole through six buildings, eight cars in the parking lot, and halfway through a hill."

"It just stopped?"

"Yes, one flash, and then it was over."

"Darn it, Lieutenant. That moron probably turned on my laser without plugging it in. He probably ruined the battery. Now I'll have to replace it too. Idiots! Didn't their mommies tell them not to play with big boys' toys?"

They both started laughing, but I didn't. When the lieutenant saw my face, she said, "I take it you're fairly angry, Freddy."

It was plain to see that I was fuming. "They set me back six months, Lieutenant. I have to order and wait for four more generators. I have to worry that they're going to try something again, and I have to start all over on a lot of work. The project I'm trying to get to next is important,

Lieutenant—very important. My arms are still tired from the work I just finished. The general has just cost me over five million dollars in ruined parts, set me back six months, and worse, he's declared war on me."

"Whoa, Freddy. I don't think he meant to declare war," said the master chief.

"Really? What would you call it? Playing games? Well, I can play games too! Lieutenant, may I borrow your phone please?" She handed me the phone, and I dialed the president's office and informed her secretary that I wanted to talk to the president right away. "You tell her that the incident in northern California at the army base was caused by the theft of my inventions," I said tersely, "and that I think her people have declared war on me. Now, you get her on a secure line, or I will answer their declaration of war." A few moments later, the president answered, and I made it clear that I was very upset. "You promised that the army would stay away from me," I said. "They stole my inventions, and then were stupid enough to try to run my equipment without instructions."

I assured the president that it was not the lieutenant's fault and that her team was doing a great job but that I wouldn't let them near my place, so they had stayed away, as requested. I ended our conversation by telling her that I had a tape of the whole thing that I would give to the lieutenant. Then I handed the phone to the lieutenant, saying, "She wants to talk to you."

The lieutenant's end of the conversation consisted primarily of "Yes, Madam President," which she said repeatedly. When the lieutenant finally hung up the phone and sat down, she was as white as a sheet. She said, "Master Chief, we're about to get new orders. Send one of the team down to the Communications Center to pull it off the system herself. I don't want anyone to see the orders before I do."

After the master chief left, the lieutenant said to me, "Freddy, the general is about to get new orders too. I need to get that tape and dispatch the ensign to the Pentagon today. It appears that the general is about to get court-martialed, along with everyone else on that tape."

"Good."

"Freddy, this will ruin the general's career."

"Your point, Lieutenant?"

"I know you're angry, but that was the first time I've ever seen you do something mean to anyone."

"Lieutenant, I've tried to warn the general. I think I've been fairly easy on him, all things considered. The man is mean, and he will continue to do whatever he wants until someone stops him. I have read about history throughout the ages, and the thing that sticks out in my mind is that people who are completely wiped out do not retaliate. The president assured me that she would wipe him out for me. It was that, or I had to harm him myself. This was the lesser of two evils. I really don't want to harm anyone. I don't ever want to start down that path. I pride myself on being a healer and a creator, not a destroyer. The general made me be a destroyer, and I don't like the feeling, but right now, I need to make you a copy of that tape and then take this stuff home. I have a lot of work to do."

"Freddy, if we could protect you at home too, this will never happen again."

"Lieutenant, if someone comes to my home uninvited again, they're going to find several very unpleasant surprises. Please keep your people away, because I don't want them harmed. The system I'm about to put up is not passive. I will develop a passive protection system while I'm waiting for the parts I now have to reorder, but for the time being, please stay away."

"I understand, Freddy."

I downloaded the information into her computer. As soon as it was ready, the ensign left for Washington, DC. We packed up everything, and I hugged them and left.

✦

The big Gray exclaimed, "Ah … this I also understand."

Everything went black, or so they thought.

"Master?"

"That poor general sacrificed his life to ensure that this evil child did not have all the power. Our color has had to do similar heroic things to obtain information from you Greens."

The Green said, "I tend to see it the same way this creature does. That general, or military Gray, was a thief and stole his equipment. Why trash the rest of his equipment, if not to cover up his theft?"

"Typical scientific Green. You're worse than the crazed moralistic Whites. Of course he had the place trashed; the creature is dangerous! I would have had him shot."

"Please pardon the slang of your color, master, but I find your militaristic Gray opinions offensive and oppressive. That is why we call you the 'pleasure killers.'"

"I take no offense in being considered your pleasure killer. In fact, I take great pleasure in removing your pleasure. Now, continue."

A Blue walked in. He was far bigger than either the Gray or the Green, and I could see the fear in the Gray's face—if I could call that a face. "I have been watching the two of you." It turned to the Gray. "You will stop with this childish prattle so that the Green can finish his job. And if I ever hear you call a Blue anything besides Great One or sire, I will have your pleasure for dinner." He turned to the Green. "Please continue."

CHAPTER 27

✦ ✦ ✦

WHOOPS, I THINK A VISIT FROM THE NAVY WOULD BE GOOD

Back at home, I made a short but wide tunnel in the side of the cliff and moved everything inside. I had plenty of time to just relax now, so I tried on the earrings that Becky had given me. They were surprisingly comfortable, and I enjoyed wearing them immensely. The bells were fun and did remind me of Becky.

I had plenty of power with the two generators that the army had not destroyed, so I continued working on setting up things. Two weeks later, the lieutenant called to tell me that a lot of equipment just had come in and that some of it was quite large. I told her I'd be right there.

I flew to the base and saw that nearly everything I'd reordered was there, plus a lot of the things I'd ordered from town. This would keep me busy for a while. Now, if I could just get my new generators. The big items were the metals that I had requested. The machines I ordered were also there. One was much bigger than I expected, but I could work with it. I thanked them and took it all home—in eight trips.

The first things I hooked up were the washers and dryers. I didn't have a house, but I had plenty of dirty clothes. I had ordered five of each so that I could get everything done quickly. Next, I unpacked the hot water heater and hooked it up. This was a new design that took up almost no room. It heated water on demand with a continuous loop. Everything worked really well, and soon I was pulling out clean clothes from the washers. They were a little small, though. I thought about that, as I had dried them on the highest heat. When I finally figured out what had happened, it was too late. I took my pants out of the dryer and could not get them on—and it was the same with almost everything else. I was sitting there in my birthday suit with nothing to wear. It occurred to me that I might need to cut the temperature on the hot water heater to below 175 degrees Fahrenheit.

I called the lieutenant to ask if she could bring me some new clothes. She said she'd be glad to shop for me and bring the clothes out to my home.

I went back to work. First, I looked up the correct temperature for a water heater and set it to 135 degrees Fahrenheit. Next, the lieutenant would need a place to land. I had the landing platforms, but they were covered with equipment while I assembled and installed the lights. These installed flush, so I had to do some tiny drilling and run a trench around in which to place the wire. Then I had to fill it with rock and compact it down, flush with the rest. I also needed to roughen the walking areas, as they were like glass and very slippery, especially when wet. Another learning experience and a sore back end.

The lieutenant called me back the next day to say that she had everything.

"Great, Susan, and a big thanks!" I said. "I'll scan the area and if it's safe, you can land your helicopter on the landing pad. I'll have it lighted for you."

"Those are the round, flat areas I saw in the tapes?"

"Yes, the center one is all clear. If the pad is lighted, then it's okay to land. Give me a few minutes to scan and turn off the protective grid."

"I'll be there in an hour," she said.

Everything scanned fine, so I turned off the grid and turned on the lights. I was wearing the few things I could piece together or that stretched enough to get on. I was determined to see Becky this week and have her teach me how to do laundry. I could use the rest anyway. Besides, I missed Becky.

In exactly one hour, the lieutenant's helicopter showed up on my warning scanner. She flew over once and then circled around and landed directly in the center of the pad. She climbed out with two others. I ran over to help her with the packages, and that's when the master chief reached out and grabbed me. She had been trying to get to me every time I was off the base since we made that bet that they could not sneak up on me. I would have detected her, but I did not use the scanner for such, and I turned it off once I was sure everything was safe. The lieutenant was surprised and yelled, "Master Chief, what are you doing?"

"Lieutenant," I said, "she was just playing with me—and she won the bet."

The lieutenant looked at us and said, "I had forgotten all about that."

"She was not supposed to come on my land, though, but now that I think back on the bet, I forgot to state that. Well, I said I would grant one thing within reason. Any idea what you want?"

"Yes," said the master chief. "Any chance we could come out here and guard you?"

"That's not within reason, Master Chief."

"Then the lieutenant and I will come up with something."

I thanked the lieutenant for bringing me some clothes and wrote her a check for the amount I owed her. As I handed it to her, she looked around with her mouth open. I could read the astonishment in her mind. "Big change, isn't it, Lieutenant?"

"Big change isn't the half of it. I could bring a division of engineers out here, and they couldn't do this in a year. It's been only three months."

"If you don't mind the mess, Lieutenant, I'd be glad to show you around. I'm leaving in an hour anyway."

"Why?" she asked. "Where to this time?"

"The Seaward Inn. I need to get someone to show me how to wash my clothes so that I don't shrink them again."

The lieutenant shook her head. "They won't be able to help you for a day or two. The boats are coming in tonight, and everyone's going to be busy. Petty Officer Smith can help you, though. She's very good at laundry. The master chief, ensign, and I will look around here, if that's all right."

"You can help me?" I asked Petty Officer Smith.

"I should think so. I come from a family of fourteen, so I know how to do laundry. I'll get you started while the others wander around for a while."

"I should show them around," I suggested.

"They can find their way around, believe me."

"Okay, but let me tell them a few things first. Lieutenant, please don't press any buttons on anything you find. If you just can't help it, and you find you have to press something, point it away from me. Aim it at the water, and if you're not absolutely sure which end the energy comes out of, then don't stand behind it."

Her eyes got wide, and she said, "Of course."

"If you fall into the water, swim to the center ramp over there," I said, pointing to it. "The others are still like glass.

I haven't had a chance to roughen them up yet. Be careful—things are slippery."

"Understood."

"Don't go into the cave over there, as I have my tunneler digging in there, and it could be very dangerous. Okay, that's all. Let's go."

As Petty Officer Smith and I headed off to do laundry, the lieutenant said, "I want to see that opening to the ocean. There seems to be a ledge going most of the way around."

"Lieutenant, take the skid if you want to do that." I pointed to where it was. Then Petty Officer Smith—Marian—and I went to my laundry area. Marian was happy to see five washers and dryers all in a row.

I had picked up a tractor beam gun—I called it a TBG—and had it close to me at all times. The TBG was my newest small invention, a tractor beam that could hold, pull, or repel. I could sense it made Marian nervous—it did look a little unfriendly. We talked and sorted clothes, and she showed me how not to turn my clothes pink or shrink them. About halfway through the wash cycle, the lieutenant and master chief returned but immediately took off to look at other sights. Marian and I were putting the wet clothes into the dryers when I saw the ensign slip on the stairway and fall over the side. I pulled out the TBG and shot at her on wide beam. I made a perfect catch—she stopped in midair. I'd had it set on "hold," and now I put it on "pull" and moved her toward us while slowly bringing it toward ground level. When the ensign was only an inch from the floor and ten feet away from us, I turned off the TBG and set it down.

I walked over to her and put my hand on her arm, using my abilities to check her out internally. She was in great shape but a little shaken up. "Ensign, please be careful. I would feel really bad if you got hurt."

She grabbed me and hugged me so tightly that I thought my eyeballs were going to pop out. The lieutenant and master chief came running up. "Are you all right, Daphne?" asked the lieutenant.

Daphne wiped tears from her eyes. "I'm okay, thanks to Freddy." She held me at arm's length and said, "You saved my life. Thank you."

"You're welcome," I said with a smile.

The lieutenant was looking at my machine. "What is this?"

Marian said, "It's some sort of tractor beam. It holds and pulls, and I would bet the other setting is for push. Right, Freddy? I'll bet these adjustments are for the intensity of the beam."

"Marian," I asked, "what academic degree do you have?"

"I have a master's in aerospace design from the University of Washington and a doctorate in physics from Stanford."

"Do you have any idea what uses this device can have?" asked the master chief as she picked up the TBG and examined it.

I reached over and took the TBG from the master chief. "I know what I need it for, and that's why I invented it," I informed her. "I needed to pull cables through little holes to get power to the lights."

The master chief asked, "How powerful is this, and what do you have powering it?"

"This isn't patented yet," I said. "Information is strictly limited. Next subject?"

No one spoke until finally, the lieutenant broke the silence. "Freddy, someday you'll come to trust us a little more."

"I let you come out here and look around. That's more trust than I've extended to anyone. I do appreciate your help, and I want this to work out, but I'm sure you're working for the government and will do whatever they tell you to do. Be honest now; you're going to report everything you saw here today, including my TBG, aren't you?"

"Yes, I am, because those are my orders."

"It's not a matter of trust, Lieutenant. I trust you to do exactly what your orders say you must do, and right now those orders include reporting everything you see or hear, correct?"

"Correct."

"Then we have a problem, don't we? And I don't think this problem will go away."

"No, it probably won't," she agreed. "Next subject. You mounted a scanner on your skid so we used it. The channel is wide enough and deep enough to allow a very large ship to enter this base. Why?"

"To bring my supplies directly here. I'm hoping that bringing supplies in by ship or barge will be simpler. Once my home is finished, I'm going to work on a project that will require a large amount of supplies."

"A project?"

"Oh yes, I have a long list of projects, but this one is extremely important. I'm going to …" I looked at them and said, "Twiddle my thumbs until you all leave so I can get back to work. Thank you very much for teaching me how to do laundry, Marian."

I showed them to the landing pad and after hugs and good-byes, I watched them take off. *Man, I need to be more careful with my information.*

✦

"So, what is the problem with not having clothes?"

Everything went a little dim.

"Master," said the Green. "This species seems to be

paranoid about showing their bodies to others of the same species." Proudly, he added, "In fact, we have found out that the politicians have made it against their laws."

"You have to be kidding."

"No, master, in most places on this planet, it is against the prescribed regulations. There are a few small areas where nudity is allowed, but those are few."

"Considering how ugly these humans are, I would have to agree with the politicians on this subject."

The Blue reached out with a tentacle and tapped the Gray very hard on the top of the head.

The Gray quickly ordered, "Continue."

CHAPTER 28

✦ ✦ ✦

YOU NEED A LICENSE FOR THE SILLIEST THINGS

Now that I had clothes to wear, I started working on the indentation for my home. One of the reasons I needed to go to South Carolina and take measurements was because I needed to ensure that the foundation would fit exactly into the indentation. When I called, I was told that the house would be ready in less than a week. My house was being built to be completely self-sufficient. It was to be up on blocks so it would be above the ground, with its own foundation of reinforced concrete, a sewage container, and everything a house would need. I had supplied the manufacturer with a platform to build it on. I had Ethan Allen do the interior in Victorian.

I used the tunneler to make the indentation that the house would sit down into. The rock on which it would sit was as solid as steel and would last forever. Mommy had taught me that to make a cake you needed a great foundation—something to put the cake on—or it would fall. I was determined that my house would not fall. Everything was built far better than federal and California state regulations. I set the place for the septic tank, and made the places, and ran cable for the power and water. The water storage tank had come in, so I planted it into the ground and connected it to the water coming from the mountain. I had great water pressure.

I connected two closed-loop, continuous water heaters, large enough to supply an army. I do tend to go overboard, but why not? It was a big house, and if I had a lot of visitors at one time, I would need the hot water. It took two weeks to get everything ready. There were a lot of little things that still had to be done—outdoor lighting, a walkway to the front door and back door, and a wood shed. When I was finished, I called the house builders, and they told me that everything was ready to go, but they had no idea how I was going to move it, as the house was far too big for the roads.

I called the lieutenant to let her know I was leaving in about an hour for South Carolina to pick up my house.

"How long are you going to stay?"

"I'm not staying. I'll just fly in, connect up, and fly out with it."

"Freddy, do you have a license to fly a house?"

I had to think about that one. "No, I don't." I giggled. "There's no such thing."

"Guess what? Yes, there is, and I have one."

"How silly, Lieutenant. Why would I need a license to fly a house, and why on earth would you have one?"

"Because I have a license to fly experimental aircraft, and a house would fall into that category."

"Oh. How long would it take me to get one of those licenses?"

"About two years, if you work hard at it."

"I don't have two years to waste trying to get a license to fly something that should never require a license."

"Where are you planning to fly?"

"About two thousand feet above the ground all the way here, in a straight line."

"Did you file a flight plan so that other planes won't be running into you? Did you check to see if the other states have regulations regarding flying over areas that might be restricted?"

"I understand, Lieutenant. Any chance I could talk you into doing a little flying for me?"

"Be happy to, Freddy, for a favor."

"What favor?"

"It will take some time to get that house back here won't it?"

"I figure about three days if we don't land."

"I want to talk to you about something, just talk. I want a chance to try to persuade you that we would be a benefit to you, not a hindrance, if we guarded you on your land."

"Lieutenant, we've already been over this."

"Not really. I do not know all your issues, and you do not know all we can do for you. You may turn me down flat, Freddy, but at least I can report that I tried, and you will be working off all the information, not just what you perceive."

I had to think about that for a minute. "Very well, Lieutenant. I hate to admit that I may not have all the issues out in the open. I will allow you to help me build a pro-and-con list."

"And if the pros outweigh the cons?"

"One thing at a time, Lieutenant. Let's buy the goat before we start counting on milk or something like that. If you're coming along, how many others are you bringing?"

"How many can you fit in the thing you're flying it with?"

"We're flying a house, Lieutenant. It can fit quite a few."

"We're going to actually fly the entire house?"

"Yes, any problem with that, Lieutenant?"

"No! No! I can do it. I think I'll bring three others."

"Very well. I'll set up air transportation to get us to South Carolina and a limo to the construction site. You get us to the airport and get clearance or whatever to fly my house home. Deal?"

"Deal."

✦

The Gray exclaimed, "Primitives! We fly houses all the time."

Everything stayed clear—not perfectly but almost there.

The Green looked at the Blue in frustration.

The Blue said, "Yes, and we've been doing it for a little over one hundred years."

The Gray proudly said, "That's correct."

Blue continued, "The problem is, Gray, that they are supposed to be thousands of years behind us still. What caused Freddy's intellect to soar so high as to bring them to our level through his inventions? Now be quiet."

CHAPTER 29

✦ ✦ ✦

PLANNING

Lieutenant James sat back and said out loud, "My God!" Ensign Morgan could see that the lieutenant was very concerned. "What's up, Susan? Was that Freddy on the phone?"

"Ensign, call assembly. Everyone's going to go running. I need to talk with them, and I don't want unauthorized ears listening. Leave the spy here to watch the building."

The group was assembled in less than five minutes. When they were far enough out, Lieutenant James explained that Freddy was just about to make the news. "He's going to fly a house from South Carolina to California at low altitude and slow speed."

"You mean he's going to pick a house up with a helicopter and then fly the helo here?"

"No, Petty Officer Summer. He's going to fly the house here, just like in *The Wizard of Oz*."

That started a lot of chatter: "You've got to be kidding"; "I've got to see this"; "This is going to make guarding him a lot harder." The lieutenant had the master chief call for attention, and then she dropped the bomb—she wanted volunteers. When she asked for three volunteers, everyone raised their hands instantly.

PO1 Colleen McMasters stepped forward. "Permission to speak for the group, ma'am."

"Go ahead, Colleen."

"If we're going to be in the news, then we need to make it known that anyone coming near Freddy is looking for trouble. I would suggest that you take an extra pilot so that you can run shifts and stay off the ground. I also recommend you take the meanest-looking people we have, and if you can fit more people into that house, do so. The rest of us need to be at Freddy's home to protect it."

Before she could respond, the lieutenant's phone rang. It was Freddy, informing her of the time for departure. Lt. James made note of the time, but then said, "Freddy, we're going to have a lot of problems. When everyone sees the house flying overhead, the media will have a lot of questions."

"I hate the media," Freddy said petulantly. "Most are nice people, but some are real butt-wipes, and they ruin it for the rest."

"I would like to take five people—seven total, including you and me—and I think it would be helpful if we knew we were coming home to a clean place."

"Clean?"

"Free of unnecessary or unwanted personnel."

"I'll arrange for seven to travel, but extra security here is not required at this time, as I have my passive protection working, Lieutenant. See you tomorrow at noon."

"One more question. Is the house powered and ready to be used, or do we need to bring a portable latrine and field rations?"

"The house is fully powered, including the kitchen, and we'll have a limited amount of onboard water storage. With seven of us, there should be enough to supply us with fresh water for eight days—longer if we watch the length of our showers."

When the Lieutenant hit "end" on her cell phone, she paused to think.

"What's up, Lieutenant?" asked the ensign.

"Freddy agreed to take five others and me with no problem, but he still won't let us guard his house. He says that his passive protective system is up, whatever that is, and he thinks that's enough. I'm sure that if he could get away with flying the house without us, he'd try. Damned independent child! That's exactly what he is—a child who assumes he knows it all. The bad thing is, he mostly does, but the good thing is, he's open to learning when he realizes that he doesn't. We're going to take advantage of that. The personnel I need for volunteers are as follows: Master Chief, you're coming, and you're in charge of security. No one comes near Freddy or the house. Make an example of anyone who tries."

"Yes, Lieutenant."

"Master Chief, I'm talking 'handle with extreme hatred.' I want a scare put into anyone who wants to get close to him. Only people with direct permission will get through, and they only get through after submitting to a complete search."

Master Chief smiled and said, "Not a problem, Lieutenant, but searches won't be necessary if Freddy lets us use his scanner."

"Good idea. We'll ask him tomorrow."

"Machinist Mate First Class Swanson, I need your ears on this one. And McMasters, I need you to mother us all, especially Freddy. Meals, bedtime—you know the routine. Don't overdo it; just get him to like having you around. Find out what his favorite foods are and anything else he may like."

"Sweet," McMasters responded. "I have KP duty."

Smith said, "We'll help, and so will Freddy. Reports say he likes to help in the kitchen."

"Smith, I want you to interest his mind while you're not on security watch," Lt. James said. "Half the time we have no idea what you're saying, Smith. You are way over our heads, so let's see if you can keep up with him."

"Yes, ma'am."

"Potter, I want you to come along as security also. If anyone comes near Freddy, I want them physically removed, and that's your job. I want you to be as mean as possible. Get real nasty if the media tries to come close. I want people to understand that this child is untouchable. Got it?"

"Yes, ma'am!"

"Ensign, your job is not going to be easy. I want you to check out his passive security system and see how good it is. Wait until we're on the plane out of here, and then take the rest of the team and check things out."

"Freddy won't like it if we snoop around while he's gone," Ensign Morgan said. "You know he'll be recording it."

"I'll clear it with Freddy. Moreover, Ensign, it is time we cut the strings to Sgt. Davies. Send her back and make it look like someone turned her in. I don't want her to be held at fault with the general. It would be good if he thought he had his own personnel leak."

"I have just the ploy, Lieutenant," Ensign Morgan replied.

"Good. I'm going to make flight plans. Master Chief, you and the volunteers make plans for a six-day stay in a house, including food and toilet paper—everything. Ensign, do the same for your assignment. We leave in thirty minutes. No one talks about this conversation after we leave this place. We gather up what we need and we pack, but we say nothing. I don't want to know what you plan, Ensign, and I don't want you to know what the master chief plans, and no one will know the flight plan except me."

"People are going to find out quickly, Lieutenant," Ensign Morgan said. "How long do you expect to keep it a secret? They'll look up the flight plan as soon as they know they can."

"Leave that to me, Ensign."

✦

"Is everything the military does public knowledge with this species?"

Everything went black after the Green reached down and adjusted something at the bottom of the tank. *Darn.* However, I could still sense everything.

A thick blue tentacle quickly wrapped around the Gray's neck and lifted it off the floor.

Green replied. "No, master. It seems that flying over civilian airspace requires the civilians to know so that they can stay out of the way of the military."

Blue said, "Pay no attention to this fool. Continue."

The Green was looking just a little afraid but smug. And Gray was turning blue from lack of air.

CHAPTER 30

✦ ✦ ✦

CHANGE OF PLANS

The next morning, the master chief and the five volunteers took off for the airport. The lieutenant and the ensign took a small helicopter to pick up Freddy. When the lieutenant was close to home, she pulled up and hovered. A light blue bubble covered the entire canyon. The ensign asked, "What's that?"

"I expect it is Freddy's passive security system," Lt. James answered.

Freddy called the lieutenant then to let her know he was opening a door in his shield. "Can you see it?" he asked.

An area about halfway up the bubble became clear.

"Yes, I see it," Lt. James said.

"Come on in then."

The lieutenant moved the craft toward the opening, which was three or four times the size of her helicopter. She flew right in and landed on the closest platform. When she looked up, she realized that the shield had disappeared.

Freddy walked up to the helicopter with only one bag. The ensign and the lieutenant climbed out and greeted him, and Freddy hugged the lieutenant. Lt. James couldn't help thinking that Freddy was a very affectionate little boy.

"Where did the shield go?" Lt. James asked. "Did you turn it off?"

"No, ma'am. I set the modulation so that it's invisible. I had the idea of a shield a few months ago, and after the army did their little thing, I decided to upgrade its priority. It's now in place, but I still have some improvements to make."

"Freddy, will this keep out the riff-raff?" Lt. James asked.

"I think so, Lieutenant, but I'm not completely sure without tests."

"Tell you what …" she said, narrowing her eyes in concentration. "The ensign is staying behind. How about if she brings a crew out here and tries to defeat your security system? That should test it fairly well, don't you think?"

"Sure, and if she gets through, she can let me know so that I can plug the gap when I get back. That's a great idea. Ensign, be really careful, please. I don't want any of you to get hurt, okay?"

"Okay, Freddy," Ensign Morgan agreed. "We'll be careful."

"Thanks. Lieutenant," Freddy said, "I thought about what you said about flying over people and the media, so I brought five portable scanners for your use, if you wish. Will that help?"

Lt. James nodded. "That will help a lot, Freddy."

"What about the media?" he asked.

"Freddy, we don't want to talk to them unless it's absolutely necessary, but if we do, then we need to be polite, if possible. The media can cause you a lot of problems."

"I know they can. Lieutenant, we have another problem. Washington needs me to do something for them, so the trip has been extended for two days. They already changed the flights for us. I just found out, or I would have let you know sooner. I hope this doesn't cause too many problems."

"I will need to change the flight plan, but I don't think it will be a problem. Ensign, contact the master chief and let her know."

"Yes, ma'am."

"Are you ready to go Freddy?"

"Yes, Lieutenant."

Freddy climbed in, and Lt. James strapped him into the backseat. She took off as Freddy remodulated and opened the security door. Then he closed the door and modulated it to "clear."

The ensign finished talking to the master chief and then took over flying while the lieutenant called several people and made changes to their flight plan. Once at the airport, Freddy saw a sleek black Lear jet on the runway, and the master chief was waiting. She gave a snappy salute to the lieutenant and then said, "Hi, Freddy. Nice day for flying. Looks like someone chartered a plane for us."

"Actually the government canceled all my flight reservations and made their own," Freddy responded. "We fly military, all the way. Could you please have everyone line up right here, including the pilots?" He turned to the lieutenant. "I updated the lie detector," he said, handing it to her. He showed her how to use it, and she held it while Freddy asked everyone on the flight crew his or her plans. The crew was okay.

He then gave Lt. James four of the five scanners. "Lieutenant, I expect to have all this equipment returned to me without tampering."

"Yes, sir. This will make our job much easier." She handed out the scanners to the master chief, who kept one and gave one to each of the others, except MM1 Katie Swanson. "Katie, I don't want you to depend on these gadgets. I trust your ears much more than I trust any scanning device."

Katie smiled and said, "Understood, sir."

Freddy could feel the way the master chief felt about being called "sir," and it was very positive. *Seems she is butch in more ways than one.* "Now I'm ready," Freddy said. "Ladies, please don't play with your new toys during takeoff and landing, and keep your seats and tray tables in their upright position."

The next day, Freddy worked for the Supreme Court, using his mind-reading ability instead of the lie detector, not remembering that Lt. James and Katie Swanson were unaware of this gift. He also healed three people, one who had third-degree burns over half her body. He was very tired afterward, as healing required a lot of his energy.

✦

Blue interjected, "Healing?"

Everything went black.

"Sire?"

"We cannot heal with a touch. This creature is powerful indeed. It seems this species has a redeeming quality that we could use."

The Gray added, "We have been hearing about his healing this entire time, and I have given it some thought. Having instant healing in war would be helpful, but it seems that he is very limited."

The Blue said, "True. Continue."

CHAPTER 31

✦ ✦ ✦

MORALS

I was half awake when I heard the master chief exclaim, "The boy can heal with his mind? That's incredible! No wonder the government wants him protected."

"The government is interested in his healing ability as well as his ability to read minds—extremely interested, but they don't want him walking around Washington reading minds," said the lieutenant. "He solved a case the Supreme Court was working on for three years. They were winning, but new evidence presented by the defense attorneys caused them to lose ground. With just a few simple questions, Freddy found out that the new evidence was false and how and where they did it—enough to put them all away for life. You can imagine what Congress would think of him on the floor of the House of Representatives. One more thing—the inventions that he's working on could throw us into a technically advanced lead that will be impossible for the rest of the world powers to overcome. Analysts say that he is working on things that are used mostly in space. They think he wants to build some sort of spacecraft, and they want first bid on the technology. They don't want it falling into the wrong hands."

"You were called away to see the president?" the master chief asked.

"Yes, and she's worried. She gave me new orders—written orders that she signed. We are now a presidential detachment with complete control over everything we do. Now, even the Pentagon can't touch us. She authorized us to set up our own base at Freddy's home, and the order gives us complete choice of personnel, equipment, and a very generous budget, along with presidential promotions for everyone. The only persons from whom we are to take orders are Dr. Anderson and the president. Ladies, the president made it very clear that Freddy's orders override hers."

"That makes Freddy our boss?" the master chief asked.

"Yes, it does. We only have one thing to overcome."

"That Freddy doesn't want us at his home?"

"That's right," I called out, slowly sitting up. "I'm sorry, but I was listening to the last four or five sentences. What did I miss?"

"Nothing much, you little sneak." Lieutenant James messed my hair while saying, "If you were listening, then you know what's going on in Washington."

"Lieutenant, if you had my abilities, then you'd know much more. For instance, the government wants to build a base on the moon, then Mars, and then other planets. In less than one hundred years, this planet is going to be full of people—very full. If they don't do something now, their children's children will have no place to live. We're not talking a space issue as much as what this planet can handle with oxygen and resources. The president took every chance she could to talk in front of me about going into space and what was needed that hasn't been invented yet. She was so obvious that I nearly laughed myself sick. They want my healing and mind-reading abilities, but you're right. I'm dangerous to them and their affiliations. Besides, being this close to so many people at once gives me a headache. I can't shut out their thoughts, and I can't think. What did she say about my staying put?"

"We are to persuade you to stay right where you are," Lt. James said. "They like your being away from everyone, but at the same time, they want us to help you as much as possible. It was made very clear that if anything happens to you, we would be held fully responsible."

"Lieutenant—or should I say Lt. Commander?"

"It's still lieutenant, sir."

"Stop the 'sir' stuff," I snapped at her. "I'm not going to run this show; you are. All orders come from you as far as I am concerned. I don't want the responsibility. For goodness' sake, I'm just a kid. You have it, Lieutenant, so take the ball and run with it. And oh yes, you're correct, you do still have that problem."

The speaker came on, and the pilot said, "Everyone strap in. We'll be landing in approximately five minutes. The transportation requested is waiting for you and will take you directly to the construction site."

I said, "Thank you, pilot."

"He can't hear you from back here," Lt. James said, but the pilot came back and said, "You're welcome, Dr. Anderson."

I said, "It's a matter of making the mind think that it heard it from the outside."

"Freddy, how often are you in our heads?" she asked.

"Seldom, Lieutenant. I rely on your outward emotions and don't need to delve any deeper. Your emotions are readable enough for me to ask questions and determine if the answer is the truth. I actually have not read any of you any deeper than your surface thoughts, except Katie."

"Why Katie?"

"She's telepathic." This surprised even Katie. "When

she started guarding me, I found her reactions to things very interesting and realized she had abilities that were above normal, so I looked deeper with her. Sorry, Katie, but I needed to protect myself."

"I understand," Katie responded, "but what did you find that makes you say I'm telepathic? I've never read minds."

"You just are. It's very minor, and you haven't developed it as much as you could, but you have the potential to send as well as receive. Watch." *Katie, I'm sorry, but I saw your life when I went deep into your mind. I know what you've been through, and I cried when I found out. I love you girls, and I won't betray you.*

Tears formed in Katie's eyes, which was not her norm. "That's all right."

No, don't say it out loud. Just say it to me in your mind.

I love you too, Freddy. You make a great little brother. You're forgiven, but don't do it again.

Okay.

"You and I can talk to each other," I said to Katie, "probably from a great distance. Your abilities are weak compared to mine but stronger than any other I've met. If you practice your ability, it will increase in power, and you may start picking up others. Think about that. If you want to do this, I can help you develop more, but it's a real pain sometimes."

"Freddy, why haven't you deep-scanned the rest of us?" asked the lieutenant.

I sat a little taller and said with just a little indignation, "It's not polite."

She smiled and gave me a big hug. "Freddy, I already think very highly of you. You're kind, nice, and easy to get along with, and you don't demand much, but my estimation and love for you just went way up."

"Why?" I asked with surprise.

"Because you have a moral side that I wish others had, and because you have all this power and know better than to use it."

"Power, yuck. Don't want it. Daddy always told me, 'the more power you have, the more you have to work to keep it. Takes up too much time.' I like to invent, and I like to build. Trying to acquire power too would take away all my inventing and building time. I couldn't care less about having power. I patent everything because I need the money to allow me to invent and build and do some nice things, but that's the only reason I need it."

"Freddy, is inventing and building your top priority?" Lt. James asked.

I said with all seriousness, "No, I'd put making friends, helping people, and things like that as my first priority, because those things make me feel really good. Don't you feel really good when you help people? I get a high from that almost as much as seeing one of my inventions work. Inventing and building are close to the top, though, and I build all my plans around that."

✦

The Blue said, "Stop there."

Everything went black.

"Sire?"

"If this creature were of our species, he would be a Red."

Green stood proud and said, "Yes, sire. He would have started out Green, but he would be Red now."

"Few Greens ever make it to Red, but this one would have. Categorize and send to the Body System that this child is Red."

"Sire, if I do that, the Yellows may become involved."

"For the child's sake, let's hope not. Send it, and continue."

CHAPTER 32

✦ ✦ ✦

WHEN IT FINALLY HITS HOME, WHO'S GUARDING YOU

The plane landed, and everyone became busy. I grabbed my bags and started to leave the plane, but the Lieutenant stopped me and asked the master chief, "What's the matter?"

The master chief said, "This scanner shows twenty armed men standing at the ready on the other side of that building." She pointed out the window to a two-story building.

The lieutenant asked, "Freddy, can you read them from here?"

I closed my eyes and reached out. "Yes, they're waiting for us to get off the plane. They think they can prove to me and to the president that they would be better at guarding me than your team. Those are their surface thoughts anyway. They're here to make you look bad, Lieutenant." This irritated me, and it showed on my face. I reached into my bag and pulled out another gadget. I again started out of the plane, but the lieutenant put her hand on my shoulder.

"Freddy, what do you think you're doing?"

"I'm going to detach the cohesiveness of their molecular DNA."

"You mean, 'disintegrate' them?"

"Yes, that's what I said."

The master chief quickly and deftly removed the toy from my hand and put it away. "This is our job, Freddy. Let us handle it. Twenty men, probably the army's finest." The master chief pointed at petty officers Smith and Potter and made a quick signal. The two left silently out the rear emergency exit. I pulled out my scanner and watched as they ran around the building.

"Lieutenant, they left their scanners behind," I said, somewhat alarmed.

"Don't worry, Freddy. They were ordered not to take them into a compromising situation."

"Initial Team to home base, we're in place. Any sign that we were seen?"

The master chief answered. "IT, this is home base. Negative. Proceed."

I watched the energy readings on the screen as the two SEALs walked up behind the troops and tore into them. It happened so quickly that most of it was a blur on the screen. In less than fifteen seconds, only three were standing—petty officers Smith and Potter and one man. They sent him on his way, and he ran quickly.

We all disembarked. The two SEALs rejoined us, and they weren't even breathing hard. The limousines pulled up after they saw that everything was okay. I scanned and questioned the drivers, and then we drove to the construction site. The lieutenant noticed that I was shaking.

"What's wrong, Freddy?"

I looked up at her with fear in my eyes. Petty Officer McMasters saw right away what was wrong. She pulled me to her, holding me very close. "Freddy, don't be afraid of us. We won't hurt you."

Hardly able to say anything, I choked out, "What ... what ... what if the president ... or the next one ... decides ... decides I'm too big a risk ... too big a risk to have around?"

"In that case, Freddy," Lt. James said simply, "you'd be dead." Petty Officer McMasters glared at the lieutenant, but Lt. James continued. "Look, I'm not going to lie to you, Freddy. You'd know I was lying anyway, wouldn't you?"

I nodded my head.

"So I'm going to lay it right on the line. Our orders are to keep you alive and well and working at all cost. The president pulled no punches when she said that the life of the planet depends on our following those orders, and if you get taken, then we had better all be dead from trying to protect you."

"The president seems very interested in letting me put in as much time on my toys as possible."

"*Toys*. Freddy, your toys could save this planet! Every person in this group would gladly die to save your life."

"Really?"

Colleen interjected, "Yes, sweetheart, we would, and not just because those are our orders but because we like you."

"That's true, kid," said the master chief. "I don't think there's even one of us who wouldn't give her life just to save yours."

The lieutenant finished. "That's what it may be. If the order came down, it would be the hardest thing we ever did, but every one of the girls would carry out her duty. You understand?"

"Yes. It would be like asking you to kill your friend. You don't want to, but your duty to country requires that you do. Will you do me a favor and let me know if I'm doing something that may worry the president? I'd stop, you know, or at least explain what I'm doing so she wouldn't be worried."

The lieutenant said, "Sure, I'd be glad to help you keep the president from getting worried. That's a great idea. If you're willing to do that, then I'm sure that no bad orders will ever come down." Then she added, smiling, "Isn't it good to know that you're protected by people who can do what they just did?"

"They were so fast!"

Petty Officer Smith asked, "Want to learn?"

I perked up and said, "You bet!"

Lt. James said, "Another great idea. Do you do much exercising, Freddy?"

"No."

"Well, exercise would be good for you, and since you put me in charge, I'm ordering one hour of exercise every day, starting when you get home. It can be in the form of training in the martial arts. You won't get a belt, but in a few years, it will be very hard for anyone to pick on you again."

I didn't want to tell her that it would be hard for anyone to pick on me now. I could use telekinesis, but I couldn't stop all of them. If they wanted me dead, then I'd be dead. I was genuinely afraid, and that bothered me. I stayed in Colleen's arms for the rest of the way, just letting her hold me and trying to calm down before I met with the construction crew. When we were almost there, I tried harder to stop shaking and was calmer but not yet recovered, so the lieutenant ordered the driver to continue on for a few miles and then ordered the team in the other limo to do recon. That gave me enough time to calm down and get the red out of my eyes and face.

I smiled gratefully at the lieutenant. "Thank you, Susan."

"You're welcome, Freddy. Ready to meet with the builders?"

I sat up straight, pulled back from Colleen, and in a strong voice said, "Ready."

✦

The Gray said, "What a crybaby!"

Everything went black.

The Blue said, "And what if I sent you to see a Yellow? Would you not cry?"

The Gray radiated instant fear. "I have done nothing to deserve that!"

The Blue quietly and with conviction said, "Raise your voice at me again and see. Green, continue, please."

CHAPTER 33

✦ ✦ ✦

FLYING MY HOME

We pulled into the construction area and were met by the sight of another twenty army personnel who were lying on the ground. I asked, "Are any of the girls hurt?"

"Yes, I think Swanson has a broken arm," Petty Officer Potter answered.

"Not Katie!" I cried.

"Calm down, Freddy," ordered the lieutenant.

"Okay. Please have her taken into my house, so I can attend to her injuries right away."

The master chief, the lieutenant, and Katie and Colleen went into my house with me, and I healed Katie's arm. It was only a slight fracture, but it was pushing on a nerve ending that also needed healing.

The lieutenant said, "Katie, pretend that your arm is still broken and that all we did was set it—at least until we're out of here."

"Yes, ma'am," Katie responded, and she and the master chief splinted it and bound it to her body.

I started inspecting the house to ensure that everything was in order. The army had installed two bugs, and I removed them. I signed the final papers and included a good bonus. This was a really great company, and I wanted the owners to be eager to contract with me again. The whole company was there to see how I was going to get the house out of the area. They had bets on a gigantic truck or several huge helicopters, but they never thought I would just fly it out. After the master chief had all her supplies on board, we shook hands, and everyone climbed up. I did one last scan and then took six gadgets from my bag. One was a remote control that looked like an old Atari video game with two controllers. The others were power disks. I made sure the controls were in neutral and set for "on ground," and then I went out. Petty Officer Denise Potter followed me. I placed the power disks into the base on which they'd built the house and then climbed back up. Petty Officer Potter helped me up and then climbed in herself.

"Everyone ready?" I asked.

They were, so I showed the lieutenant the controls. "This button labeled 'U' is 'up.' The one—"

She took over. "The one labeled 'D' is down, 'F' is forward, 'B' is back, 'L' is left, and 'R' is right. What is 'SK'?"

"Station keeping."

"And the five strings of lights are power levels?"

"Power left in the disks. They are all lit right now, but if they start going down, then we may need to land so that I can replace them. I have spares."

"This is going to be easy. How do I increase speed?"

"Hold any button down. The longer you hold it, the faster we'll go in that direction. When you release it, we'll continue at that speed and in the same direction for approximately one hour, or until you press another button.

If you fail to do anything in an hour, then it goes to station keeping."

"How do we see what's around us? I don't want to run into anything. What if there's fog?"

"You have scanners."

"We can use them safely?"

"Transmissions from other sources will not affect this unit. This is not an antiquated plane. This is a house, and we will be moving slowly. If the unit fails, then everything goes to station keeping. It would be hard to mess up, as long as you pay attention, but anyone can fly it. I didn't ask you before because I didn't want to bore you with this mundane task."

"Even at a crawl, I would hardly call this a mundane task. Flying a house has to be a first."

"Well, it's all yours, Lieutenant. Good flying!"

I went into the living room and started working. Colleen came in to ask me what I wanted for lunch.

"Do you have anything with a lot of carbohydrates and fats?" I asked.

She looked shocked. "Why?"

I said rather absentmindedly, "When I do healing, like I did yesterday and today, I burn up fat. When I run out of fat, I burn carbohydrates. No fat in the body means headaches, and a decrease in carbohydrates causes muscle fatigue. I can't concentrate when I have a headache, and I need to go to the restroom so often that it's hard to get anything done. I need to do some work to get the last-minute changes ready for installation, so I really need to concentrate."

"I think I know just what will help," she said.

I gave her a most sincere thank-you smile. I could hear the lieutenant and a hundred others whoop with joy as the building lifted smoothly off the ground. I could also hear Colleen shush the other girls in the house, letting them know that I had a headache—and why. Everyone was very quiet after that. I fell asleep.

✦

Gray said, "Good. They are placing limits on him."

Everything went black.

Green exclaimed, "What is so good about that?"

Blue laughed. "Remember Dexes 2? All life was destroyed by plague that a Green started."

Gray added, "Or how about Parandum. We had to destroy everything on the planet after a Green turned all things evil."

"Point taken. I will continue."

CHAPTER 34

✦ ✦ ✦

STEPPING OVER THE LINE

Colleen woke me up for lunch. We had some kind of pasta with a thick, sweet white sauce. I loved it and ate seconds and thirds. My body knew this is what it needed. After lunch, I hugged Colleen and helped her clean up, and then I checked on our progress. I could look through any window and see that we were moving, but I had no idea where we were.

The lieutenant took time off for lunch but was back at the controls when I entered the office.

"How are we making out, Susan?" I said in greeting. "Is everything okay?"

"The power levels haven't changed, and the controls are working fine," she said, though she raised an eyebrow, adding, "Even though they are a bit juvenile. We're traveling about fifty miles an hour. We could go faster, but I don't want to take chances."

I ignored the "juvenile" remark. "Fifty miles an hour for a little over twenty-five hundred miles will put us in the canyon in just over two days."

The lieutenant said, "Not quite. The path we're taking will put us over the Pacific Ocean in about five days and then another day up to the canyon."

"Six days to get home? You must be taking a very roundabout way, Susan."

"I'm staying over government land as much as possible—no-fly zones, military-only fly zones, restricted zones, that kind of thing. We can't stay out of the public's view forever, but we can keep out of their reach nearly all the way to the ocean. I expect we'll get some company from the different militaries at several places along the way. The navy already has two F-18s watching us at high range and directly behind us." She showed me on the scanner.

"Want to have some fun?" I asked.

She looked at me skeptically. "Depends on what you call fun."

I flipped up another device and powered it up, after attaching it into the flying controls. It had two buttons marked S and I.

"I hate to ask," Susan said warily, "but what does S stand for?"

"Shields. It would drain the power fairly quickly, and we would need to change power disks soon after running them or we'd crash, but we should be able to get an hour out of it on high shields and four or five hours on low. The lights above tell you the level. One light is low and two is high."

"And the I button?"

"Invisibility. Cool, isn't it? Hit that button." I reached over as if to push it, but she stopped me.

"Invisibility?"

"Sure. It puts out a shield that really isn't very good at stopping anything but modulates in such a way as to make light, radar, and all frequency-based signals pass right around us. Therefore, we're invisible to the unaided eye and any radar system the military has."

"Are we invisible to your scanners?"

"Not a chance. Nothing we have is invisible to my scanners. I know, because I tried to fool them. Only someone sneaky, like the master chief, can get past them and then only when you're not looking for it."

She looked worried. "Freddy, you just stepped over the line."

"What? I'm sorry I said that about the master chief, but I think she likes being sneaky."

"Not the master chief. The president would be very much afraid if she thought that this technology could possibly get into someone's hands before we had it."

"Uh-oh."

"Very big time uh-oh. If another country had this technology before we had good scanners, and we were not aware of their having invisibility so we could watch for them, then …" She paused to think. "Well, let's just say we could be speaking a different language very soon."

"No problem. Let's talk the admiral into allowing us to test the bigger scanning unit on the base, that way, they can see anything using the invisibility shield."

"What about the two types of shielding units?" she asked.

"Not a chance. I have to patent them first. I have sort of a patent on the scanner."

Her eyebrows shot up. *"Sort of?"*

I put my hands on my hips and glared at her with righteous indignation. "It's done all the time. Why do you think people can buy up patented items, and no one can copy them? I sent all the documentation into the patent office but left out some important requirements. It won't work without some of my other technologies—things that I have not yet patented—and I told them so. They understand protecting all of my other ideas and had no problem with that. There are several things I simply did not patent, as that would give away how to make the other inventions."

"So no one else can make them?"

"I don't want other countries to copy my inventions and undersell me, like they do with electronics and music. I also don't want bad copies on the market that don't work well. It would ruin my reputation … when I finally have one."

"Is that why I haven't seen anyone using the antigravity disks like you do?" I must have turned red, as she started laughing. "Thought so."

"Can you protect me from the oil cartels?" I asked.

She sat up straighter at that question. "Why?"

"Running the antigravity disks requires a lot of power. That means you need *my* power disks. If I patented the parts, including the power disks, then it would put the oil people out of business very quickly. Each disk can run a car for four years and a semi truck, fully loaded, for six months or better."

"That's amazing."

"They cost about twenty cents to make, once the equipment is set up and paid for, and they're made out of a very cheap, renewable source. I'd patent them, but I'm afraid that I'd end up disappearing or worse. I would sell the patent to them if I thought that they would use it, but I don't think they will, at least not until they use up all the oil in the world."

"Who else knows about this?" Susan asked.

"Just us."

"Keep it that way for now, and let me think about it. We can protect you, but it would become very dangerous for everyone we love, so let's try to avoid that. Do the generators at the base have the energy to run the big scanners?"

"Yes, but they won't need to, because I can install one of the bigger scanners at the radar site and connect it into my own generators. I would never see the power drain. I have so much energy that I need to bleed it off sometimes. It's no problem to install a couple of monitors in the base control center."

"I think the admiral would be happy about that. How's your headache?"

"It's gone, thanks to Colleen."

"Good, but you're looking tired. Try to get some sleep before dinner. I may need you refreshed if anything happens."

"Aye-aye, Lieutenant." I turned to leave.

She smiled, thinking, *Now where did he learn that?* "Freddy, please have Marian come in here."

✦

"Interesting issue," said Green.

Everything went black.

Blue took the bait and asked, "Why?"

Green said, "The Greens have had several ideas lately that have ended up in Greens missing. It would appear that this species has the same corruption problem."

Blue looked sad for a second. I could tell, because his entire body went limp as a leaf, with arms to the sides, and his cheeks were drooping. "The Yellows have traced down the corruption problem and sent the Blues that started it for mind wipe."

Green turned to Blue and said, "That was only one instance. We have asked Yellows to follow up and correct the others." Green turned back.

Blue, looking nauseated, said, "Please continue."

CHAPTER 35

✦ ✦ ✦

ATTACKED AGAIN

The lieutenant asked, "You've seen the possibilities in this and its capabilities. Do you think he can run the base on this fuel?"

"Yes, he could," answered Petty Officer Smith. "The base, his planes, helicopters, cars, trucks—anything that requires energy to make it run. It would cost a good penny to convert things over, but I'm sure Freddy would split the cost for a written understanding of ownership."

"You're saying we could run an F-18 off these disks?"

"Faster and with a much greater range."

"We need …" That was the last thing she said before blacking out.

I was lying in my bed when my body started acting strange. I checked it and realized that I was being gassed. I used my mind to touch the shield button and replace all the oxygen in the house with some from two miles away, and then I staggered to the office. Lt. James and Marian were out, just like the rest I had passed on the way. I checked the status of the house, and it was still flying straight. I checked the shield status, and it was operational. I checked the scanners while laying a hand on the lieutenant. As she started to cough and wake up, I noticed that there was a helicopter coming up out of the mountain behind us.

"What happened?" Lt. James asked.

"We're under attack, Lieutenant."

She became fully awake and totally alert and took over flying. "Freddy, can you wake the others?" I already had a hand on Marian, and she was coming around.

"No, Lieutenant. I don't have enough energy left. I had to use it to clear the air. We were hit with a knockout gas, probably from that helicopter coming up behind us."

"Okay, so it's just the three of us. I see the shields are up. Good job. Can they see them?"

"No, ma'am."

"If they try to land on us, what will happen?"

"The shield won't give, but the rotors on the helicopter will."

Marian was now awake and standing, ready to protect me.

"That's an option," said Lt. James, "but that leaves us with them thinking that the gas may have worked and the house is on automatic pilot."

"Lieutenant, how far can that radio of yours be heard?" I asked.

"At this altitude, about three hundred miles."

"Far enough for any friendly bases to pick us up? And where did the F-18s go?"

"They left about thirty minutes ago, Freddy. This is army airspace."

"Would the navy hear the radio call?"

"Yes, it would, but they're too far away to respond in time."

I smiled and said, "We don't need them to respond. I

have this." I showed her the disintegration toy. "I took it back from the master chief." I explained my plan to the lieutenant, and she smiled really big. "Marian, are you a good shot?" I asked.

"Very good."

I handed her the toy, with the setting on "max."

The lieutenant pressed the talk button on the radio. "Unknown army helicopter, this is the commander of Flight F127. We have an important civilian passenger on board. Back off and do not try to land. Our sensors show that we were attacked with an unknown gas, and we are in a full defensive posture. Please do not try to land, as we will consider it a hostile act and destroy you."

"I don't believe you have anything on board that could possibly harm us. Lieutenant, this is Captain Craftman, and I have twenty fully armed and armored Black Berets on board. We're coming in, Lieutenant. Prepare to be boarded."

Lt. James looked at Marian, who motioned that she was ready.

"Captain Craftman, please look at the hill off to your right. See that rock on the top?"

"Yes, I see it."

She pointed to me, and I dropped the shield. She pointed to Marian, who fired my gun, sending a blue beam of energy so hot that it removed the entire top of the mountain. The lieutenant's eyebrows shot up, and she looked at me accusingly. I turned the shields back on. The lieutenant turned back to the radio and said, "Now you don't see the rock or the mountain top it was on, do you, Captain? I strongly suggest you back off now. You have ten seconds to start moving away and one minute to get out of range before I let my gunner loose. She really doesn't like people trying to gas her."

The helicopter changed directions and beat it out of

there. Not another transmission was sent to or received from them.

"Lieutenant Commander James, this is General Swetser. Are you in need of assistance?"

"Not at this time, General, but I would like you to please forward a message to the president of the United States that the army has attacked us three times now."

"I'll send the message. You are about to get an escort. I don't care if it is over army property. Expect it to show up in less than five."

"Thank you, General."

I watched my expanded screen and saw two aircraft lift off from a base only ninety miles away. The scanners identified them as Air Force F-14s.

"That air force general is a friend of Admiral Bates. They play chess over the Internet," Lt. James said.

I watched the F-14s coming up fast. When they were close, I could see they were fully armed. They looked impressive.

"Commander of Flight F127, this is Captain Robert Curran. We will be your escort for the next several hours, and then others will take our place. You won't be left alone again."

"Welcome along, Captain—and thanks."

I readjusted my sensors for detecting gasses and any other change in the area that could affect our health. I turned off the shield and let the lieutenant know. Then I went back to see what I could do to help the others. I thought that the master chief was going to be really mad.

✦

"Why did they give warning? I would have fired directly on them."

Everything went black.

Blue's eyes turned around in its head, sort of like we roll our eyes, except sideways. "Gray, attack is not always the answer."

"A lot of issues would be resolved much quicker if attack first was the answer," Gray said.

Green looked sick for a second, "Like the removal of the Gigipods. A completely peaceful species that had technology we needed but now don't exist for us to ask them. And how about the Mortrans. Asking us for help fighting the Armetts, and Grays went in and wiped out the wrong side. *And to fix things, wiped out the other species also! Is that what you mean*?"

I was falling, and Blue looked shocked, saying, "Don't let it touch the sides!"

Green turned back to me and gently lifted me back up. Then it said, "I am sorry, but war for no reason is a sore point with us Greens."

"It is with us Blues also. Gray, you will refrain from any further shows of stupidity while Green is trying to work. Green, please continue."

CHAPTER 36

✦ ✦ ✦

ALL CONS

On the second day, I was just coming out of the kitchen, where I'd had a wonderful breakfast, when I ran into the lieutenant, and she asked if I was ready.

"Ready for what, Susan?"

"That pro-and con discussion you promised me."

"Sure, do you have someone to take notes?"

"Colleen will be in here in just a minute."

"Who's flying the house?" I asked.

"Petty Officer Smith. She has a pilot's license."

Colleen entered with a note pad and said in a sing-song way, "I'm ready, Freddy."

I smiled at her and saw she was grinning from ear to ear. "Let's get started, then. Colleen, please make a list of the pros and cons. I will assign them a number between one and ten to show what I believe is the level of impact, ten being the worst."

Colleen said, "Fire away."

"Let's start with my professional concerns for not wanting the government at my home. Now, this is off the top of my head, so please forgive me if our talks bring out other reasons that I simply have not considered."

The lieutenant smiled and said, "Leaving any doors open, Freddy?"

"Lieutenant, I've thought about this for a long time, and I'm keeping an open mind. If, after hearing my reasons, you can persuade me, then I will gladly go with the best option available. I do not toss out ideas just because I may not like them. If I closed my mind that much, I'd never invent anything. First, in the con section, the government would have increased knowledge and influence regarding my projects. Rate that a five. Second—"

"Wait," said the lieutenant. "May I interject in between each of your concerns?"

"Susan, you can ask anything you want to get clarification, but please hold your arguments until I'm done. It may be to your advantage if you do so."

"Agreed, but I don't see how this could be an issue, as we've already seen your inventions. We know all about the energy bars, the tractor beam, power disks, lasers, sensors, shields—"

"No, Lieutenant, you don't. You've seen them, but you don't have any knowledge about how to make them. If you were living with me, you would gain that information too, but that's not the reason I'm saying this. I don't mean to be to blunt, but those are just toys and small tools to help me with my real projects."

✦

"Amazing. These are just toys to him?"

Everything went black.

Two blue tentacles shot out and slammed into the Gray. "Don't interrupt!"

✦

The lieutenant's eyes widened, and Colleen sat up much straighter.

"Second, under cons—security risks. Since I can develop and secure my own home, as I'm sure the ensign has told you by now, I don't want the human factor of possible security risks. The military changes personnel every two to three years. Even if I allowed your team, whom I do trust, to start guarding me, in three years, it would be a completely new team. People are transferred and reassigned, and that includes SEAL teams. The army is trying to prove that they can do a better job, so that they can force a replacement. I cannot allow that type of political mess to screw up my home security and waste my time. Not only that, but when people transfer out, they may talk about what they have seen. I stand to lose a lot if other companies patent my inventions before I do. If this happens, then I won't be able to afford to build the bigger projects. Rate that an eight."

"Eight, Freddy?" Lt. James questioned. "I would have thought it would be a ten."

"It would hamper me from doing what I came out here to do—invent and build—so it's a high priority but not that high. Third, also con—human interference. Every person, every mind, every emotion is a possible distraction to me. Noise, both on the audible level and mind noise, can prevent me from thinking. Also, taking care of people, their entertainment, food, cooking, laundry, housing, cleaning, storage—the list goes on, Lieutenant. Taking care of one is bad enough and takes too much time out of my day. Taking care of a dozen people is unacceptable. Rate it eight. Fourth, con—lack of control. I would have no control over people and guests who live at or visit my home. This is partly a big security risk but also could be somewhat of an irritation. Give that a five.

"Okay, now let's go to a more personal level. Fifth,

con—teasing, laughing, and disgust. These are things that can really bother me. Your team members are very good and understanding. I really think that they would not care if I decided to run around in my birthday suit. They'd just report when and for how long, and that's that, but as I've said, people transfer out and replacements come in. Even if something is not said aloud, I still hear it. Emotions cannot be so easily stopped. If I want to try different things, like swimming in the nude, I could not help but feel the emotions of everyone who saw me. Rate that three."

"Not too high a grade on that one," said Colleen.

"Not that important what others think," said the lieutenant.

"Very good, Susan. That's exactly right," I said.

"Sixth, con—my abilities. I would have no privacy. I don't want the president to know just what my mental abilities can achieve. That's no one's business but mine. That's a nine."

"They already know, Freddy."

I slowly shook my head and said sadly, "No, Lieutenant, they don't know. They only know what I've allowed them to see. I need to practice my abilities so that I can extend and control them. I can't hide them all the time, as I might lose them."

"I understand, Freddy."

I smiled before telling this next one. "Seventh, still con—there would be witnesses to my little pranks. Rank that as two."

Colleen and the lieutenant smiled at that. Colleen said, "There would also be people to let you know if you're taking them too far."

"Yes, well … good argument. Eighth—and this is pro—the only way to keep the media and their freedom of the press, or as I like to put it, 'freedom to depress,' off my back is for my projects to become national security issues. Give that one a ten. As much as I hate the idea of government involvement, the pressures are mounting, and I don't need out-for-profit, snoopy people causing problems. Last, but not least, nine is another con—getting attached to people. I can't help getting attached to people, especially the girls on your team. Lieutenant, I can't stop thinking about losing one if she died. It's causing me no end of trouble. I'm so worried that one will die that I can't sleep, and it messes up my thinking. Ten."

"We'll all die, Freddy," said Susan.

"I know, I know. I've lost everyone I have ever loved, Lieutenant. I told myself that I would never love anyone again, and here I am with a big crush on Becky, love for her mother and family, and you. I'm developing love for all your team, and if one of you dies, especially because of me, I don't think I could stand it. It's part of being empathic; I can't help but love."

Colleen put a motherly arm around my shoulders. "We understand, sweetheart, but you must understand that this is God's way. We all die. If we didn't, then the world would sure be crowded. I've lost several friends and a brother, and I don't want anyone else to die either, but it's going to happen. Where are we most likely to die, Freddy? Out there, where we can get into accidents, and there's no one with your abilities to heal us; where there's cancer and AIDS and every other kind of disease; or right here with you? I think our chances are better guarding you than driving in traffic, where a drunk driver could run us over, and we would never even know why we died. We love doing what we do. Sure, it's dangerous, but we're the best, and chances are, we won't die any time soon. If we do, then we did it doing what we love. I want you to think about that for a while. The lieutenant and I are going to talk, and we'll get back with you."

"Okay." I gave her a hug and left for my bedroom. What they didn't know was that time was getting short, and I needed help, or all this would be for nothing. They were going to find it very easy to talk me into letting them sign on—but not too easy, or they'd get suspicious. Fact is, the world emergency was forcing me to need them.

The lieutenant took the list and said, "Let everyone know we're going to have a meeting this afternoon, and get the president on the line."

✦

The Gray said, "I don't understand. What emergency? We never detected any emergency."

Everything went black. I was getting tired of that and wished the Gray would shut up.

The Blue answered, "And we will never find out if you don't keep quiet! Green, continue."

CHAPTER 37

✦ ✦ ✦

REFUELING

On the third day, we had company. The media had tried to get to us several times that morning, but our escorts chased them off before they could get pictures. This time, they settled themselves on the top of some hills and waited for us to reach them. Leave it to the media to never give up. Within minutes, we were on television, and by the next morning, we were plastered all over the papers.

The lieutenant's plan was working, and no one could come near us. We stayed over military and government land for almost the entire trip. On the fourth day, while we were over Nevada, I asked the lieutenant to land.

"Lieutenant, the power does not seem to have drained much, but soon we're going to be out over the ocean, and we'll have plenty of company. We may need to go shielded, and that will take more power. I have the replacement disks ready to install and would like to change them out."

"We're over government land, and we're in the middle of the desert. We should be able to land right now. Master Chief, scan the area and find us a landing place away from prying eyes."

"Yes, ma'am."

"Petty Officer Smith, contact our escorts and let them know we're going to land for refueling. How long will this take, Freddy?"

"About two hours."

She looked at me hard. "That's a long time to be sitting out in the open, powered down."

"I'm sorry, Lieutenant, but I really wasn't planning to be out here this long."

"Understood."

"Lieutenant, there's a base where we could land at Area 51," said Master Chief Uniceson. "We'd need clearance, but it's the safest place."

"Lieutenant, I have an incoming call from the area commander," said Petty Officer Smith. "He's going to allow our escort to land and refuel. He'd like to extend the same courtesy to us."

"Tell him that I appreciate the courtesy, and we'd be happy to accept." She started the turn toward the base only a few miles away. Our escort stayed up until we landed.

The base was out in the middle of nowhere, and the scanners showed that a lot of it was underground. There were some interesting elements stored below that my scanners could not identify. After we landed, I went right to work. The entire group was armed and watching to ensure that we had no issues with this commander. He did show up and asked the lieutenant if she needed anything. Shortly after he left, a jeep drove up with her request. She checked it and took it inside.

I finished the replacement in just under the two hours, and we immediately took off. Once we were in the air, our escorts also took off and resumed following us.

"Master Chief, please check that those F-14s following us are manned by the same pilots."

She had her new equipment out and set up in the flight

office. She turned it on and called Admiral Bates, telling him, "Place your phone on 'scramble,' please."

"We're on scramble now, Lieutenant," Bates confirmed. "What's going on? I'm getting all kinds of orders requiring me to lend you every possible courtesy. Seems you're no longer attached to my base."

"I'll fill you in when we return, Admiral. It's a long story, but you're right. We now work directly for Dr. Anderson."

Both my eyes went wide in shock. "I thought—"

The lieutenant put a finger to her lips, letting me know to be quiet.

"I'm sorry, Lieutenant. I had no idea this was going to become such a permanent situation. My condolences," said the admiral.

She smiled, but I was frowning and placed my arms across my chest. I was ready to read him the riot act, but she shook her head, so I held back.

"I think I can handle the orders, Admiral. I will need to use part of your base as a staging area. We should be there in three days. We have an escort of two fighters that will need refueling."

"I understand, Lieutenant. I'll prepare my people."

"Thank you, sir."

"What's it like, flying a house, Lieutenant?"

"Slow, sir, very slow."

He laughed. "You know it's all over the news. The whole town is in an uproar. The media knows it's coming, and they're here in flocks."

"Thanks for the warning, Admiral. I'll take measures to that effect."

"Good luck, Lieutenant. If you need anything, just let me know." He hung up.

"Condolences, indeed," I grumbled. "Why didn't you let me give him a piece of my mind?"

"Because we're going to need him," Lt. James said. "That's why."

"Why did you say that you work for me? I know what the president said, but that's crazy! He can't believe that."

"Smith, take over the controls and keep to the plan. Let me know if anything happens. Freddy, we need to talk."

✦

"Interesting. Their Blues gave a Red power over Grays."

Everything went black.

Gray said, "Disgusting!"

Green said, "Not so. If we need Grays on a scientific mission, we have to bother the Blues so that we can keep the Grays in line and not destroy the subject. It would be far easier if we had some control."

Blue said, "Yes, something we have not thought about or tried. We may, though."

Gray looked at Blue, with total shock registering in rippling shades of gray.

Blue said, "Continue."

CHAPTER 38

✦ ✦ ✦

THE ANSWERS TO THE CONS—SEEMS SIMPLE, DOESN'T IT?

Lt. James and I went into the living room and sat down. Everyone was there except Petty Officer Smith and the master chief. They had the flight watch.

The lieutenant started. "Freddy, you've made your concerns known to me, and now I'm ready to give my arguments. Colleen, please place the chart of his concerns on the wall." After I read them over, she asked, "Are these correct?"

I agreed that they were.

"Let's take the first one: increased government knowledge and influence regarding your projects, which you rated five. I've thought about this and realize that you're limiting yourself. You're tying your own hands and making it harder for you to complete your projects."

"How's that, Lieutenant?"

"I talked with several people. The best way—and the only *good* way—to market products like the power inserts, which are very volatile to politics, would be to fully test them. After they've been completely tested and proven, patent them, and let the government run the contract out to everyone. You'd get the profits you need, and at the same time, you'll be hidden so deep in red tape that no one would find you. Even if they did find you, they would not care, because killing you would not affect the process. Also, if the president doesn't know what's going on, she'll get nervous, and you don't want that. You already have government involvement on moving your home. A fighter escort would never be given to just Freddy Anderson. You have a presidential detachment flying this house and therefore, you get every courtesy the government can possibly give. Without us, you wouldn't have gotten twenty miles before the FAA had you brought down. You need our protection."

She waited for me to dispute this, but I just looked at her and said, "So the ensign found a way in?"

"Yes, she did, and she said it wasn't all that hard. In fact, she found three ways in." I must have turned red, as she said, "Nothing to be embarrassed about, kid. She's the best there is at escaping—that's the main reason she's on the team. She just reversed the process and tried to escape into your home. She's been there, camping out, since the first day. Oh, by the way, when we get back, Maggie would like to know if you'd fix her broken leg."

I stood up, surprised by the amount of concern I was feeling. Colleen placed a hand on my arm and pulled me back down. "She'll be okay," Colleen said. "It's just a leg, and she's young."

"Tell her I would be happy to heal her leg."

"I already did, dear."

I looked at Colleen and smiled.

"You see, Freddy," said Lt. James, "it's that kind of concern that makes it hard for us not to want to protect you. You're the kid brother we all wish we had. Let's go on."

"Two: security risk—the personnel changes and people

who transfer out who may talk about what they've seen. You rated that an eight. I talked with the president about this, so she called an emergency closed session with the House and Senate. By unanimous vote, it was decided and a bill was signed into law for the creation of a special presidential detachment for the protection of Freddy Anderson." She pulled out a piece of paper and read from it. "'The detachment will be fully funded by a special fund from the office of the president of the United States. The detachment's sole purpose is to protect Dr. Freddy Anderson and his work from adverse private and political situations and to take all actions necessary for the continued development of technological inventions by Dr. Anderson. Furthermore, no person, including the president, will have control to override Dr. Anderson's orders, as long as the leader of the detachment believes that such orders do not jeopardize the security of the United States.' There's a lot more, and you need to read it. It gives you full authority to select people to fill the positions. It gives you the right to reject or replace personnel for no reason at all. They know you can read emotions and expect you to screen everyone who joins the group. That seems like it puts a lot on your shoulders, but if you can trust the person you put in charge—and yes, you get to select that person too—then that person can use that lie detector of yours to screen people for you, and you'll only need to be notified of the decisions."

"I can't believe that Congress signed that into law," I said. "Do they understand what they just gave me? They must want something from me."

"Yes, they do, Freddy. They want your inventions. They have done several studies of you and think you're going to build a spaceship or at least invent everything needed to build one." There's no way she could miss the guilty look on my face. "Freddy, you're not hard to read, and anyone who got his hands on you could easily get information out of you. How far along are you?"

"I have the plans for a shuttle and most of the plans for a destroyer now. I was hoping that after I get my house in place, I would have time to build it."

"Destroyer?"

"You know, a ship with the ability to protect my interests."

"We'll talk about this later. Therefore, it's this detachment's job to ensure you get that time. Let's continue, shall we? Number three: human interference and mental distractions, which you rated an eight. Freddy, I can't control the fact that there will be people around, but you get to screen each one, and if anyone leaks too much emotion and disturbs you, you can have that person transferred. With regard to your taking care of them, they can take care of themselves. They will be *your* cooks, *your* housekeepers, *your* personal shoppers for supplies or do anything else you need or want them to do. They'll even take care of the grounds, be your gardeners, if necessary. You won't have to take care of them, and you won't have to take care of yourself; they'll do that for you."

"Why do you keep saying 'they'? If I am to choose someone to stay with me, it will be your team, and you will be in charge, so stop with the third-party stuff."

Her emotions peaked, but she showed nothing. "Very well. Number four: lack of control, which you rated five. I think we already hit on that one. You get your choice. Number five: teasing, laughing, and disgust. You rated this a three. You want to try different things, like swimming in the nude. If you run around nude, then expect to be laughed at. We would all get used to it, but you're going to receive adverse emotions every time you're somewhere other than within your own property. I can't help the fact that you're empathic, but ordering people to hold back would be unproductive. It's contrary to human nature. You've got another problem—what about love and crushes? All of these emotions will come out eventually. You're growing up, and people will start looking at you differently. Don't you think you'd better get used to it in a controlled environment, so that it won't surprise you when you visit other places, like Washington, DC?"

"Yes, well … that does make sense," I said.

"Number six: lack of privacy. You rated this high—a nine. But realize that if everyone knows about your abilities, then they won't be as afraid of what you can do, because their minds will be on what you can do for them instead. They know that you can read minds, but they also know that you won't do so without permission or if you're threatened. They tried to bribe you into doing things for them, didn't they?"

"Yes, they did!" I said with contempt."

"Well, they believe that moral stance of yours makes you harmless, now that they know that you refuse to use your abilities to do bad things. As long as you remain steadfast in that stance, then they won't care. As long as they don't think you're after them, then everything's fine. Number seven: witnesses to your little pranks. This obviously isn't very important to you, since you gave it a two, but it is a worry for me. You're dangerous, and I want to know about any pranks you might want to pull before you do them. I don't want to wake up to find myself floating on my bed in the middle of the ocean, or something worse." She pursed her lips and gave me a stern look.

I said innocently, "Okay, I'll be good."

She looked skeptical but continued. "Number eight: projects to become national security issues. This you rated ten. When I talked to the president, she nearly had a fit, telling me that your projects already *are* national security issues. She emphasized that I am ordered to do anything possible to ensure that the media does not get hold of information related to anything you are doing."

"That attitude may save the world, Lt. James," I said, and everyone stared at me for a second.

"Continuing on … number nine: getting attached to people and their dying. This one you gave your highest priority—ten. Do you remember what Colleen said?"

"Yes."

"Have you thought about it?"

"Yes, I have," I said. "It comes down to this: no matter what life brings, it's not worth living if you don't love. That includes your family, your friends, your job, everything. It's not my fault that God decided to let my mother and father die, and it's not God's fault that it happened. It's no one's fault. I'll concede number nine on the grounds that I need to love and that with life comes death. I should rejoice in one and expect the other."

"That's very true, sweetheart," Lt. James said kindly. "What about the other eight?"

"I'll concede numbers two and four, on the grounds that I can scan each person and select the ones I think will work, and I can change my mind at any time about that person. I'll concede number three, gladly, if you can take some of the mundane work off my hands. Numbers five and seven are small issues, and you're right. Number eight is important, and I hope the president is telling the truth, as the media can cause a lot of pressure, and she may buckle. Numbers one and six … we still need to talk about those. I'm not convinced that the government will give up control so easily."

We talked for hours and finally, I gave in, on the condition that this was a tentative plan for a trial period of one year. I wanted to make it on a day-to-day basis, but the lieutenant said that would not be fair to anyone, so I agreed to a one-year trial. If it worked out, then I would extend it for five more years. She agreed that was fair. By the time we were finished, it was late and time for bed.

✦

Green took a deep breath.

Everything went black.

Blue asked, "What is wrong, Green?"

"I am becoming tired. This child's mind is stronger than mine, and he is fighting. I am afraid that he will learn as much from us as we learn from him."

Blue thought on that for a turn. "Green, let him look and learn."

Green and Gray looked astonished.

Blue added, "I will take full responsibility. Don't fight him. A Green to a Red of another species. You should be able to pass information to him, and he may actually understand. Give him mostly history. He will be so busy trying to assimilate the information that he will not have a chance to grab technology or the way to get out of his present situation. In addition, you will be able to work longer."

"Very good idea," said Green.

"Please continue."

CHAPTER 39

✦ ✦ ✦

I STILL THINK PLOWING THROUGH WAS A BETTER IDEA

First thing the next morning, the master chief called us to come to the flight office. The lieutenant got there just in front of me. "Report, Master Chief."

"Look at the scanners." The scanners showed at least twenty aircraft traveling along the borders between government land and public property. We had to cross that area to get out over the ocean. "Can they see us yet Freddy?" Master Chief asked.

"Yes, and they do, ma'am—they're all converging on the area we'll be crossing shortly."

"The crossing between this site and the last one before the ocean is about one hundred miles, Lieutenant."

"That's two hours out in the open. Do you think they'll try to block our passage, Master Chief?" Lt. James asked.

"I believe that's their plan, ma'am."

I thought for a second. "Lieutenant, what's the maximum altitude capability of those aircraft?"

"Why, Freddy?"

"Just a thought, Lieutenant."

"The helicopters have a hover ceiling of 10,200 feet. The small planes can hit up to 27,000 feet, and that larger plane is rated up to 51,000 and higher, if necessary—and the pilot has guts."

I smiled. "Great. Let's go up, Master Chief." I started adjusting the shields.

"What are you planning, Freddy?"

"We go over them. I'll turn the shields on low and at maximum distance, and then keep them at that distance. Now, the pressure outside will decrease, but I can maintain pressure inside by regulating the size of the shield. We will have plenty of air, as I can use another ability to ensure that our interior air stays fresh. This is a well-insulated house, and we can turn on the heat, so that's not a problem. Lieutenant, if we wanted to, I could fly this house to the moon, except we'd run out of food and water and possibly air and fuel by then."

"Okay, Freddy, I trust you," said Lt. James. "Master Chief, take her up, but keep us going forward too. I want to hit 80,000 feet at about the same time we hit the border."

The master chief looked at me skeptically but then answered, "Yes, ma'am."

"I understand your concerns, Master Chief, but don't worry. I can do this easily," I said.

We started climbing, and Colleen turned up the thermostat. The shield was in place and was holding the interior pressure and maintaining air quality. When we were getting close, several helicopters dropped out of the chase. Even closer, the other helicopters and several small planes dropped out, and just before we hit the border, the rest of the planes dropped out. Most of the other SEALs were climbing into the office. "Hey, we're a long ways up!" someone said.

Colleen took them out and explained it to them. I could hear several cuss words, and then Katie said, "We should be doing our job, not complaining. Watch the windows." They scattered. We drifted for several hours, with the armada right behind us. When we reached government land again, they turned around and left.

"Master Chief, get us down quickly," I said.

"Sure thing, Freddy."

We came down softly but very quickly. The gravity was almost free-fall but not quite. When we hit one thousand feet, she stopped our descent and asked, "How's that?"

"Great!" I took the shields off and looked at the lights that told the readings of the power disks. All were one down from full. "Good job, Master Chief. Nice even burn."

She smiled and said, "Thanks, Freddy."

The lieutenant gave orders to watch for a possible return of our pursuers and to do a complete check of the house, top to bottom. I watched the scanners and soon saw that our escort was back. I let the lieutenant know that they were the same pilots.

"We should be getting a call any time now for violating FAA regulations regarding exceeding the altitude stated in our flight plan," Lt. James said.

"Really? How are they going to call us?"

"Good point." The lieutenant's SEAL phone rang. We all stared at it as the lieutenant picked it up. "Lt. James here."

"Hello, Lieutenant. This is Captain Curran. Nice piece of flying. Is everyone all right?"

"Yes, Captain. we're doing fine. It was pretty scary, but it worked out well."

"It's amazing that you didn't die from lack of oxygen. You can sure hold your breath a long time!"

"Practice, Captain—that's all it takes."

I could hear him laughing. "What are you going to do

once you get out over the ocean? We can't attack civilians out there—no jurisdiction. We can't even threaten them."

"I expect that I'll have no choice but to plow my way through. I'll give them plenty of warning, but you may want to have the coast guard ready for search and rescue."

"Will your shields hold up for that?"

She held her breath. He knew. I looked at her with concern. She said, "Captain, I can neither confirm nor deny the existence of shields."

With a laugh, he said, "Then you'd better check your television, as the shield around his canyon is making big news."

She asked, "How long do we enjoy the protection, Captain?"

"Until you're three miles out. Anything more takes presidential authority."

It was now the lieutenant's turn to smile. "Check code alpha, gamma, niner, niner, five, one, four."

"Hold on."

A few seconds later, I heard a whistle. "Looks like we're all yours until you're home, Lieutenant. In fact, the boss is scrambling up several Scorpions to break up your welcoming committee. He's impressed, and that's hard to do!"

"Thank you, Captain."

"My pleasure, Lt. Commander James. Over and out."

I looked at her with a questioning look. She said, "As a presidential detachment, we've been given the highest priorities, Freddy."

✦

"Interesting."

Blue asked, "Why did he not expect this?"

Everything went black.

Green said, "The Greens of their species do not work with government much. They study and let something called 'managers' and 'directors' do the interface with politicians."

"Do you know why?"

"Yes, sire. Too many politicians and not enough scientists, so the Greens have created another class so they can continue to work without the interference."

"For some reason, I think you have that wrong. Continue."

CHAPTER 40

✦ ✦ ✦

MEDIA DILEMMA

"We need to contact the ensign to see how she's doing, Freddy," said Lt. James. "You keep her steady while the master chief gets some breakfast." Lt. James dialed, and Ensign Morgan answered right away."

"I thought you'd be calling, Lieutenant," the ensign said. "We have company."

"Have they breached the shields?"

"No. We plugged those possibilities, but they're right outside the shield."

I put a hand on the lieutenant's arm. "May I make a suggestion, Lieutenant?"

"Go ahead." She handed me the phone.

"Ensign, what style of transportation do you have, and what do they have?" I asked.

"We flew in and parachuted down into the forest south of here, so we have no transportation. They packed in on horseback, but the scanner shows they have cars and trucks only three miles from here."

"Great, that means they're on my land, and I can use the parts. Ensign, I saw several busses on the base. The master chief told me that they were used to bring drunken military personnel back from the town. I think she called them 'cattle cars'—am I right?"

"Yes."

"If the lieutenant approves of my plan, we will contact the admiral and have them waiting for you at the location where their transportation is waiting. Can you possibly arrest every one of them, or will that be too difficult for the personnel you currently have with you?"

"Are you kidding? We may have to get nasty, but it would be a cinch. Parks has that broken leg, but that leaves four others, including me."

"Ensign, this may be a diversionary tactic, so keep back Petty Officer Parks and one other. I don't want that base compromised," ordered the lieutenant.

"Yes, ma'am."

"This is what I want you to do," I said. "Arrest every one of them. Walk them to their vehicles. When they get there, have them placed into the cattle cars and driven into town. I'm confiscating all their equipment. It's on my land and therefore belongs to me. I'll contact my lawyers so they know what's going on and can handle any problems that may arise as a result of my decision. Do not purposely harm anyone, but if anyone tries anything, make an example of them. I want it known that I don't accept visitors and will prosecute all trespassers to the max. Call the local police station, and let them know that you're bringing them in. Is this plan okay with you, Lieutenant?"

She smiled. "If you think you can get it to stand up in court, Freddy, it's okay by me."

"Not a problem, as long as we don't cause any physical harm to anyone unless absolutely needed."

"Got that last part, Ensign?" asked Lt. James.

"Yes, ma'am."

"Then carry out your orders."

"Yes, ma'am."

"Ensign, are you on live broadcast?" I asked.

"I think so, Freddy."

"Good. Make sure that you are seen arresting every one of them. Be nice and apologetic about it while you're on TV. I want them treated nicely, but I also don't want them coming back. Let them know that I will be suing every one of them for trespass and invasion of privacy. And the government is prosecuting for breaking national security. If anyone attacks you, please defend yourselves."

The next call was to the admiral. There would be no problems there. We then called the sheriff. He said he could handle the increase in cellmates, that it would be nice to have the jail full. Finally, I called my lawyers. I warned them about what I was going to do, so they could be prepared. They were ecstatic about suing the media and jumped on the case immediately. They also told me that legally, I might not want to do anything with the equipment until after the judge awarded me damages. Then I could seize their equipment to satisfy my judgment against them.

"It's going to be costly, Dr. Anderson, but we can easily win an injunction against them to make them stay away from your home entirely, for national security reasons especially."

"I want the injunction to cover all their affiliates too. I prepared a package for you. Open it, but don't release the information yet. I want to use it to let these media people know that I can afford to play the same games. If they want to ruin my privacy, then they should expect the same in return. Try to keep me out of this lawsuit as much as possible. The media will try to drag me into court to get more pictures and sensationalize this whole thing."

"We'll try to keep your participation down to a minimum, Dr. Anderson. The first thing we'll ask for is closed hearings.

One thing, though, as long as you're going to fly houses around, you've got to realize that the media is going to be on your case every second."

"I understand, and I'll take care of that." We covered other items, and then he hung up.

Lt. James sat back and said, "I have several questions about what you're planning, Freddy. The first is just for my own curiosity. What's in the package you left with your lawyers?"

I smiled and said, "It's not hard to realize that I was going to be in the news again, so I did some investigation first. I hired several detective agencies, and they became close to the top people in the different media groups. They learned about their illegal dealings and where the supporting evidence might be, and then they stored the data away for when I might need it. I have enough information on all of them to put them in prison for years. I plan to let them know that if they make my life an open book, theirs will be too. Of course, the information was gathered anonymously and will be given out incognito to a member of the press we can trust. Due to freedom of the press laws, a reporter can report on anything from an anonymous source. It's all perfectly legal, but I don't want to use the information, because it would ruin their lives. However, I may need to make an example of a few of them." My smile broadened. "I got just as nasty as they did, and I dogged their families too. You wouldn't believe some of the things their kids have done."

"You seem to have a plan about how to handle the media. Want to let me in on it?"

We talked for the better part of that day. Finally, I said, "It comes down to this: I'm going to jealously protect my home, the town, and the base. When I'm out in the open, I won't say anything to provoke anyone, but if I get harassed, I'll have my lawyers harass back. I will be good to the media as long as they are good to me. When I'm going to do something, like flying a house across country, I will let them know and may entertain the notion of having them join in the fun from time to time. I have lots of fun things planned. It's inevitable that they will find out about a few of them, but most of the time, the media won't even know about my activities unless I decide to tell them. It'll be their choice—respect the townspeople's privacy and mine and enjoy great coverage, or press the issue and have no coverage at all."

"They can't stop the little independent groups, like the sleaze magazines."

"They own the sleaze magazines, Lieutenant. Don't let them fool you. They need to start policing their own, and if they don't, then I can't trust them."

"Where do you want to land to start this game?"

"This is not a game, Susan. I know you sometimes think of me as a kid, but if I don't set limits with the press, then it will cause me problems for the rest of my life."

"I understand, Freddy. It's just that I don't think the president will like this."

"On the contrary, I had a talk with the president about this exact situation. In fact, she brought it up. She was the one who gave me the parameters that I need to set. She knows I'm going to do something like this, just not what or when. In fact, she told me the sooner, the better. I understand that this will make it even harder to guard my inventions, and I'm sorry about that, but there's nothing else I can do."

The master chief asked, "Freddy, you're thinking about landing this house and talking to the media before going home, aren't you?"

"Yes, sir, I am."

"Then I would like to have that favor I won from you."

"I remember, Master Chief. What would you like?"

"That we don't land until we get you home. Then you

can go into town and hold a meeting with them later, after we can get some security set up first."

"Done. You know you just wasted a favor."

"How's that?"

"You're in charge of security under the lieutenant. If you feel that it's too risky to make a surprise landing, then that's your call, and we wouldn't have done it." The master chief and the lieutenant looked at each other, and I said, "What? Were you two worried that I wouldn't listen to you?"

"Actually, yes, we were," said the lieutenant.

"Look, Susan, my expertise is inventing and building, and I know very little about security matters. Your expertise is with people and security, and you know very little about inventing. I'll leave the security to you, and you leave the inventing to me. Deal?"

"You got it, Freddy," said the lieutenant. "Master Chief, the flight plan stands. Have the ensign set up a meeting in town on Friday."

"Lieutenant, you know my needs regarding the media. Are you willing to take care of setting up a meeting and carrying it out?" I asked.

"Yes, Freddy. I can do that."

I gave her a big smile and said, "This may work out after all. I hate doing this kind of junk. Great, I can go back to my inventing! It's all yours." I went back into the living room.

The lieutenant looked at the master chief and said, "Something's wrong. This is too easy."

"I know what you mean," the master chief agreed. "Something's up, but keel haul me if I can tell what he's planning. I'll give it some thought, but you're better at this than I am. I really don't feel like I'm being used … more like I'm on trial."

"That's it, exactly."

"What's it?"

"The little rascal thinks he's giving us just enough rope to hang ourselves. I bet all his bigger projects will be hidden."

"And I bet he lets us have the run of everyplace else."

The lieutenant smiled. "Warn the rest of the team. We're taking on the care and feeding of Freddy, and he's going to let us. Make sure they know he's testing us."

Petty Officer Smith came in a couple of hours later to ask the lieutenant to come into the living room. "You're going to want to see this."

On the satellite television was a news broadcast about the arrest of all media around Freddy's property:

"Repeating our top story, all of the reporters at the Anderson shield have been captured at gunpoint. Their equipment has been destroyed. All reports are that they are being taken away at this moment. Some may be dead, but reports are that at least one is wounded, and there could be other injuries, but no medical help has been requested. Here is the last broadcast from the shield site …"

The image changed to a forest view with the canyon in the background. The ensign's voice could be heard clearly as she came into view.

"My extreme apologies, but you have been warned several times to vacate these premises. You have been told that this is private land and that you are trespassing and breaking national security. I have asked you three times to leave, and each time you have told me that you have a right to be here. Well, you're wrong about that. You are breaking the law, and I am arresting you in the name of the United States government and on behalf of the owner of this land, Dr. Freddy Anderson. You have the right to …" She read off their rights and asked if they understood them.

"We understand, young lady. Now you get this." A male reporter was stabbing Ensign Morgan in the chest with his finger. "We have a right to be here, and there's nothing you can do about it. If you want to remove me, then it's going to have to be by force."

"As you wish, sir." She shot him in the arm. He looked shocked. "Do I need to use more force?" She was looking at the others when someone tried to jump her from behind. She moved so fast that it was hard to see. The outcome was plain to see. The man who attacked her was on the ground, and it was hard to tell if he was dead or alive.

"Denise, is he dead?" I asked.

"No, Freddy. She simply knocked him out. It's a simple move that anyone with training would see."

It looked like everyone else was cooperating fully, including the wounded man. The ensign reached up and turned off the camera and then ordered everyone to do the same. All complied except one jerk who left his on, so she shot the camera. That was the end of the report. I sat back and thought about the outcome. I saw nothing wrong with her actions, as she was under attack, but then again, I was not the expert. The lieutenant, however, was the expert, and she was smiling. "So what do you think, Susan?" I asked.

"I think that went very well. First, she tried to be polite, and she got it on TV that she had warned them three times. That's a good job, as it made him agree that he'd been warned. She only shot him in self-defense and in the line of duty, because he was hitting her in the breast."

I opened my mouth in shock, but she was right. Hitting a woman in the breast was not a good thing to do, especially if she was carrying a gun. Every woman in the world would be on her side in a court battle, so no problem there.

"Then she was physically attacked, and although some might think she killed him, they will soon learn that she only knocked him out. This is going to make the media look really bad. It will show that they will go to any lengths, even breaking the law and attacking people who are trying to do their duty, just to get a story. She could beat the crap out of every one of them from here on out, and no one will say a thing. She won't, though, because her orders are to get them to the admiral and then to jail without harming anyone more than necessary."

"It's a long walk to the vehicles, Lieutenant, and she looked like she was running out of patience."

"You have a point." The lieutenant went into the flight office and called home base. They relayed a message to the ensign that she'd done really well and also to let her know that the lieutenant said not to harm anyone else. She replied in the affirmative.

Later that evening, the news showed all of the reporters as they came out of the cattle cars and went into the jail. They showed a doctor going into the jail to take care of the wounded. When the doctor emerged, they had her on live broadcast.

"No one was seriously injured," said Dr. Karen Jenson. "In fact, the news people let me know that they were all treated very nicely after they started cooperating. They were given plenty of rest periods, food, and water. The man who was knocked to the ground was very apologetic for attacking the ensign and was glad that she had only knocked him out. The man the ensign shot sustained only a flesh wound. These people attacked trained killers—navy SEALs, the best of the best. It's good for everyone that Dr. Anderson does not wish to see anyone harmed, and his orders were to not use any more force than absolutely necessary. These young women were very capable of killing them all; that they held back is more than I would have done. The ensign has bruises on her breast that will take months to heal and could lead to cancer. If I were her, I'd press charges. You people are pathetic. I would suggest you don't trespass on any of our properties. We're just looking for an excuse to shoot you ourselves, and we don't shoot as straight as the ensign does."

The lieutenant said, "I love that woman."

The reporter went on to say that the local court was just as hostile toward the media but that it had no authority in the matter, because Dr. Anderson's home was private land that was controlled by the federal government. The local judge had said earlier that he wanted to ask the governor if he could reinstate hanging as capital punishment.

The federal judge in Sacramento had no comment, but a US attorney stated that he would prosecute all of the trespassers to the fullest extent of the law if Dr. Anderson requested it. He stated that it was apparent that the media was trespassing on Dr. Anderson's land, which was forbidden due to national security issues, and they had used violence against a legal and authorized authority. Their crimes could put them away for a long time, and after viewing the TV broadcast, he would have to say that it was an open and shut case.

The news story was repeated all night long.

✦

"Why is the media not following the laws and doing what the military and politicians are requesting? They should all be shot."

Everything went black, but this time I let it.

Blue answered, "This species gives the report groups full rights to do as they want."

Gray exclaimed, "That's insane!"

Green smiled. "For once I agree with you."

Blue said, "Continue."

CHAPTER 41

✦ ✦ ✦

MAKING WAR ON THE MEDIA

When we finally reached the ocean on the morning of our fifth day, there was no media to be seen, just two helicopters that Colleen called "gunboats." They were painted dark gray and had wings that were loaded with all kinds of weapons. I couldn't help but think it was a bad design. It had to cut down on maneuverability and left the weapons out in the open and unprotected. It looked heavy and probably could not travel fast.

I went back to work. I was trying to figure out a way to house the SEAL detachment. Around eleven in the morning, I made a call to the contractor we had left five days ago. I asked him how long it would take to design eight huts that were fully enclosed, just like my house. We talked about what they needed, and he told me he'd have a design ready in a couple of days. With that taken care of, I started working on finishing the plans for the new ship.

About noon I received a call from my lawyers that a federal judge had signed a restraining order, stating the media had to stay five miles away from my home and that any breach of that five-mile limit would constitute a violation of my rights and a be considered a national security issue. The judge ordered the coast guard to enforce the removal of media vessels from the surrounding waters. He also said that the ensign should be given a commendation for her actions. It played right into our hands and placed public sympathy on our side. The lawyers also said that the media had sent threats, which the lawyers had published.

"Freddy, we want to use some of your information now. Putting some of the media's dealings in the limelight would send a message to the rest of them that this is a war they can't win, and it will take some pressure off you by making you old news."

I looked at the lieutenant, and she said, "Do it. Use all of it."

"Great. We'll get moving on it. Thanks."

As soon as they hung up, the lieutenant called the White House and soon was talking to the president. "I'd like the media to see that the FBI and others are watching and looking into their dealings," Lt. James said. "I want all possible pressure brought to bear, everything all at once. The point is, we want them to be afraid of touching Freddy in any way without permission."

"Consider it done, Commander," said the president.

When they hung up, I asked the lieutenant, "Aren't we going just a little overboard?"

"I've been thinking about that, Freddy. If you want them to stay away for good, then we need to make them aware that this is war. We make it very costly to them to upset you. When they realize they can't beat us, then they may back off. If they do that, then we have a chance to control the situation; otherwise, it'll be in the tabloids constantly."

"Very well, Lieutenant."

✦

"I'm starting to like this Red better."

Everything went black.

Blue asked, "And why would a Gray like a Red?"

"This Red actually listens to the Gray and does what she says. He also looks up to her as if she were smarter than he is. No Green or Red I have ever met looked to a Gray for information."

Green said, "None of our Grays are that intelli—"

A Gray tentacle with some kind of weapon pointed at the Green, and Blue quickly took it away from the Gray. Blue said, "Green, you go too far. Be careful. Continue."

CHAPTER 42

HOME

We continued up the coast, well out of sight of land. At the appropriate point, we moved inward toward where the scanners showed my home site. We passed over a coast guard cutter, and the captain gave us a call. I pulled out several items and mounted them on the porch to enable me to see better. I was just outside the flight office, and the window was open so that I could communicate with the lieutenant. The ensign was on a portable communicator, talking directly to the lieutenant from home base.

As we pulled up to my home site, I had the lieutenant stop just short of the shield. We scanned the area; everything was "green light" to let the shield down. I communicated with the computer and had it lower the shields. As soon as the shields were dropped, we moved in and settled over the indentation I had made for the house. It had leaves and other debris in it—I hadn't anticipated that. I used my own telekinesis to levitate down to the surface and after shaking hands with the ensign, I took care of the first priority. I went right to the tent and healed Maggie's broken leg. As we walked out together, I told her to be careful on that leg for the next week. "Give the bone time to harden some, and then you can use it normally."

The lieutenant and the master chief noted how quickly I tossed all other things out of my mind to help Maggie. The master chief said, "Note, Lieutenant, that he needed no help dropping down over forty feet to the ground. He knew exactly where Maggie was and went directly to her before worrying about this multimillion-dollar house that he painstakingly planned out and had built. I wonder just how much of that was his empathic abilities and how much was just plain old-fashioned concern for a friend."

"I'll bet he cares much more for Maggie and any of the rest of us than all the money or inventions he has."

"No bet, Lieutenant. I think you're right."

I walked around with Maggie, watching to be sure that she wasn't in pain and that I had healed her leg correctly. Then it hit me that I had a house hovering and people waiting. I looked up and said, "Sorry, I'll be right there. Have to go Maggie. Take it easy."

"Thanks, Freddy. I will."

I took the tractor beam gun over to the hole. I put it on wide beam, very low power, and raised everything in the hole up and moved it out. It was autumn, and winter was coming fast. There were a lot of leaves. Then, to the lieutenant's horror, I jumped down into the hole under the house and checked for any other problems.

"Freddy, what are you doing? Get out of there now!"

"Lieutenant, I need to clean the hole before I set the house into it. Also, I need to set up the connections. If they're not clean, then we could leak, and that would be a bad thing."

Dirt had gotten into the quick connects for the water and the main power. I had a bag over the special power source, and it came off with the leaves. The big black disk did not miss the lieutenant's attention.

"What's that?" she asked.

"Backup power, enough to run everything for two years if someone cuts off my main power. Lieutenant, please drop down my pocket scanner." I levitated out of the hole. She dropped the scanner down to my hand, and I said, "Okay, ready." I set the scanner for matching the hole to the base of the house, and it was a perfect match. *So far, so good.* Now I had to orient the house so that it would drop directly down on the connectors and automatically hook itself up. I was using a new material that I had developed for both connectors that was totally impervious to weather. "Ensign, please stand back and tell the lieutenant to let go of the controls." I levitated up and turned on my other equipment. Four lasers shot down, looking for their match. I moved the house over the holes until I got the first one to match up and locked it in. Then I simply told the computer to match up the rest. The computer took over and moved slowly until all at once, all four lasers' green lights lit up. I then used the scanner to ensure that I had good alignment. It was within one two-thousandths of an inch. I told the computer to lower until it connected. The house started dropping slowly down. Just at the point where the porch touched the ground, I heard several connectors lock into place, and the green lights for all of them came on. The house was finally in place, so I turned the equipment off.

I went inside and disconnected the flying equipment and then went to the operator's room, which had been inspected very closely by the SEALs beforehand. From there, I powered up the house, turned on the water and the continuous-loop water heating system. I also turned on the climate control and set the computer for protection and continuous monitoring. Next, I connected this computer into the existing temporary computer and set the controls for setup.

"Everyone here, Lieutenant?"

"No, we have two girls watching the town."

"Computer on."

"Welcome, Freddy. I see you are not alone. Please enter the proper code words."

I said the correct words and the computer said, *"Accepted. Continue with setup?"*

"Yes. Please scan all personnel and show them on the screen, one at a time."

I had previously trained the computer and set it up so that it recognized each member of the SEAL team. I had it scan the town, find the two there, and add them. I then set security levels.

I gave the lieutenant a level 1-B and told her that she could set the levels for the rest of her people. I showed her how to do that and what the other levels meant.

"Freddy, what is level 1-A? It's a menu choice on the screen that's blanked out for me."

"That's the owner's security level. Don't worry; if you don't have access to something, the computer will let you know. Level 1-B gives you 'near owner' access. The differences are very minor." I left it at that. "Computer?"

"Yes?"

"Lt. Susan James needs to spend time learning your software, and then she needs to learn the abilities that I built into you. She will need to train all her people also. Please bring up a list of all the things that the lieutenant will need to know, according to her access level." A long list appeared on the screen. "Make the list into a check-off table, and do the same for each person who is given access to you. Keep this list as a training matrix for everyone to access but that only you and the lieutenant can change. As each person completes a level of training, please check the person off on the list so that we can see who is qualified to do what. Understood?"

"Understood ... Working ... Completed."

The list changed to an Excel file that had check-offs.

"It's all yours, Lieutenant. Have fun! Computer, please restore the shield to full operation and warn us if any human approaches within two miles."

"Compliance."

"If you need any help, Lieutenant, I'll be checking the working functions of the rest of the house. I need to run the water for a few hours to clean out the system. We already know that the electricity works, and the inside water is fine, but the pipes leading to the house have had water sitting in them for weeks, so they need bleeding. I also need to set the anchors—little things that can really bite us if we forget."

"Very well, Freddy. Petty Officer Donet, please go with Freddy and learn all you can. Petty Officer Parks, you're with me."

I looked at Maggie Parks. "Computer expert?"

"That's right, Freddy."

"Please don't try to break into my computer programming. It's physically protected. You'll get a warning if you do. Heed it!" I turned and left for the kitchen, with Betsy Donet right behind me.

Setting the anchors took a long time. The house missed aligning with the anchor holes by about three inches. *Can't do everything perfect!* I thought.

Betsy thought it was funny and said so. I had to drill new holes and plug the old ones. Then I had to set the locking pins and plug the new hole. Each one took twenty minutes when it should have taken only one or two minutes. I had finished eight of the anchors but had twelve to go. It was getting late, and although I had no problem working until the job was done, Colleen called from the house, saying that dinner was ready and that I was to get myself to the table right away.

Dinner was great, and I felt sleepy afterward, so I told Betsy we could finish the job tomorrow, as I was going to bed early.

✦

The Blue used a tentacle to motion for the Green to stop.

Everything went black for only a second and then became crystal clear.

Blue said, "Well, other than this Oz house from some place called Kansas, this is a first for this species."

Green said, "It is interesting. Several things to note: the power units that flew the house are more powerful than ours, his use of telekinesis is far greater than our best Yellow, and though he is a pacifist, like most Greens and Reds, he is willing to use his ability for protection."

Gray said, "I see no conflict in that attitude. Protection from others is the number one reason we developed space travel and hundreds of other technologies."

Blue said, "True. Continue."

CHAPTER 43

SHOP

The next day was Friday. When I got up, the computer said, *"Freddy, you have two messages."*

"Go ahead, computer."

"First message from Susan James. Freddy, your meeting with the media is scheduled for 1:00 p.m. this afternoon. It will be held in the Crescent City Elk Middle School at Crescent City. End of message."

"Computer, acknowledge receipt and then delete first message."

"Acknowledged. Deleted. Second message from Susan James. Freddy, your lawyers would like to talk to you before you go to the meeting this afternoon. End of message."

"Computer, acknowledge receipt and then delete second message."

"Acknowledged. Deleted. End of messages."

I looked at the time, and it was only four in the morning, so I decided to go outside, finish anchoring the house, and work in my workshop. I dressed and headed downstairs. Petty Officer Patricia Henderson was on watch and saw me on the scanners, moving about. She was nice enough to make sure that I saw her, so I wouldn't be startled. After finishing the house, I said hello to her.

"Hi, Dr. Anderson. Where are you going?" asked Patricia.

"It's 'Freddy,' and I'm going to work for a couple of hours in my workshop. I'll be back for breakfast. Just have the computer call me when it's ready. Thanks."

I walked out, knowing that she was watching my every step. I really didn't care, as they were all going to see sometime anyway. I walked up to the side of the cliff and mentally touched the button inside. I was instantly challenged by the computer and scanned.

"Good morning, Freddy."

"Good morning. Shop, please report." I started walking directly through the wall of the cliff. I could feel Patricia's emotions, and she was freaking out. I knew the lieutenant was about to be awakened early.

"Everything is secure. The project has been completed, and the robots are awaiting further instructions."

"Home?"

"Yes, Freddy?"

"What time did the lieutenant go to sleep last night?"

"She did not, Freddy. She stayed up until just an hour ago."

"That's not good. Oh well, it's not my problem. They all need to get used to me." I walked back into the workshop, and it was exactly as I planned. The problem was—my plans were wrong, and so I started setting the robots to make some changes.

I heard Katie in my head. *"Are you all right, Freddy?"*

"Yes," I answered, and I raised my mental shields.

Getting the robots set for the changes took about an hour, and I couldn't do much while that was going on, so I decided to grab some breakfast. When I exited the cliff, several people were standing there, watching.

"Hello, Freddy."

"Hi, Patricia. You still on watch?"

"No. Betsy is in the computer room, watching the scanners. She has the watch. Where were you?"

"In my workshop. Why?"

"We could not detect your presence in the area. We were worried and more than a little concerned when I saw you walk into a mountain. When I ran out here, the wall was just that—a wall."

Maggie added, "The scanners don't reach into your workshop, Freddy. That part of the mountain seems to be blanked out. Even the portable scanners won't penetrate the cliff. Everyone was worried, except the lieutenant. She said, 'He'll come out,' and Katie said that you were okay."

"I'm sorry, but you'll have to admit that the lieutenant was right again. I came out. My workshop is protected from all energy emissions, so the toy scanners that I'm letting you use are useless. No one can see into or enter my workshop without my direct permission. I'm not ready to let you have use of one of the high-level scanners, at least not yet."

"How will we know when you're in your workshop or off somewhere else, then?"

"Simple. Home?"

A big voice sounded directly above them. ***"Yes, Freddy?"***

"If any of the people with level 2-D or above clearance need to know if I'm in my workshop, or if they need to talk to me due to an emergency or to know my condition, please contact Shop and get them the information. Understand?"

"Understood."

"Did you catch that, Shop?"

The sweetest motherly voice sounded. *"Yes, Freddy, and I will provide the following information upon request: whether you are or are not in the workshop. If you are in the workshop, upon request I will provide your physical and mental condition and allow communication if it is an emergency. Is this correct?"*

"Yes, that is exactly what I want. Thank you."

"You're welcome, Freddy."

They all looked stunned. Patricia said, "Your workshop computer seems to be more advanced than your home computer."

"Very much so, but we can talk about that later. Right now, I'm hungry, so I'm going to get myself something to eat. Anything else?"

"No, that should do it. Thank you, Freddy."

"You're welcome." As I was walking away, I could feel the emotion and at least one had a little fear. I touched that fear, and it was about the workshop computer. She had a fear of intelligent computers—strange. I could also hear them examining the wall. I said a little mental "good luck, girls" and walked into the house.

✦

Blue said, "If he knew what we know, he would have fear of intelligent computers also."

Everything went black.

Green smiled. "He knows now. I just gave him that memory, and the Body System reinforced it with information of their own."

Blue looked pleased. "Good. Continue."

CHAPTER 44

✦ ✦ ✦

THE OFFICE

Colleen was in the kitchen, preparing breakfast for everyone—bacon, spicy potatoes, and eggs, just the way I liked them. I asked Colleen how long she was going to have to do KP duty. "Are you being punished? You don't seem to enjoy it much, although you are very good at it."

"The lieutenant has already requested that additional people be screened for the cook and other positions. Moreover, I'm not being punished. Someone has to do the job until we get a regular cook, and everyone here knows that I can cook, so I was volunteered. The cooking is not the part I like or dislike. It's the cleanup."

I smiled. "I like the cleanup. I have a brain block to cooking. I tend to make it way too complicated and try to reinvent each recipe. It seldom comes out very good." I said in a low tone, "In fact, sometimes it comes out very badly from both ends." On a cheerier note, I added, "Cleaning up takes no mental abilities at all, and I can think and plan while I'm doing it. I like having my hands in the hot water while washing dishes, and the talk that usually goes along with two or more people in the kitchen can be fun."

She smiled. "I'm getting enough help. It's a nice offer,

Freddy, and you're a good kid," she said, ruffling my long hair, "but the lieutenant already assigned people to help with cleanup. They are on KP duty."

"Really? What'd they do wrong?"

"That's not for me to say. Ask the lieutenant. The orders are to give you all the time you need to work on your projects."

"I see." I know I sounded a little disappointed.

"What's the problem?"

"Susan is a very intelligent person. She knows that if I allow her to take over everything and do little or nothing for myself that I will end up being dependent on the team. That's not the type of situation I want to be in." I sighed, deciding to call my lawyers. "Thanks for breakfast. It was excellent. I liked the spicy potatoes a lot. They taste really good mixed in with the egg yolk." I left the kitchen, knowing full well that Colleen would report our conversation to the lieutenant the moment I was out of sight.

I went into the office and opened a line to my lawyers at Zimmer and Venski. We had a good discussion about what I should say at today's meeting, and Venski informed me that Jeff Zimmer was already there to represent me and protect my interests. The biggest thing he emphasized was not to talk about the lawsuit. After we concluded our conversation, I went to see Lt. James.

"Home, where is the Lieutenant?"

"She has made an office out of the closet next to the computer room."

"Thank you." I thought, *Interesting. I need to see this. That room is really too small to be an office.* My office was in my room and in my workshop, so I had no need for this one. It was a nice office, though. I had stuffed it with loads of goodies. I had to set this straight right now, and I had to do it tactfully. "Home, is she alone?"

"No, she has four others with her."

"Thank you. Well, that lets out paging her to her office." I got up and went over to the computer room. As I went by the closet, four people were standing outside, talking to someone inside. The closet was too small for more than one person at a time. I approached, and everyone parted. "Lieutenant, there you are. I was just in your office, looking for you. Are you turning this into a watch room or something?"

She looked at me and said very honestly, "No, Freddy, I'm turning this into my office."

"Why?"

"Because I didn't think you wanted me in your office."

I sat down on her two foot by two foot desk. "Look, Lieutenant. I have a problem with this. I plan on entertaining people, possibly the admiral and definitely people from the town. I may need to invite some members of the media at one point or another. How's it going to look when they find out that the person in charge of this place sits in a closet? You're the boss. My life is in your hands, as well as that of the team's. You make all the decisions. You're my liaison to the base. You're the only person, short of the president of the United States, who I trust to control my life and teach me how to be independent, as far as knowing how to do everyday things. I should be calling you Mother. You think I would put my mother in a closet? You want to embarrass my girlfriends"—I motioned around me at the team—"and me like that?" I was purposely acting like I was spinning up, getting madder and madder.

She stood up and put her arms around me. "Okay, all right. I'll move into the office. I'd be honored. I should have asked, but I thought you wanted it for yourself."

"I already have two offices. Why do I need a third?"

"What two offices?"

"The one hidden in my bedroom and the one in my workshop."

She frowned at the mention of the workshop. "Freddy, I've been informed about your workshop."

"Wasn't it nice of me to give the girls access to information about me when I'm working? I didn't want them to worry."

She looked at me as if I had just ruined her approach on the subject, which was exactly what I was trying to do, but I could see the subject was not closed.

The Gray said, "Crafty little creature."

Everything went black. Darn.

The Green said, "I bet you like that about it."

"Actually, yes I do." He looked up at the Blue and hastily said, "Continue."

CHAPTER 45

✦ ✦ ✦

TOWN COUNCIL PLUS A FEW

"I talked to my lawyers and one of them is going to meet us in town. His name is Jeff Zimmer."

Susan looked impressed. "Zimmer—of Zimmer and Venski?"

"Yes. Do you know them?"

"I've heard of them. They took the government on in a case over women in combat situations and won."

"Yep, that's them. They helped me gain my emancipation. My father always said, 'Hire the best for the job, and you can expect to get the best job done.'"

"Is that why you hired that construction company? They were a long way away from here."

"Yes, they're the best for single construction projects, and they're very honest."

"Well, they did a great job—not a single crack after traveling three thousand miles. You do realize that this house is bulletproof."

"Of course. I designed it. And who shot at my house?"

"No one. It was just an examination. My apologies; I temporarily forgot you designed it."

"That's okay. When are we leaving for town? I'd like to stop in and say hello to Mrs. Crain and my friends before the meeting. I'd like to get their call on the activity in their town before I make my final decision on what to say to the media."

"That's a good idea. I've had two people in town, watching. I think you should also talk to them to see where the support and nonsupport lies."

"Great. Can you bring them in, or should we meet them there?"

"We'll meet them in town, so we need to leave in about an hour."

"Okay. I'll call Mrs. Crain and see if we can have lunch at the inn. I'm sure she'll let us hold a meeting there. How many for lunch?"

"Lunch at the inn is out. Right now, it's full of media people."

"Yes, I guess it would be. Sorry, I didn't think."

"You get yourself ready, and I'll contact the watchers to set up something else."

"Please include Betty Caster, Devin Miles, and Karen Jenson, if possible."

"I'll try, but they are all really busy. The entire town is busy."

"I understand, but let them know that I'd like to have their input before I make a decision that could affect them."

"Put it that way, and I don't see how they could refuse."

At ten o'clock, the lieutenant had the computer call me downstairs. Everything was ready. A helicopter was sitting on the left pad with the rotors idling. The designated group boarded, and off we went. The helicopter took the ocean route, and the trip was very quick. I did have time to notice the dozens of sea lions and hundreds of birds that were on or near the surrounding beaches.

"Yes," said the lieutenant in a soft voice filled with wonder, "no matter what else you do, that"—she pointed to the beach—"justifies your existence."

I whispered back with wonder in my voice too, "You haven't seen anything yet."

She put her arm around me, and we watched the beaches all the way into town.

We landed in the back lot of the lumberyard, left the helicopter, and went into the Town Hall. The meeting was already in progress, and I guessed that most of the top people were there, including Captain Mike Crain and Captain Bob Allen. Captain Crain came right up to me and picked me up. Katie moved ten feet to his side and touched his neck before the lieutenant could give her a quick hand signal that it was all right. Rubbing his neck, he looked back at me with a smile that went from ear to ear. He said in a voice that everyone could hear, "This is the child who's bringing fishing back to the southern shores. Three cheers for Freddy!"

Everyone cheered, "Hip, hip, hooray! Hip, hip, hooray! Hip, hip, hooray!"

Captain Crain held me on his shoulder until we reached the table, and everyone quickly sat down. I had the seat at the center, and the lieutenant was next to me. The rest of the team was dispersed to check security, except Katie. She was standing there looking as if she would kill anyone who so much as looked at me the wrong way. Everyone saw the lieutenant motion to her not to react to the captain, and they knew that without that signal, she would have killed him. Consequently, many of them were looking at Katie instead of me. Normally, this would have been fine with me, but I needed their attention, so I used telepathy to tell her, *"Katie, you've frightened them all."* She smiled and went over to the captain. She put out her hand and said, "I'm sorry, sir. It's just that you surprised me. No hard feelings?"

The captain took her hand and said, "None at all, young lady," as he smiled his big, friendly smile. "I don't think I could ask for anyone better to protect one of our town members."

That settled everyone down, and we discussed the town and what would be best for everyone. I was surprised at their answers. They wanted to have the media there. It was good for business and with all the attention I was attracting, it would likely cause a boom in the population, and that would create more jobs, more revenue for the stores, and spark an increase in the price of their catches.

"Are you sure this is what you want? This is such a nice town, and you all get along so well and work together wonderfully. Do you really want to expand?"

I got a resounding yes from everyone, except Betty Caster. I asked her what her reservations were.

"I come from a big city. I moved out here to get away from the crime."

Mayor Devin Miles patted her on the back. "It's going to stay crime-free, Betty. Isn't it, Lieutenant?"

"With Freddy's permission, it will."

I looked at her and asked, "What permission?"

"I want to use your lie detector in the local court. It's a good way to test it out, and it will give this town one of the best courts in the country. Instant knowledge of the truth will make it so people won't be able to get away with anything."

"That's a good thing for keeping crime down, but it would be bad if you started using it for checking to see if your husband was cheating on you or to settle arguments with your kids."

"Why?" asked a shocked Mayor Miles.

"How do people react if they know a person can read their minds? They stay away from that person. They become paranoid, and they eventually move away. It could be simple little things that aren't even a crime, like asking, 'Did you make it to home base last night with your girlfriend? What were you doing out with your neighbor's wife last night? Is your kid really as good as you say? Did you really bake this yourself?'"

"Freddy, I think we get the point. The unit will need to be monitored very carefully and used for the express purpose of solving crimes or major disputes."

"Yes, and to that effect, I haven't patented it yet, so I will need assurance that it will be kept in control of someone who reports to us on a regular basis. It will have to be one of the SEAL team who uses it and keeps it."

"Can't you trust someone from the town?" asked Betty.

"I trust you a lot, but I don't want to put your life in jeopardy."

"My life?"

"Yes. People may come here to conduct espionage. Just one of my inventions could make someone a multimillionaire. Some people would kill or hire someone to kill for them for such a chance."

Betty turned red. "I think you're right, Freddy. It would be better if one of the SEAL team handled the unit."

"Good, as long as the lieutenant agrees to that stipulation, then it's not a problem."

Susan nodded her head. "That will also give us daily reports on the whereabouts of the unit. If it was stolen, then Freddy could patent it before anyone else could take it apart and figure out how it works."

"Well … if they take it apart," I said sheepishly, "I hope they're in a bomb shelter so that no one else gets hurt. Many of my devices are booby-trapped with very powerful explosives."

Betty said nervously, "We need the unit, and I have no

problem with one of the lieutenant's people doing *all* the handling of it."

Captain Crain sat back and laughed. "What? No guts, Betty?"

"Not for blowing my brains out, no."

"Well, it's time for Freddy and his companions to eat before he takes on the media. We can work out the details over lunch," said Mayor Miles.

Lunch was catered by Betty's Diner, and it was great. We had to hurry, though, as the time to leave for the meeting was getting close. Everyone except the mayor and Captain Crain had already left for Crescent City and would meet us there.

✦

Blue looked thoughtful. "That's very interesting."

Everything went black.

"Sire?" both the Gray and Green said at the same time.

"Instead of running to the Blues, the Yellow, and sometimes the Whites the moment he thinks he has any possibility of a breakthrough, this one hides his inventions and traps them so they cannot be stolen before he has them completely ready."

"Yes, sire. That is their way. They work on an incentive program called money. It is an ingenious program. You need money to eat, and the more money you have, the better you can eat. However, the more money you have, the more you need to keep what you have. It is a vicious circle that forces them to work harder. Of course, a few have found a way to beat the program, and they hold most of the money."

Blue looked shocked. "If we stay in contact with this species, we will correct that greed."

Gray said, "I certainly hope so."

Blue said, "Please continue."

CHAPTER 46

✦ ✦ ✦

PRESS CONFERENCE

At exactly 12:30 p.m., we walked into the lumberyard and climbed back into the helicopter. The trip only took twenty-five minutes, but it was a wonderful trip. We stayed close to the shoreline, and I received a good look at all the wildlife that was starting to return to my land—seals and sea lions, fish, whales, and dolphins. Captain Crain pointed out sea birds, grasses, and different types of seaweed that were growing back rapidly. He also pointed out the areas that were going to take a lot longer to restart. He patted me on the back, saying, "I owe you a lot. The whole town owes you."

In a humble voice, I answered, "Just doing what's right, sir."

The helicopter took a turn to the left and headed inland, just before an island with a lovely old lighthouse. The lieutenant set the helicopter down in the parking lot of the Elk Middle School. The parking lot was jammed with media and spectators. There was a sign that read, "The Cougars Welcome You, Freddy." I smiled and waved to several young people who looked about my age. They smiled and waved and shouted greetings back. My mind was wide open, and I instantly took a liking to these people. Crescent City seemed very friendly, and the spectators seemed to be good, friendly, down-to-earth people. I couldn't say the same for all the media. Most were good people, but some caused me to put my mental shields up.

We had a police escort. All looked like the kind of people you could trust and respect. In addition, several dozen people who looked like the president's Secret Service were monitoring our progress. One of these walked up to the lieutenant and introduced himself by showing his badge.

"The president sends her greetings and wishes us to extend any help you deem necessary, Lieutenant."

Without taking her eyes off the crowd, she said, "Thank you, Special Agent Howard. I would ask that you do your best to keep people away from Dr. Anderson. My team is getting nervous and may inadvertently kill someone. Understand that no one, including your men, is to come near him without my direct permission."

The rest of the team met us there, except the two that the Lieutenant left on watch at home base. Three SEALs were stationed around the helicopter, and the rest stayed very close to me. I could hardly see past them to the throng of people pressing in. All of a sudden, we came to a stop, and then people backed up quickly. A few seconds later, I saw why, when we passed five media people who were on the ground, moaning. The lieutenant said, "They'll be all right. Just a little warning. There's been no real or permanent harm." She'd hoped that use of force wouldn't be necessary, but they simply wouldn't get out of the way. She motioned to the police, and they took care of the five people on the ground. We were now in a roped-off area, so our progress toward the entrance was much better.

The school was small, but it had a big room that could seat over one thousand people. It had a stage that the SEAL team had checked thoroughly before we reached there, and I could see other people arranged around the room where they would be most useful. I looked up at the lieutenant and asked, "How many of these people are ours?"

"Temporarily, nearly thirty," was her quick response.

I was taken to the stage, where I met the mayor of Crescent City, the governor of California, two congressmen, and a female senator, as well as several other people, including Mr. Zimmer. When I shook hands with the governor, I asked, "All this because we flew a house across the country?"

"Not exactly, Dr. Anderson, but that's a part of it."

I took the seat offered, and the mayor stood up to make the introductions. "Ladies and gentlemen, I'm sure you know the governor of the great state of California." People applauded. I did too, out of politeness, even though I really hate politics. "And the distinguished senator from the county of Humboldt to our south." More applause. "And our own congressmen from the great county of Del Norte." More clapping.

I looked at the lieutenant and whispered, "What is this? I'm not into politics."

"Patience, Freddy. They've got to get their introductions out of the way. You're big news up here, and they want to be part of it."

"Judge Francis Moyer and the chairwoman of our local wives club." More clapping and a few cheers from a group of women on the left. "And last but not least, Dr. Freddy Anderson." There was a lot of clapping and cheering, and most people stood up, I guess maybe to get a better look at me. I started feeling funny inside and hoped I could keep my lunch down. I was getting awfully nervous. The lieutenant saw this and took hold of my hand. I was trembling.

"I don't think I can go through with this," I said.

"Freddy, what you're experiencing is stage fright. It's natural. Just go with it."

"You come with me."

"I'll be right next to you the whole time."

I squeezed her hand and tried to calm myself down.

The governor got up and said a few words about this and that before I heard him say, "I'd like to introduce Dr. Freddy Anderson," and he turned and motioned for me to come to the podium. I was scared to death. I was sure that my entire body was going to shake to pieces in front of everyone.

With the lieutenant's help, I made it to the podium. Mr. Zimmer was right next to us. A three-foot stepladder was placed in front of it for me to stand on. I stepped up and looked out. There had to be twenty microphones on the podium. I said into them, "I'm sorry. I'm so scared right now that I can't remember what I was going to say. Maybe we can start with some questions. Lt. James will select the people I'm to answer, if that's okay."

It became really quiet, and the lieutenant picked a man in the front, holding his hand up.

"Dr. Anderson, can you explain how you could fly a house across country?"

I repeated the question into the microphones, like I remembered seeing my father do. Then I answered, "I used several antigravity skids that I patented two years ago. I rigged up controls to gang them together for movement on the X, Y, and Z axis." At this point, I became really technical and went into physics and chemical formulas. I ended about ten minutes later with, "It was simple, really. The lieutenant here has a license to fly experimental aircraft, and she was kind enough to obtain the necessary permission, file a flight plan, and fly my house home. All I did was use technology that's out there, ready for you or anyone else to use when someone wants to buy the patent rights. Did you want me to go into more technical detail, sir?" We could be here for days, just on that one question.

There was general laughter from the crowd. "No, let's keep this on a level we can all understand. So you used existing technology? How did you power the skids?"

"I developed a fuel that has limited applications at this time. I have to admit that the fuel worked well for its first try, but it has a long way to go before it can be used for anything commercial. Since it's not patented yet, I don't wish to go into any further detail about it."

"Is the shield around your home existing technology?"

I wanted to say, *"If it exists, then it's existing technology,"* but instead, I said, "It's not patented technology. I expect to patent it as soon as it's been tested more thoroughly."

"There's a rumor that you have a good lie detection device. Is this true?"

"Yes, but again, it is not patented yet, so I cannot talk about its workings."

"What about a working laser that can shoot holes through mountains?"

"If you're referring to the incident on the army base earlier this year, then yes, that was my laser. It was not supposed to be where it was, and it was not supposed to be activated by the person who activated it."

Mr. Zimmer touched my shoulder and whispered to me.

I said out loud, "The government is investigating that incident and has made sure it will not happen again. I can't say any more than that until the investigation is complete."

The lieutenant pointed to a woman.

"Dr. Anderson, are you responsible for the cleanup of the shoreline across your property, as well as the general wellness that we are experiencing, now that the mess is cleaned up? If so, how did you manage it?"

I explained exactly how I did it and the tools I used and let them know that I would be happy to teach others how to handle the equipment when necessary, after I had everything patented, of course. When I was finished, I got a standing ovation.

When things quieted down, the lieutenant pointed to another man.

"Dr. Anderson, you seem to be quite open about your discoveries. Why did you have the media arrested at your home? Why have you declared war on the media?"

Mr. Zimmer gave me a brief warning that this could be a setup to trip me.

I looked sadly at the person who asked the question. "I really hated to have them arrested. We tried to warn them. We told them several times that they were trespassing and interfering in national security issues, but they refused to listen. My home is a testing ground for my inventions. I have many experiments that the pressure of being watched would cause me either to not develop the product or not test it completely. No, I definitely cannot have people watching me, and I cannot have them giving away my secrets before I get them patented. I could lose billions. I love my privacy and will guard it jealously. I don't mind holding press conferences once in a while with select media groups, thereby letting the press in on what I'm doing or inviting some to come along with me when we do something new, but only when I'm ready to do that. Until then, I cannot and will not allow anyone to invade my privacy."

"You cannot stop the media. You have to invite us all."

Mr. Zimmer stood up and said, "Wrong! Dr. Anderson can give exclusives. And in so doing, he can legally exclude all others. It's done all the time. Of course, you could try to sue us over this issue. I would love the chance to either win outright or remove the possibility of exclusives from all media." His tone emphasized that the big media players would not like that idea.

Someone yelled out, "But you're a celebrity now. Everyone has the right to know everything about you."

"Please do not take offense, but that is the silliest statement I have ever heard in my entire life. I am sure that someone in the media coined that phrase and pushed it through the courts, but I doubt that it was a celebrity. I do not wish to be a celebrity, and I assure you that if this is really the case in this country, then I will move to a country that will protect my God-given right to privacy. I don't believe this is the case, though. I believe you have the right to know what others are doing if it affects you or the populace but not the right to know information that would be damaging to my ability to complete my work, would give away my work before I have it patented, or would cause national security issues. Check the laws. I don't have to tell you anything, and I don't have to show you anything. Sure, you may find out some things through spies or disgruntled people, like you do in Washington, but the information will be sketchy at best."

That statement started a roar of protests and arguments. I held up my hand, and it became quiet again. "Next question."

The same person asked, "Would you really leave the United States over something so elementary?"

I answered, "Do you know the meaning of the word 'oppression'? Would you live in a country where you experience fear and oppression? I find it oppressive that there is constant slamming by the media, lies, exaggerations, and things taken out of context or worded to have multiple meanings and then taken completely wrong by the masses. When I was younger, I was a victim of the media, with headlines about me like 'Super Boy—Human or Alien?' and

'Alien born of human mom has super intelligence,' which I'm sure sold lots of newspapers, but they also caused many of my friends to not play with me anymore. Kids at the playground would throw rocks at me, tease me, and beat me up. It ruined my outlook on life at a time when I was just developing the ability to play and communicate appropriately with others. I cannot block the media entirely, but I can invite only reporting groups that I trust, and give them an exclusive. I have that right. Actually, I think I am being very generous by allowing select media to hear about my inventions and possibly attend the testing of some of them, but unless the media starts policing its own, or the courts start slamming the media hard and putting some completely out of business, I don't think I will be in a trusting mood. Don't get me wrong; I strongly believe in the constitutional right to freedom of the press and therefore free speech, but lying, misleading, and telling half truths in a story in order to sway public opinion is not free speech. It's using the pen to destroy lives and ruin the integrity of this country. It's not done for the love of this country or the higher standards for which our country should be known; it's done for the almighty dollar. So please forgive me when I don't see the media as the country's pulse on life. I see reporters as employees of a business, a reporting firm that has not proven to me that I can trust it to be honest and aboveboard in its dealings. If I were going to build something, I would not choose a company that I cannot trust. No successful manufacturing company in the world would. So here's a question for all of you. What makes you think that I should select your reporting firm as the one to whom I should give my exclusives? Base your answer on proven integrity, honesty, and unbiased opinion in reporting, and send it to the lieutenant here. She is the person who will select the firms who will represent me. I would also ask the general public to do one thing too, but only if they want to."

"What's that, Dr. Anderson?"

"Boycott the media until they stop lying about people. Next question, please."

It was quiet for a second, but then a hand went up in the back. The lieutenant pointed and said, "Your question?"

A little girl asked, "Do you have a girlfriend?"

I must have turned three shades of red, and the laughter was uproarious.

"That's hard to answer, young lady. I would have to say no, as I have not asked anyone to be my girlfriend, but there is a girl who I am extremely interested in." I wondered what Becky was thinking or if she was watching.

Another hand went up in front, and the lieutenant picked that one.

"What are your plans for the future?"

"There is a need that I must take care of immediately. I am working on that issue first, and it is not up for discussion. After that, I have a goal that I am moving toward. I have split that goal into hundreds of smaller goals and those into even smaller goals and have prioritized them. I will be working on achieving all of those goals over the next few years."

"What is your big goal?"

I turned to the lieutenant and whispered, "Would it be bad if I told them my overall goal?"

"Depends on what it is."

"To colonize other planets."

Her eyes widened considerably. "Yes, that would be bad to tell them, not because you couldn't do it but because they will think you're nuts. Do you have a smaller goal you can share with them?"

"How about the first step—to establish a city on the moon?"

"That would certainly be more believable. After you

achieve that goal, then letting them in on the next step would be okay, but let's take it one step at a time."

I turned back to the crowd. "First, I must address this one issue, and then the goal I will be working toward is to establish a city on the moon."

That provoked another loud uprising. When things quieted down, the question was asked. "What are you going to call it?"

I smiled. "I actually have two possible answers, one derived from a book I've read by a wonderful and imaginative writer—Lunar City, from Robert Heinlein's *The Moon Is a Harsh Mistress*—and my own thought is First Base."

"First Base. Sounds like that's only the first step."

"It is," I said with a hint of mysteriousness. "If you want to ride along, then play nice."

At that, I stepped down, and we left. Mr. Zimmer said that I did very well, and then he took off.

Several questions were yelled at us while we were heading to the helicopter, but I answered only one. It was a surprise, and I decided that it was worth answering. Someone yelled, "Dr. Anderson, if the media asks for a truce, are you willing to talk?"

I stopped and turned to the reporter who asked the question. "It would be a shame if the media were to ask for a truce after I've dropped only one little bomb." I pretended to think for a second. "In truth, I don't really need or like the distraction from my work." I thought for another second and said, "I must admit that the prospects of dropping my next bomb and eventually getting to some of the big ones are looking more and more possible, but then I don't enjoy destroying people's lives and putting thousands of people out of jobs, so yes. I suppose I would be interested in hearing what they have to say, but only if my lawyers and the lieutenant here say I should."

We climbed into the helicopter and left.

✦

"Red!"

Everything went black.

"Sire?"

"That is the Red's stance on the Whites (media) and Blues (politicians) to an exactness that is near amazing. This boy is as close to one of our Reds (top scientists) as I have ever seen in another species."

Green smiled and said with pride, "Yes, sire, he is."

Gray mumbled, "With a hint of Gray."

Blue and Green turned toward Gray with a look of shock, and Blue said, "Green, continue."

CHAPTER 47

✦ ✦ ✦

STRAIGHTENING THINGS OUT

Susan said, "That was an interesting answer to the question, Freddy."

"But it's true. I would listen, and if they came up with a workable plan that would be beneficial, I might even entertain the idea of calling off the war. We didn't start it to destroy the entire media world. We started it to set parameters, and if we achieve that goal, then there's no need to continue with the war."

"Be careful not to end it too quickly or seem too willing."

"Okay, but an end to it and a smooth relationship would be good for us all."

"Not if they think they might be able to get away with things that seem little now but may be big sometime down the road. For instance, don't promise that they can come along on every test ride."

"I won't. Thanks."

The trip back was uneventful except that we had escorts from the base. We stopped in town first to let Captain Crain off so that he could head back out to sea.

When we sat down on the beach at the inn, a lot of people were there.

The captain asked, "What you said about being extremely interested in a girl … was that my Becky?"

"Yes, sir, it was. I know we're young and all, but I do have a crush on her."

He smiled. "Well, if you don't hold her for a while and tell her she's the one you were talking about, Mrs. Crain is going to have a very upset little girl on her hands." He pointed to Becky up at the inn. She was crying.

"Lieutenant …"

"I see her, Freddy. I understand." She cut the engines while giving hand signals to the team. The SEALs spread out for protection. Katie stayed next to me as my bodyguard. I climbed out and ran to Becky. We hugged, and I asked if she'd watched the meeting on television.

"Yes, I watched."

I lowered my head and shyly asked, "You're not mad at me for telling the world that I have a crush on you, are you?"

She threw her arms around my neck and kissed my face all over. Then she planted one right on my lips that was really very nice. I heard a loud clearing of someone's throat, and she quickly pulled away. Captain Crain was standing there. He looked over at Mrs. Crain and said, "Watch these two," and then he looked back at me and added, "Real close." I must have been as red as a beet, and I could hear laughter from a place that caught me off guard—heaven?

With a loving look at her husband and at us, Mrs. Crain said, "I will, my captain."

"It's time for me to go. Becky, how about tossing some of those kisses my way?" the captain asked.

Becky jumped up and ran to her daddy. Something was wrong, but I couldn't put a finger on it. They hugged, and he carried her and Annabelle out to the docks. After many hugs and kisses, the crew climbed aboard and cast off. Becky and I held hands as they left, and then I let her know I needed to get home but that I'd try to come to see her again soon.

She took a defensive stance and asked, "How soon? You go away for weeks and weeks and never say a word. I can't even write you a letter because you have no address. How do you get your mail? What about e-mail? Do you have an e-mail address?"

I looked up at the lieutenant, and she said, "I'll remind him. He can always call, but his e-mail is off-limits. I don't want that getting out."

I held my arm around her waist and kissed her on the cheek. "Becky, once again you've pointed out something that I've completely overlooked. What would I do without you?" I turned to the lieutenant and said, "She has a point. I need to set up an address to get mail."

"It's a good point. The SEALs need a way to get mail also. Petty Officer Parks will take care of it."

"Yes, ma'am, I'm on it," said Parks. "It's getting a little crowded here, don't you think?"

"Yes, we need to go anyway," I agreed. "I have a lot of work to do. Bye, Mrs. Crain, Johnny, Carroll." I knelt down and kissed Annabelle on the forehead. "Bye, Annabelle."

She wrapped her arms around me and gave me a big hug. "Bye, Freddy."

I straightened up and gave Becky one more hug and kiss on the cheek and said, "See you soon."

✦

Everything went black.

The Green said, "We need to stop here. The creature is strong, but if we continue without rest, we could burn it out. We can start up again in a few days."

Gray said, "I don't care if we burn it out. I want that information!"

Blue picked the Gray up by the top of the head and said, "If it burns out, fool, then we will never have the information." It turned to the Green and said, "Two days."

Then it left, with the Gray squirming in its grasp.

To be continued …